RESORTING TO MURDER

HOLIDAY MYSTERIES

EDITED AND INTRODUCED BY
MARTIN EDWARDS

D0002856

THE BRITISH LIBRARY

First published in 2015 by

The British Library
96 Euston Road
London NW1 2DB

Cataloguing in Publication Data
A catalogue record for this book is available from the British Library

ISBN 978 0 7123 5748 7

Typeset by IDSUK (DataConnection) Ltd
Printed and bound in England by TJ International

CONTENTS

INTRODUCTION

Holidays offer us the luxury of getting away from it all. So, in a different way, do detective stories. Yet another means of enjoyable escapism involves taking a glance at the past, especially where it seems (if perhaps deceptively) to have been a simpler time than the present. *Resorting to Murder* is an anthology which combines these three forms of pleasure-taking. It presents vintage stories written over a span of roughly half a century, and which have the backdrop of a holiday. This straightforward unifying theme is counterpointed by the stories' sheer diversity.

Holiday mysteries are as popular today as they have ever been, probably because they are as infinitely variable as holidays themselves. Look at the body of work of today's crime writers, British or foreign, and you will find that holidays play a part in rather more stories than you might expect. Why is this? I can suggest a couple of reasons. First, when authors themselves visit an unfamiliar and intriguing location on holiday, it often serves to inspire them to write. Second, our lives change pace on holiday. We are more receptive than usual to fresh experiences. And sometimes, people take risks on holiday that lead them into danger, and even into crime.

This book focuses on the work of British writers, although with a wide variety of settings. But the holiday mystery has an appeal internationally to readers and writers alike. To take one story almost at random, Patricia Highsmith's *The Two Faces of January* illustrates how a crime committed on holiday can fascinate readers and movie audiences over a fifty-year span. The book, first published in 1964, but not filmed until 2014, derives not only its storyline but also much of its power from the premise that the conman Chester and his wife are two Americans enjoying Greece when they become embroiled in murder and a strange relationship with a fellow American. Chester is a long way out of his comfort zone, and his sense of isolation contributes to the panicky decisions he makes, with fatal consequences.

There is nothing new about the holiday-based mystery. A notable, if eccentric, example is B. C. Skottowe's *Sudden Death* (1886) in which crucial action takes place during an extended visit to Homburg made by the wealthy narrator, Jack Buchanan. The exotic (by Victorian standards) foreign setting adds to the air of mystery that pervades a strange book boasting an ahead-of-its-time subtext about sexual ambiguity. Skottowe's more illustrious contemporaries, Arthur Conan Doyle and E. W. Hornung, also explored the holiday mystery, as this anthology reveals.

The post-war turmoil experienced in Britain after the Armistice was succeeded by the misery of an economic slump, and then by the growing threat posed from overseas by Nazism and Fascism. It is no coincidence that the Twenties and the Thirties became the 'Golden Age of Murder', when novelists such as Agatha Christie, Dorothy L. Sayers and Anthony Berkeley crafted complex and original puzzles of whodunit, howdunit, and whydunit that tested readers' wits and earned their authors fame and fortune. There was something unashamedly escapist about much detective fiction written during the Golden Age, but it is also true to say that the better books reveal far more about the society of the time than critics have acknowledged. That escapism regularly took engaging but wildly unlikely forms, with impossible crimes taking place within locked rooms, vital clues being hidden by way of complex cryptograms, and mysterious 'dying messages' uttered by murder victims who could never bring themselves to take the more obvious step of simply naming their killers.

Christie and her colleagues found that stories with holiday settings helped to create a sense of distance and unreality that made it possible to dispense with (or at least limit the use of) their creakier plot devices. Sayers' *The Five Red Herrings* sees Lord Peter Wimsey visiting an artists' colony in Galloway, where she and her husband had enjoyed several holidays, and the real-life background lends a welcome touch of authenticity to an otherwise prosaic mystery. More vivid is *Have His Carcase*, which opens with the novelist Harriet Vane's walking tour through the south of England being rudely interrupted by her discovery of a man's corpse. The dead man proves to be a foreign gigolo who has been working locally, at a hotel, the Resplendent, whose ambience Sayers captures wonderfully.

Christie loved holiday mysteries, and Hercule Poirot's travels had an uncanny habit of leading him into close encounters with murder most ingenious. *Peril at End House* and *Evil Under the Sun* are set in tourist destinations in the south of England, but her most memorable holiday mysteries were set overseas. *Murder on the Orient Express* and *Death on the Nile* remain two of the most successful whodunits ever written. Christie never lost enthusiasm for holiday mysteries; as late as 1964, she took Miss Marple away from St Mary Mead to an exotic island on the other side of the world, and a televised version of *A Caribbean Mystery* enjoyed as much success as the book when it was screened in 2013.

This anthology contains its share of stellar names from the past – Arnold Bennett and G. K. Chesterton, for instance – and stories that have won acclaim over the years, but I was also keen to unearth previously hidden gems. 'Razor Edge' by Anthony Berkeley – whose brilliance with plot had even Christie in raptures – is represented by a story so (undeservedly) obscure that even the British Library did not have a copy. The stories by Phyllis Bentley and Helen Simpson are almost equally rare, despite the success which both writers achieved, while those by H. C. Bailey, Leo Bruce and the little-known Gerald Findler have seldom been reprinted.

The stories in *Resorting to Murder* are presented broadly (but not precisely) in chronological order, reflecting the way in which the holiday mystery evolved over the years. My hope is that readers will find the book is rather like the best kind of holiday – enjoyable and relaxing, with nice touches of the unexpected, and offering memories to look back on with a good deal of pleasure.

Martin Edwards
www.martinedwardsbooks.com

THE ADVENTURE OF THE DEVIL'S FOOT

ARTHUR CONAN DOYLE

Arthur Conan Doyle (1859–1930) needs no introduction to enthusiasts for classic detective fiction. This story of 'the Cornish horror' was one of the later Sherlock Holmes stories, following the great man's dramatic escape from doom at the Reichenbach Falls, and was first published in 1910, although set thirteen years earlier. As so often happens to holidaying sleuths, Holmes' 'rest-cure' is interrupted by crime.

Conan Doyle's unforgettable portrait of the eccentric but brilliant consulting detective is at the heart of our eternal fascination with Holmes, but it is not the only reason why the stories have stood the test of time. Conan Doyle's taste for the macabre and sensational is on display here, and proves as enticing as ever. And, without wasting too many words on description, he captures both the splendour and the menace of his Cornish setting.

*   *   *   *   *

IN RECORDING from time to time some of the curious experiences and interesting recollections which I associate with my long and intimate friendship with Mr. Sherlock Holmes, I have continually been faced by difficulties caused by his own aversion to publicity. To his sombre and cynical spirit all popular applause was always abhorrent, and nothing amused him more at the end of a successful case than to hand over the actual exposure to some orthodox official, and to listen with a mocking smile to the general chorus of misplaced congratulation. It was indeed this attitude upon the part of my friend and certainly not any lack of interesting material which has caused me of late years to lay very few of my records before the public. My participation in some of his adventures was always a privilege which entailed discretion and reticence upon me.

It was, then, with considerable surprise that I received a telegram from Holmes last Tuesday—he has never been known to write where a telegram would serve—in the following terms:

Why not tell them of the Cornish horror—strangest case I have handled.

I have no idea what backward sweep of memory had brought the matter fresh to his mind, or what freak had caused him to desire that I should recount it; but I hasten, before another cancelling telegram may arrive, to hunt out the notes which give me the exact details of the case and to lay the narrative before my readers.

It was, then, in the spring of the year 1897 that Holmes's iron constitution showed some symptoms of giving way in the face of constant hard work of a most exacting kind, aggravated, perhaps, by occasional indiscretions of his own. In March of that year Dr. Moore Agar, of Harley Street, whose dramatic introduction to Holmes I may some day recount, gave positive injunctions that the famous private agent lay aside all his cases and surrender himself to complete rest if he wished to avert an absolute breakdown. The state of his health was not a matter in which he himself took the faintest interest, for his mental detachment was absolute, but he was induced at last, on the threat of being permanently disqualified from work, to give himself a complete change of scene and air.

Thus it was that in the early spring of that year we found ourselves together in a small cottage near Poldhu Bay, at the further extremity of the Cornish peninsula.

It was a singular spot, and one peculiarly well suited to the grim humour of my patient. From the windows of our little whitewashed house, which stood high upon a grassy headland, we looked down upon the whole sinister semicircle of Mounts Bay, that old death trap of sailing vessels, with its fringe of black cliffs and surge-swept reefs on which innumerable seamen have met their end. With a northerly breeze it lies placid and sheltered, inviting the storm-tossed craft to tack into it for rest and protection.

Then come the sudden swirl round of the wind, the blustering gale from the south-west, the dragging anchor, the lee shore, and the last battle in the creaming breakers. The wise mariner stands far out from that evil place.

On the land side our surroundings were as sombre as on the sea. It was a country of rolling moors, lonely and dun-coloured, with an occasional church tower to mark the site of some old-world village. In every direction upon these moors there were traces of some vanished race which had passed utterly away, and left as its sole record strange monuments of stone, irregular mounds which contained the burned ashes of the dead, and curious earthworks which hinted at prehistoric strife. The glamour and mystery of the place, with its sinister atmosphere of forgotten nations, appealed to the imagination of my friend, and he spent much of his time in long walks and solitary meditations upon the moor. The ancient Cornish language had also arrested his attention, and he had, I remember, conceived the idea that it was akin to the Chaldean, and had been largely derived from the Phœnician traders in tin. He had received a consignment of books upon philology and was settling down to develop this thesis when suddenly, to my sorrow and to his unfeigned delight, we found ourselves, even in that land of dreams, plunged into a problem at our very doors which was more intense, more engrossing, and infinitely more mysterious than any of those which had driven us from London. Our simple life and peaceful, healthy routine were violently interrupted, and we were precipitated into the midst of a series of events which caused the utmost excitement not only in Cornwall but throughout the whole west of England. Many of my readers may retain some recollection of what was called at the time "The Cornish Horror," though a most imperfect account of the matter reached the London press. Now, after thirteen years, I will give the true details of this inconceivable affair to the public.

I have said that scattered towers marked the villages which dotted this part of Cornwall. The nearest of these was the hamlet of Tredannick Wollas, where the cottages of a couple of hundred inhabitants clustered round an ancient, moss-grown church. The vicar of the parish, Mr. Roundhay, was something of an archæologist, and as such Holmes had made his acquaintance. He was a middle-aged man, portly and affable, with a considerable fund of local lore. At his invitation we had taken tea at the vicarage and had come to know, also, Mr. Mortimer Tregennis, an independent gentleman, who increased the clergyman's scanty resources by taking rooms in his large, straggling house. The vicar, being a bachelor, was glad to come to such an arrangement, though he had little in common with his lodger, who was a thin, dark, spectacled man, with a stoop which gave the impression of actual, physical deformity. I remember that during our short visit we found the vicar garrulous, but his lodger strangely reticent, a sad-faced, introspective man, sitting with averted eyes, brooding apparently upon his own affairs.

These were the two men who entered abruptly into our little sitting-room on Tuesday, March the 16th, shortly after our break-fast hour, as we were smoking together, preparatory to our daily excursion upon the moors.

"Mr. Holmes," said the vicar in an agitated voice, "the most extraor-dinary and tragic affair has occurred during the night. It is the most unheard-of business. We can only regard it as a special Providence that you should chance to be here at the time, for in all England you are the one man we need."

I glared at the intrusive vicar with no very friendly eyes; but Holmes took his pipe from his lips and sat up in his chair like an old hound who hears the view-halloa. He waved his hand to the sofa, and our palpitating visitor with his agitated companion sat side by side upon it. Mr. Mortimer Tregennis was more self-contained than the clergyman, but the twitching of his thin hands and the brightness of his dark eyes showed that they shared a com-mon emotion.

"Shall I speak or you?" he asked of the vicar.

"Well, as you seem to have made the discovery, whatever it may be, and the vicar to have had it second-hand, perhaps you had better do the speaking," said Holmes.

I glanced at the hastily clad clergyman, with the formally dressed lodger seated beside him, and was amused at the surprise which Holmes's simple deduction had brought to their faces.

"Perhaps I had best say a few words first," said the vicar, "and then you can judge if you will listen to the details from Mr. Tregennis, or whether we should not hasten at once to the scene of this mysterious affair. I may explain, then, that our friend here spent last evening in the company of his two brothers, Owen and George, and of his sister Brenda, at their house of Tredannick Wartha, which is near the old stone cross upon the moor. He left them shortly after ten o'clock, playing cards round the dining-room table, in excellent health and spirits. This morning, being an early riser, he walked in that direction before breakfast and was overtaken by the carriage of Dr. Richards, who explained that he had just been sent for on a most urgent call to Tredannick Wartha. Mr. Mortimer Tregennis naturally went with him. When he arrived at Tredannick Wartha he found an extraordinary state of things. His two brothers and his sister were seated round the table exactly as he had left them, the cards still spread in front of them and the candles burned down to their sockets. The sister lay back stone-dead in her chair, while the two brothers sat on each side of her laughing, shouting, and singing, the senses stricken clean out of them. All three of them, the dead woman and the two demented men, retained upon their faces an expression of the utmost horror—a convulsion of terror which was dreadful to look upon. There was no sign of the presence of anyone in the house, except Mrs. Porter, the old cook and housekeeper, who declared that she had slept deeply and heard no sound during the night. Nothing had been stolen or disarranged, and there is absolutely no explanation of what the horror can be which has frightened a woman to death and two strong men out of their senses. There is the situation, Mr. Holmes, in a nut-shell, and if you can help us to clear it up you will have done a great work."

I had hoped that in some way I could coax my companion back into the quiet which had been the object of our journey; but one glance at his intense face and contracted eyebrows told me how vain was now the expectation. He sat for some little time in silence, absorbed in the strange drama which had broken in upon our peace.

"I will look into this matter," he said at last. "On the face of it, it would appear to be a case of a very exceptional nature. Have you been there yourself, Mr. Roundhay?"

"No, Mr. Holmes. Mr. Tregennis brought back the account to the vicarage, and I at once hurried over with him to consult you."

"How far is it to the house where this singular tragedy occurred?"

"About a mile inland."

"Then we shall walk over together. But before we start I must ask you a few questions, Mr. Mortimer Tregennis."

The other had been silent all this time, but I had observed that his more controlled excitement was even greater than the obtrusive emotion of the clergyman. He sat with a pale, drawn face, his anxious gaze fixed upon Holmes, and his thin hands clasped convulsively together. His pale lips quivered as he listened to the dreadful experience which had befallen his family, and his dark eyes seemed to reflect something of the horror of the scene.

"Ask what you like, Mr. Holmes," said he eagerly. "It is a bad thing to speak of, but I will answer you the truth."

"Tell me about last night."

"Well, Mr. Holmes, I supped there, as the vicar has said, and my elder brother George proposed a game of whist afterwards. We sat down about nine o'clock. It was a quarter-past ten when I moved to go. I left them all round the table, as merry as could be."

"Who let you out?"

"Mrs. Porter had gone to bed, so I let myself out. I shut the hall door behind me. The window of the room in which they sat was closed, but the blind was not drawn down. There was no change in door or window this morning, nor any reason to think that any stranger had been to the house. Yet there they sat, driven clean mad with terror, and Brenda lying dead of fright, with her head hanging over the arm of the chair. I'll never get the sight of that room out of my mind so long as I live."

"The facts, as you state them, are certainly most remarkable," said Holmes. "I take it that you have no theory yourself which can in any way account for them?"

"It's devilish, Mr. Holmes, devilish!" cried Mortimer Tregennis. "It is not of this world. Something has come into that room which has dashed the light of reason from their minds. What human contrivance could do that?"

"I fear," said Holmes, "that if the matter is beyond humanity it is certainly beyond me. Yet we must exhaust all natural explanations before we fall back upon such a theory as this. As to yourself, Mr. Tregennis, I take it you were divided in some way from your family, since they lived together and you had rooms apart?"

"That is so, Mr. Holmes, though the matter is past and done with. We were a family of tin-miners at Redruth, but we sold out our venture to a company, and so retired with enough to keep us. I won't deny that there was some feeling about the division of the money and it stood between us for a time, but it was all forgiven and forgotten, and we were the best of friends together."

"Looking back at the evening which you spent together, does anything stand out in your memory as throwing any possible light upon the tragedy? Think carefully, Mr. Tregennis, for any clue which can help me."

"There is nothing at all, sir."

"Your people were in their usual spirits?"

"Never better."

"Were they nervous people? Did they ever show any apprehension of coming danger?"

"Nothing of the kind."

"You have nothing to add then, which could assist me"

Mortimer Tregennis considered earnestly for a moment.

"There is one thing occurs to me," said he at last. "As we sat at the table my back was to the window, and my brother George, he being my partner at cards, was facing it. I saw him once look hard over my shoulder, so I turned round and looked also. The blind was up and the window shut, but I could just make out the bushes on the lawn, and it seemed to me for a moment that I saw something moving among them. I couldn't even say if it was man or animal, but I just thought there was something there. When I asked him what he was looking at, he told me that he had the same feeling. That is all that I can say."

"Did you not investigate?"

"No; the matter passed as unimportant."

"You left them, then, without any premonition of evil?"

"None at all."

"I am not clear how you came to hear the news so early this morning."

"I am an early riser and generally take a walk before breakfast. This morning I had hardly started when the doctor in his carriage overtook me. He told me that old Mrs. Porter had sent a boy down with an urgent message. I sprang in beside him and we drove on. When we got there we looked into that dreadful room. The candles and the fire must have burned out hours before, and they had been sitting there in the dark until dawn had broken. The doctor said Brenda must have been dead at least six hours. There were no signs of violence. She just lay across the arm of the chair with that look on her face. George and Owen were singing snatches of songs and gibbering like two great apes. Oh, it was awful to see! I couldn't stand it, and the doctor was as white as a sheet. Indeed, he fell into a chair in a sort of faint, and we nearly had him on our hands as well."

"Remarkable—most remarkable!" said Holmes, rising and taking his hat. "I think, perhaps, we had better go down to Tredannick Wartha without further delay. I confess that I have seldom known a case which at first sight presented a more singular problem."

*　　*　　*　　*　　*

Our proceedings of that first morning did little to advance the investigation. It was marked, however, at the outset by an incident which left the most sinister impression upon my mind. The approach to the spot at which the tragedy occurred is down a narrow, winding, country lane. While we made our way along it we heard the rattle of a carriage coming towards us and stood aside to let it pass. As it drove by us I caught a glimpse through the closed window of a horribly contorted, grinning face glaring out at us. Those staring eyes and gnashing teeth flashed past us like a dreadful vision.

"My brothers!" cried Mortimer Tregennis, white to his lips. "They are taking them to Helston."

We looked with horror after the black carriage, lumbering upon its way. Then we turned our steps towards this ill-omened house in which they had met their strange fate.

It was a large and bright dwelling, rather a villa than a cottage, with a considerable garden which was already, in that Cornish air, well filled with spring flowers. Towards this garden the window of the sitting-room fronted, and from it, according to Mortimer Tregennis, must have come that thing of evil which had by sheer horror in a single instant blasted their minds. Holmes walked slowly and thoughtfully among the flower-plots and along the path before we entered the porch. So absorbed was he in his thoughts, I remember, that he stumbled over the watering-pot, upset its contents, and deluged both our feet and the garden path. Inside the house we were met by the elderly Cornish housekeeper, Mrs. Porter, who, with the aid of a young girl, looked after the wants of the family. She readily answered all Holmes's questions. She had heard nothing in the night. Her employers had all been in excellent spirits lately, and she had never known them more cheerful and prosperous. She had fainted with horror upon entering the room in the morning and seeing that dreadful company round the table. She had, when she recovered, thrown open the window to let the morning air in, and had run down to the lane, whence she sent a farm-lad for the doctor. The lady was on her bed upstairs if we cared to see her. It took four strong men to get the brothers into the asylum carriage. She would not herself stay in the house another day and was starting that very afternoon to rejoin her family at St. Ives.

We ascended the stairs and viewed the body. Miss Brenda Tregennis had been a very beautiful girl, though now verging upon middle age. Her dark, clear-cut face was handsome, even in death, but there still lingered upon it something of that convulsion of horror which had been her last human emotion. From her bedroom we descended to the sitting-room, where this strange tragedy had actually occurred. The charred ashes of the overnight fire lay in the grate. On the table were the four guttered and burned-out candles, with the cards scattered over its surface. The chairs had been moved back against the walls, but all else was as it had been the night before. Holmes paced with light, swift steps about the room; he sat in the various chairs, drawing them up and reconstructing their positions. He tested how much of the garden was visible; he examined the floor, the ceiling, and the fireplace; but never once did I see that sudden brightening of his eyes and tightening of his lips which would have told me that he saw some gleam of light in this utter darkness.

"Why a fire?" he asked once. "Had they always a fire in this small room on a spring evening?"

Mortimer Tregennis explained that the night was cold and damp. For that reason, after his arrival, the fire was lit. "What are you going to do now, Mr. Holmes?" he asked.

My friend smiled and laid his hand upon my arm. "I think, Watson, that I shall resume that course of tobacco-poisoning which you have so often and so justly condemned," said he. "With your permission, gentlemen, we will now return to our cottage, for I am not aware that any new factor is likely to come to our notice here. I will turn the facts over in my mind, Mr. Tregennis, and should anything occur to me I will certainly communicate with you and the vicar. In the meantime I wish you both good-morning."

It was not until long after we were back in Poldhu Cottage that Holmes broke his complete and absorbed silence. He sat coiled in his armchair, his haggard and ascetic face hardly visible amid the blue swirl of his tobacco smoke, his black brows drawn down, his forehead contracted, his eyes vacant and far away. Finally he laid down his pipe and sprang to his feet.

"It won't do, Watson!" said he with a laugh. "Let us walk along the cliffs together and search for flint arrows. We are more likely to find them than clues to this problem. To let the brain work without sufficient material is like racing an engine. It racks itself to pieces. The sea air, sunshine, and patience, Watson—all else will come.

"Now, let us calmly define our position, Watson," he continued as we skirted the cliffs together. "Let us get a firm grip of the very little which we *do* know, so that when fresh facts arise we may be ready to fit them into their places. I take it, in the first place, that neither of us is prepared to admit diabolical intrusions into the affairs of men. Let us begin by ruling that entirely out of our minds. Very good. There remain three persons who have been grievously stricken by some conscious or unconscious human agency. That is firm ground. Now, when did this occur? Evidently, assuming his narrative to be true, it was immediately after Mr. Mortimer Tregennis had left the room. That is a very important point. The presumption is that it was within a few minutes afterwards. The cards still lay upon the table. It was already past their usual hour for bed. Yet they had not changed their position or pushed back their chairs. I repeat, then, that the occurrence was immediately after his departure, and not later than eleven o'clock last night.

"Our next obvious step is to check, so far as we can, the movements of Mortimer Tregennis after he left the room. In this there is no difficulty, and they seem to be above suspicion. Knowing my methods as you do, you were, of course, conscious of the somewhat clumsy water-pot expedient by which I obtained a clearer impress of his foot than might otherwise have been possible. The wet, sandy path took it admirably. Last night was also wet, you will remember, and it was not difficult—having obtained a sample print—to pick out his track among others and to follow his movements. He appears to have walked away swiftly in the direction of the vicarage.

"If, then, Mortimer Tregennis disappeared from the scene, and yet some outside person affected the cardplayers, how can we reconstruct that person, and how was such an impression of horror conveyed? Mrs. Porter may be eliminated. She is evidently harmless. Is there any evidence that someone crept up to the garden window and in some manner produced so terrific an effect that he drove those who saw it out of their senses? The only suggestion in this direction comes from Mortimer Tregennis himself, who says that his brother spoke about some movement in the garden. That is certainly remarkable, as the night was rainy, cloudy, and dark. Anyone who had the design to alarm these people would be compelled to place his very face against the glass before he could be seen. There is a three-foot flower-border outside this window, but no indication of a footmark. It is difficult to imagine, then, how an outsider could have made so terrible an impression upon the company, nor have we found any possible motive for so strange and elaborate an attempt. You perceive our difficulties, Watson?"

"They are only too clear," I answered with conviction.

"And yet, with a little more material, we may prove that they are not insurmountable," said Holmes. "I fancy that among your extensive archives, Watson, you may find some which were nearly as obscure. Meanwhile, we shall put the case aside until more accurate data are available, and devote the rest of our morning to the pursuit of neolithic man."

I may have commented upon my friend's power of mental detachment, but never have I wondered at it more than upon that spring morning in Cornwall when for two hours he discoursed upon celts, arrowheads, and shards, as lightly as if no sinister mystery were waiting for his solution. It was not until we had returned in the afternoon to our cottage that we found a visitor awaiting us, who soon brought our minds back to the matter in hand. Neither of us needed to be told who that visitor was. The huge body, the craggy and deeply seamed face with the fierce eyes and hawk-like nose, the grizzled hair which nearly brushed our cottage ceiling, the beard—golden at the fringes and white near the lips, save for the nicotine stain from his perpetual cigar—all these were as well known in London as in Africa, and could only be associated with the tremendous personality of Dr. Leon Sterndale, the great lion-hunter and explorer.

We had heard of his presence in the district and had once or twice caught sight of his tall figure upon the moorland paths. He made no advances to us, however, nor would we have dreamed of doing so to him, as it was well known that it was his love of seclusion which caused him to spend the greater part of the intervals between his journeys in a small bungalow buried in the lonely wood of Beauchamp Arriance. Here, amid his books and his maps, he lived an absolutely lonely life, attending to his own simple wants and paying little apparent heed to the affairs of his neighbours. It was a surprise to me, therefore, to hear him asking Holmes in an eager voice whether he had made any advance in his reconstruction of this mysterious episode. "The county police are utterly at fault," said he, "but perhaps your wider experience has suggested some conceivable explanation. My only claim to being taken into your confidence is that during my many residences here I have come to know this family of Tregennis very well—indeed, upon my Cornish mother's side I could call them cousins—and their strange fate has naturally been a great shock to me. I may tell you that I had got as far as Plymouth upon my way to Africa, but the news reached me this morning, and I came straight back again to help in the inquiry."

Holmes raised his eyebrows.

"Did you lose your boat through it?"

"I will take the next."

"Dear me! that is friendship indeed."

"I tell you they were relatives."

"Quite so—cousins of your mother. Was your baggage aboard the ship?"

"Some of it, but the main part at the hotel."

"I see. But surely this event could not have found its way into the Plymouth morning papers."

"No, sir, I had a telegram."

"Might I ask from whom?"

A shadow passed over the gaunt face of the explorer.

"You are very inquisitive, Mr. Holmes."

"It is my business."

With an effort Dr. Sterndale recovered his ruffled composure.

"I have no objection to telling you," he said. "It was Mr. Roundhay, the vicar, who sent me the telegram which recalled me."

"Thank you," said Holmes. "I may say in answer to your original question that I have not cleared my mind entirely on the subject of this case, but that I have every hope of reaching some conclusion. It would be premature to say more."

"Perhaps you would not mind telling me if your suspicions point in any particular direction?"

"No, I can hardly answer that."

"Then I have wasted my time and need not prolong my visit." The famous doctor strode out of our cottage in considerable ill-humour, and within five minutes Holmes had followed him. I saw him no more until the evening, when he returned with a slow step and haggard face which assured me that he had made no great progress with his investigation. He glanced at a telegram which awaited him and threw it into the grate.

"From the Plymouth hotel, Watson," he said. "I learned the name of it from the vicar, and I wired to make certain that Dr. Leon Sterndale's account was true. It appears that he did indeed spend last night there, and that he has actually allowed some of his baggage to go on to Africa, while he returned to be present at this investigation. What do you make of that, Watson?"

"He is deeply interested."

"Deeply interested—yes. There is a thread here which we have not yet grasped and which might lead us through the tangle. Cheer up, Watson, for I am very sure that our material has not yet all come to hand. When it does we may soon leave our difficulties behind us."

Little did I think how soon the words of Holmes would be realized, or how strange and sinister would be that new development which opened up an entirely fresh line of investigation. I was shaving at my window in the morning when I heard the rattle of hoofs and, looking up, saw a dog-cart coming at a gallop down the road. It pulled up at our door, and our friend, the vicar, sprang from it and rushed up our garden path. Holmes was already dressed, and we hastened down to meet him.

Our visitor was so excited that he could hardly articulate, but at last in gasps and bursts his tragic story came out of him.

"We are devil-ridden, Mr. Holmes! My poor parish is devil-ridden!" he cried. "Satan himself is loose in it! We are given over into his hands!" He danced about in his agitation, a ludicrous object if it were not for his ashy face and startled eyes. Finally he shot out his terrible news.

"Mr. Mortimer Tregennis died during the night, and with exactly the same symptoms as the rest of his family."

Holmes sprang to his feet, all energy in an instant.

"Can you fit us both into your dog-cart?"

"Yes, I can."

"Then, Watson, we will postpone our breakfast. Mr. Roundhay, we are entirely at your disposal. Hurry—hurry, before things get disarranged."

The lodger occupied two rooms at the vicarage, which were in an angle by themselves, the one above the other. Below was a large sitting-room; above, his bedroom. They looked out upon a croquet lawn which came up to the windows. We had arrived before the doctor or the police, so that everything was absolutely undisturbed. Let me describe exactly the scene as we saw it upon that misty March morning. It has left an impression which can never be effaced from my mind.

The atmosphere of the room was of a horrible and depressing stuffiness. The servant who had first entered had thrown up the window, or it would have been even more intolerable. This might partly be due to the fact that a lamp stood flaring and smoking on the centre table. Beside it sat the dead man, leaning back in his chair, his thin beard projecting, his spectacles pushed up on to his forehead, and his lean dark face turned towards the window and twisted into the same distortion of terror which had marked the features of his dead sister. His limbs were convulsed and his fingers contorted as though he had died in a very paroxysm of fear. He was fully clothed, though there were signs that his dressing had been done in a hurry. We had already learned that his bed had been slept in, and that the tragic end had come to him in the early morning.

One realized the red-hot energy which underlay Holmes's phlegmatic exterior when one saw the sudden change which came over him from the moment that he entered the fatal apartment. In an instant he was tense and alert, his eyes shining, his face set, his limbs quivering with eager activity. He was out on the lawn, in through the window, round the room, and up into the bedroom, for all the world like a dashing foxhound drawing a cover. In the bedroom he made a rapid cast around and ended by throwing open the window, which appeared to give him some fresh cause for excitement, for he leaned out of it with loud ejaculations of interest and delight. Then he rushed down the stair, out through the open window, threw himself upon his face on the lawn, sprang up and into the room once more, all with the energy of the hunter who is at the very heels of his quarry. The lamp, which was an ordinary standard, he examined with minute care, making certain measurements upon its bowl. He carefully scrutinized with his lens the talc shield which covered the top of the chimney and scraped off some ashes which adhered to its upper surface, putting some of them into an envelope, which he placed in his pocket-book. Finally, just as the doctor and the official police put in an appearance, he beckoned to the vicar and we all three went out upon the lawn.

"I am glad to say that my investigation has not been entirely barren," he remarked. "I cannot remain to discuss the matter with the police, but I should be exceedingly obliged, Mr. Roundhay, if you would give the inspector my compliments and direct his attention to the bedroom window and to the sitting-room lamp. Each is suggestive, and together they are almost conclusive. If the police would desire further information I shall be happy to see any of them at the cottage. And now, Watson, I think that, perhaps, we shall be better employed elsewhere."

It may be that the police resented the intrusion of an amateur, or that they imagined themselves to be upon some hopeful line of investigation; but it is certain that we heard nothing from them for the next two days. During this time Holmes spent some of his time smoking and dreaming in the cottage; but a greater portion in country walks which he undertook alone, returning after many hours without remark as to where he had been. One experiment served to show me the line of his investigation. He had bought a lamp which was the duplicate of the one which had burned in the room of Mortimer Tregennis on the morning of the tragedy. This he filled with the same oil as that used at the vicarage, and he carefully timed the period which it would take to be exhausted. Another experiment which he made was of a more unpleasant nature, and one which I am not likely ever to forget.

"You will remember, Watson," he remarked one afternoon, "that there is a single common point of resemblance in the varying reports which have reached us. This concerns the effect of the atmosphere of the room in each case upon those who had first entered it. You will recollect that Mortimer Tregennis, in describing the episode of his last visit to his brother's house, remarked that the doctor on entering the room fell into a chair? You had forgotten? Well, I can answer for it that it was so. Now, you will remember also that Mrs. Porter, the housekeeper, told us that she herself fainted upon entering the room and had afterwards opened the window. In the second case—that of Mortimer Tregennis himself—you cannot have forgotten the horrible stuffiness of the room when we arrived, though the servant had thrown open the window. That servant, I found upon inquiry, was so ill that she had gone to her bed. You will admit, Watson, that these facts are very suggestive. In each case there is evidence of a poisonous atmosphere. In each case, also, there is combustion going on in the room—in the one case a fire, in the other a lamp. The fire was needed, but the lamp was lit—as a comparison of the oil consumed will show—long after it was broad daylight. Why? Surely because there is some connection between three things—the burning, the stuffy atmosphere, and, finally, the madness or death of those unfortunate people. That is clear, is it not?"

"It would appear so."

"At least we may accept it as a working hypothesis. We will suppose, then, that something was burned in each case which produced an atmosphere causing strange toxic effects. Very good. In the first instance—that of the Tregennis family—this substance was placed in the fire. Now the window was shut, but the fire would naturally carry fumes to some extent up the chimney. Hence one would expect the effects of the poison to be less than in the second case, where there was less escape for the vapour. The result seems to indicate that it was so, since in the first case only the woman, who had presumably the more sensitive organism, was killed, the others exhibiting that temporary or permanent lunacy which is evidently the first effect of the drug. In the second case the result was complete. The facts, therefore, seem to bear out the theory of a poison which worked by combustion.

"With this train of reasoning in my head I naturally looked about in Mortimer Tregennis's room to find some remains of this substance. The obvious place to look was the talc shield or smoke-guard of the lamp. There, sure enough, I perceived a number of flaky ashes, and round the edges a fringe of brownish powder, which had not yet been consumed. Half of this I took, as you saw, and I placed it in an envelope."

"Why half, Holmes?"

"It is not for me, my dear Watson, to stand in the way of the official police force. I leave them all the evidence which I found. The poison still remained upon the talc had they the wit to find it. Now, Watson, we will light our lamp; we will, however, take the precaution to open our window to avoid the premature decease of two deserving members of society, and you will seat yourself near that open window in an armchair unless, like a sensible man, you determine to have nothing to do with the affair. Oh, you will see it out, will you? I thought I knew my Watson. This chair I will place opposite yours, so that we may be the same distance from the poison and face to face. The door we will leave ajar. Each is now in a position to watch the other and to bring the experiment to an end should the symptoms seem alarming. Is that all clear? Well, then, I take our powder—or what remains of it—from the envelope, and I lay it above the burning lamp. So! Now, Watson, let us sit down and await developments."

They were not long in coming. I had hardly settled in my chair before I was conscious of a thick, musky odour, subtle and nauseous. At the very first whiff of it my brain and my imagination were beyond all control. A thick, black cloud swirled before my eyes, and my mind told me that in this cloud, unseen as yet, but about to spring out upon my appalled senses, lurked all that was vaguely horrible, all that was monstrous and inconceivably wicked in the universe. Vague shapes swirled and swam amid the dark cloud-bank, each a menace and a warning of something coming, the advent of some unspeakable dweller upon the threshold, whose very shadow would blast my soul. A freezing horror took possession of me. I felt that my hair was rising, that my eyes were protruding, that my mouth was opened, and my tongue like leather. The turmoil within my brain was such that something must surely snap. I tried to scream and was vaguely aware of some hoarse croak which was my own voice, but distant and detached from myself. At the same moment, in some effort of escape, I broke through that cloud of despair and had a glimpse of Holmes's face, white, rigid, and drawn with horror—the very look which I had seen upon the features of the dead. It was that vision which gave me an instant of sanity and of strength. I dashed from my chair, threw my arms round Holmes, and together we lurched through the door, and an instant afterwards had thrown ourselves down upon the grass plot and were lying side by side, conscious only of the glorious sunshine which was bursting its way through the hellish cloud of terror which had girt us in. Slowly it rose from our souls like the mists from a landscape until peace and reason had returned, and we were sitting upon the grass, wiping our clammy foreheads, and looking with apprehension at each other to mark the last traces of that terrific experience which we had undergone.

"Upon my word, Watson!" said Holmes at last with an unsteady voice, "I owe you both my thanks and an apology. It was an unjustifiable experiment even for one's self, and doubly so for a friend. I am really very sorry."

"You know," I answered with some emotion, for I had never seen so much of Holmes's heart before, "that it is my greatest joy and privilege to help you."

He relapsed at once into the half-humorous, half-cynical vein which was his habitual attitude to those about him. "It would be superfluous to drive us mad, my dear Watson," said he. "A candid observer would certainly declare that we were so already before we embarked upon so wild an experiment. I confess that I never imagined that the effect could be so sudden and so severe." He dashed into the cottage, and, reappearing with the burning lamp held at full arm's length, he threw it among a bank of brambles. "We must give the room a little time to clear. I take it, Watson, that you have no longer a shadow of a doubt as to how these tragedies were produced?"

"None whatever."

"But the cause remains as obscure as before. Come into the arbour here and let us discuss it together. That villainous stuff seems still to linger round my throat. I think we must admit that all the evidence points to this man, Mortimer Tregennis, having been the criminal in the first tragedy, though he was the victim in the second one. We must remember, in the first place, that there is some story of a family quarrel, followed by a reconciliation. How bitter that quarrel may have been, or how hollow the reconciliation we cannot tell. When I think of Mortimer Tregennis, with the foxy face and the small shrewd, beady eyes behind the spectacles, he is not a man whom I should judge to be of a particularly forgiving disposition. Well, in the next place, you will remember that this idea of someone moving in the garden, which took our attention for a moment from the real cause of the tragedy, emanated from him. He had a motive in misleading us. Finally, if he did not throw this substance into the fire at the moment of leaving the room, who did do so? The affair happened immediately after his departure. Had anyone else come in, the family would certainly have risen from the table. Besides, in peaceful Cornwall, visitors do not arrive after ten o'clock at night. We may take it, then, that all the evidence points to Mortimer Tregennis as the culprit."

"Then his own death was suicide!"

"Well, Watson, it is on the face of it a not impossible supposition. The man who had the guilt upon his soul of having brought such a fate upon his own family might well be driven by remorse to inflict it upon himself. There are, however, some cogent reasons against it. Fortunately, there is one man in England who knows all about it, and I have made arrangements by which we shall hear the facts this afternoon from his own lips. Ah! he is a little before his time. Perhaps you would kindly step this way, Dr. Leon Sterndale. We have been conducting a chemical experiment indoors which has left our little room hardly fit for the reception of so distinguished a visitor."

I had heard the click of the garden gate, and now the majestic figure of the great African explorer appeared upon the path. He turned in some surprise towards the rustic arbour in which we sat.

"You sent for me, Mr. Holmes. I had your note about an hour ago, and I have come, though I really do not know why I should obey your summons."

"Perhaps we can clear the point up before we separate," said Holmes. "Meanwhile, I am much obliged to you for your courteous acquiescence. You will excuse this informal reception in the open air, but my friend Watson and I have nearly furnished an additional chapter to what the papers call the Cornish Horror, and we prefer a clear atmosphere for the present. Perhaps, since the matters which we have to discuss will affect you personally in a very intimate fashion, it is as well that we should talk where there can be no eavesdropping."

The explorer took his cigar from his lips and gazed sternly at my companion.

"I am at a loss to know, sir," he said, "what you can have to speak about which affects me personally in a very intimate fashion."

"The killing of Mortimer Tregennis," said Holmes.

For a moment I wished that I were armed. Sterndale's fierce face turned to a dusky red, his eyes glared, and the knotted, passionate veins started out in his forehead, while he sprang forward with clenched hands towards my companion. Then he stopped, and with a violent effort he resumed a cold, rigid calmness, which was, perhaps, more suggestive of danger than his hot-headed outburst.

"I have lived so long among savages and beyond the law," said he, "that I have got into the way of being a law to myself. You would do well, Mr. Holmes, not to forget it, for I have no desire to do you an injury."

"Nor have I any desire to do you an injury, Dr. Sterndale. Surely the clearest proof of it is that, knowing what I know, I have sent for you and not for the police."

Sterndale sat down with a gasp, overawed for, perhaps, the first time in his adventurous life. There was a calm assurance of power in Holmes's manner which could not be withstood. Our visitor stammered for a moment, his great hands opening and shutting in his agitation.

"What do you mean?" he asked at last. "If this is bluff upon your part, Mr. Holmes, you have chosen a bad man for your experiment. Let us have no more beating about the bush. What *do* you mean?"

"I will tell you," said Holmes, "and the reason why I tell you is that I hope frankness may beget frankness. What my next step may be will depend entirely upon the nature of your own defence."

"My defence?"

"Yes, sir."

"My defence against what?"

"Against the charge of killing Mortimer Tregennis."

Sterndale mopped his forehead with his handkerchief. "Upon my word, you are getting on," said he. "Do all your successes depend upon this prodigious power of bluff?"

"The bluff," said Holmes sternly, "is upon your side, Dr. Leon Sterndale, and not upon mine. As a proof I will tell you some of the facts upon which my conclusions are based. Of your return from Plymouth, allowing much of your property to go on to Africa, I will say nothing save that it first informed me that you were one of the factors which had to be taken into account in reconstructing this drama—"

"I came back—"

"I have heard your reasons and regard them as unconvincing and inadequate. We will pass that. You came down here to ask me whom I suspected. I refused to answer you. You then went to the vicarage, waited outside it for some time, and finally returned to your cottage."

"How do you know that?"

"I followed you."

"I saw no one."

"That is what you may expect to see when I follow you. You spent a restless night at your cottage, and you formed certain plans, which in the early morning you proceeded to put into execution. Leaving your door just as day was breaking, you filled your pocket with some reddish gravel that was lying heaped beside your gate."

Sterndale gave a violent start and looked at Holmes in amazement.

"You then walked swiftly for the mile which separated you from the vicarage. You were wearing, I may remark, the same pair of ribbed tennis shoes which are at the present moment upon your feet. At the vicarage you passed through the orchard and the side hedge, coming out under the window of the lodger Tregennis. It was now daylight, but the household was not yet stirring. You drew some of the gravel from your pocket, and you threw it up at the window above you."

Sterndale sprang to his feet.

"I believe that you are the devil himself!" he cried.

Holmes smiled at the compliment. "It took two, or possibly three, handfuls before the lodger came to the window. You beckoned him to come down. He dressed hurriedly and descended to his sitting-room. You entered by the window. There was an interview—a short one—during which you walked up and down the room. Then you passed out and closed the window, standing on the lawn outside smoking a cigar and watching what occurred. Finally, after the death of Tregennis, you withdrew as you had come. Now, Dr. Sterndale, how do you justify such conduct, and what were the motives for your actions? If you prevaricate or trifle with me, I give you my assurance that the matter will pass out of my hands forever."

Our visitor's face had turned ashen gray as he listened to the words of his accuser. Now he sat for some time in thought with his face sunk in his hands. Then with a sudden impulsive gesture he plucked a photograph from his breast-pocket and threw it on the rustic table before us.

"That is why I have done it," said he.

It showed the bust and face of a very beautiful woman. Holmes stooped over it.

"Brenda Tregennis," said he.

"Yes, Brenda Tregennis," repeated our visitor. "For years I have loved her. For years she has loved me. There is the secret of that Cornish seclusion which people have marvelled at. It has brought me close to the one thing on earth that was dear to me. I could not marry her, for I have a wife who has left me for years and yet whom, by the deplorable laws of England, I could not divorce. For years Brenda waited. For years I waited. And this is what we have waited for." A terrible sob shook his great frame, and he clutched his throat under his brindled beard. Then with an effort he mastered himself and spoke on:

"The vicar knew. He was in our confidence. He would tell you that she was an angel upon earth. That was why he telegraphed to me and I returned. What was my baggage or Africa to me when I learned that such a fate had come upon my darling? There you have the missing clue to my action, Mr. Holmes."

"Proceed," said my friend.

Dr. Sterndale drew from his pocket a paper packet and laid it upon the table. On the outside was written "*Radix pedis diaboli*" with a red poison label beneath it. He pushed it towards me. "I understand that you are a doctor, sir. Have you ever heard of this preparation?"

"Devil's-foot root! No, I have never heard of it."

"It is no reflection upon your professional knowledge," said he, "for I believe that, save for one sample in a laboratory at Buda, there is no other specimen in Europe. It has not yet found its way either into the pharmacopoeia or into the literature of toxicology. The root is shaped like a foot, half human, half goatlike; hence the fanciful name given by a botanical missionary. It is used as an ordeal poison by the medicine-men in certain districts of West Africa and is kept as a secret among them. This particular specimen I obtained under very extraordinary circumstances in the Ubangi country." He opened the paper as he spoke and disclosed a heap of reddish-brown, snuff-like powder.

"Well, sir?" asked Holmes sternly.

"I am about to tell you, Mr. Holmes, all that actually occurred, for you already know so much that it is clearly to my interest that you should know all. I have already explained the relationship in which I stood to the Tregennis family. For the sake of the sister I was friendly with the brothers. There was a family quarrel about money which estranged this man Mortimer, but it was supposed to be made up, and I afterwards met him as I did the others. He was a sly, subtle, scheming man, and several things arose which gave me a suspicion of him, but I had no cause for any positive quarrel.

"One day, only a couple of weeks ago, he came down to my cottage and I showed him some of my African curiosities. Among other things I exhibited this powder, and I told him of its strange properties, how it stimulates those brain centres which control the emotion of fear, and how either madness or death is the fate of the unhappy native who is subjected to the ordeal by the priest of his tribe. I told him also how powerless European science would be to detect it. How he took it I cannot say, for I never left the room, but there is no doubt that it was then, while I was opening cabinets and stooping to boxes, that he managed to abstract some of the devil's-foot root. I well remember how he plied me with questions as to the amount and the time that was needed for its effect, but I little dreamed that he could have a personal reason for asking.

"I thought no more of the matter until the vicar's telegram reached me at Plymouth. This villain had thought that I would be at sea before the news could reach me, and that I should be lost for years in Africa. But I returned at once. Of course, I could not listen to the details without feeling assured that my poison had been used. I came round to see you on the chance that some other explanation had suggested itself to you. But there could be none. I was convinced that Mortimer Tregennis was the murderer; that for the sake of money, and with the idea, perhaps, that if the other members of his family were all insane he would be the sole guardian of their joint property, he had used the devil's-foot powder upon them, driven two of them out of their senses, and killed his sister Brenda, the one human being whom I have ever loved or who has ever loved me. There was his crime; what was to be his punishment?

"Should I appeal to the law? Where were my proofs? I knew that the facts were true, but could I help to make a jury of countrymen believe so fantastic a story? I might or I might not. But I could not afford to fail. My soul cried out for revenge. I have said to you once before, Mr. Holmes, that I have spent much of my life outside the law, and that I have come at last to be a law to myself. So it was now. I determined that the fate which he had given to others should be shared by himself. Either that or I would do justice upon him with my own hand. In all England there can be no man who sets less value upon his own life than I do at the present moment.

"Now I have told you all. You have yourself supplied the rest. I did, as you say, after a restless night, set off early from my cottage. I foresaw the difficulty of arousing him, so I gathered some gravel from the pile which you have mentioned, and I used it to throw up to his window. He came down and admitted me through the window of the sitting-room. I laid his offence before him. I told him that I had come both as judge and executioner. The wretch sank into a chair, paralyzed at the sight of my revolver. I lit the lamp, put the powder above it, and stood outside the window, ready to carry out my threat to shoot him should he try to leave the room. In five minutes he died. My God! how he died! But my heart was flint, for he endured nothing which my innocent darling had not felt before him. There is my story, Mr. Holmes. Perhaps, if you loved a woman, you would have done as much yourself. At any rate, I am in your hands. You can take what steps you like. As I have already said, there is no man living who can fear death less than I do."

Holmes sat for some little time in silence.

"What were your plans?" he asked at last.

"I had intended to bury myself in central Africa. My work there is but half finished."

"Go and do the other half," said Holmes. "I, at least, am not prepared to prevent you."

Dr. Sterndale raised his giant figure, bowed gravely, and walked from the arbour. Holmes lit his pipe and handed me his pouch.

"Some fumes which are not poisonous would be a welcome change," said he. "I think you must agree, Watson, that it is not a case in which we are called upon to interfere. Our investigation has been independent, and our action shall be so also. You would not denounce the man?"

"Certainly not," I answered.

"I have never loved, Watson, but if I did and if the woman I loved had met such an end, I might act even as our lawless lion-hunter has done. Who knows? Well, Watson, I will not offend your intelligence by explaining what is obvious. The gravel upon the window-sill was, of course, the starting-point of my research. It was unlike anything in the vicarage garden. Only when my attention had been drawn to Dr. Sterndale and his cottage did I find its counterpart. The lamp shining in broad daylight and the remains of powder upon the shield were successive links in a fairly obvious chain. And now, my dear Watson, I think we may dismiss the matter from our mind and go back with a clear conscience to the study of those Chaldean roots which are surely to be traced in the Cornish branch of the great Celtic speech."

A SCHOOLMASTER ABROAD

E. W. HORNUNG

Ernest William Hornung (1866–1921), known as 'Willie' to friends and family, was Arthur Conan Doyle's brother-in-law, and an accomplished author in his own right. Doyle described him as 'a Dr Johnson without the learning, but with a finer wit. No one could say a neater thing, and his writings, good as they are, never adequately represented the powers of the man, nor the quickness of his brain.' Today, Hornung is remembered as the creator of A. J. Raffles, the amateur cracksman, whose equivalent of Dr Watson is Harold 'Bunny' Manders, who had fagged for him when they were at public school.

The enduring popularity of the Raffles stories is deserved, but has obscured Hornung's other work. His detective characters included Stingaree the Bushranger (Hornung lived in Australia at one time) and Dr John Dollar, who ventures to Switzerland in this story. Dollar sees himself as a 'crime doctor', someone whose mission is to prevent crime by 'treating' prospective criminals by 'saving 'em from themselves while they're still worth saving'. This is a notion which, in different forms, continues to provoke interest. It is a pity that, after producing a single book about Dollar's cases, Hornung's literary career faltered due to a combination of bereavement and poor health. His work is still worth seeking out.

* * * * *

I

IT is a small world that flocks to Switzerland for the Christmas holidays. It is also a world largely composed of that particular class which really did provide Dr Dollar with the majority of his cases. He was therefore not surprised, on the night of his arrival at the great Excelsior Hotel, in Winterwald, to feel a diffident touch on the shoulder, and to look round upon the sunburnt blushes of a quite recent patient.

George Edenborough had taken Winterwald on his wedding trip, and nothing would suit him and his nut-brown bride but for the doctor to join them at their table. It was a slightly embarrassing invitation, but there was good reason for not persisting in a first refusal. And the bride carried the situation with a breezy vitality, while her groom chose a wine worthy of the occasion, and the newcomer explained that he had arrived by the afternoon train, but had not come straight to the hotel.

"Then you won't have heard of our great excitement," said Mrs Edenborough, "and I'm afraid you won't like it when you do."

"If you mean the strychnine affair," returned Dollar, with a certain deliberation, "I heard one version before I had been in the place an hour. I can't say that I did like it. But I should be interested to know what you both think about it all."

Edenborough returned the wine-list to the waiter with sepulchral injunctions.

"Are you telling him about our medical scandal?" he inquired briskly of the bride. "My dear doctor, it'll make your professional hair stand on end! Here's the local practitioner been prescribing strychnine pills warranted to kill in twenty minutes!"

"So I hear," said the crime doctor, drily.

"The poor brute has been frightfully overworked," continued Edenborough, in deference to a more phlegmatic front than he had expected of the British faculty. "They say he was up two whole nights last week; he seems to be the only doctor in the place, and the hotels are full of fellows doing their level best to lay themselves out. We've had two concussions of the brain and one complicated fracture this very week. Still, to go and give your patient a hundred times more strychnine than you intended——"

And he stopped himself, as though the subject, which he had taken up with a purely nervous zest, was rather near home after all.

"But what about his patient?" adroitly inquired the doctor. "If half that one hears is true, he wouldn't have been much loss."

"Not much, I'm afraid," said Lucy Edenborough, with the air of a Roman matron turning down her thumbs.

"He's a fellow who was at my private school, just barely twenty-one, and making an absolute fool of himself," explained Edenborough, touching his wine-glass. "It's an awful pity. He used to be such a nice little chap, Jack Laverick."

"He was nice enough when he was out here a year ago," the bride admitted, "and he's still a sportsman. He won half the toboggan races last season, and took it all delightfully; he's quite another person now, and gives himself absurd airs on top of everything else. Still, I shall expect Mr Laverick either to sweep the board or break his neck. He evidently wasn't born to be poisoned."

"Did he come to grief last year, Mrs Edenborough?"

"He only nearly had one of his ears cut off, in a spill on the ice-run. So they said; but he was tobogganing again the next day."

"Dr Alt looked after him all right then, I hear," added Eden-borough, as the champagne arrived. "But I only wish *you* could take the fellow in hand! He really used to be a decent chap, but it would take even you all your time to make him one again, Dr Dollar."

The crime doctor smiled as he raised his glass and returned compliments across the bubbles. It was the smile of a man with bigger fish to fry. Yet it was he who came back to the subject of young Laverick, asking if he had not a tutor or somebody to look after him, and what the man meant by not doing his job.

In an instant both the Edenboroughs had turned upon their friend. Poor Mr Scarth was not to blame! Poor Mr Scarth, it appeared, had been a master at the preparatory school at which Jack Laverick and George Edenborough had been boys. He was a splendid fellow, and very popular in the hotel, but there was nothing but sympathy with him in the matter under discussion. His charge was of age, and in a position to send him off at any moment, as indeed he was always threatening in his cups. But there again there was a special difficulty: one cup was more than enough for Jack Laverick, whose weak head for wine was the only excuse for him.

"Yet there was nothing of the kind last year," said Mrs Edenbor-ough, in a reversionary voice; "at least, one never heard of it. And that makes it all the harder on poor Mr Scarth."

Dollar declared that he was burning to meet the unfortunate gentleman; the couple exchanged glances, and he was told to wait till after the concert, at which he had better sit with them. Was there a concert? His face lengthened at the prospect, and the bride's eyes sparkled at his expense. She would not hear of his shirking it, but went so far as to cut dinner short in order to obtain good seats. She was one of those young women who have both a will and a way with them, and Dollar soon found himself securely penned in the gallery of an ambitious ball-room with a stage at the other end.

The concert came up to his most sardonic expectations, and he resigned himself to a boredom only intensified by the behaviour of some crude humorists in the rows behind. Indifferent song followed indifferent song, and each earned a more vociferous encore from those gay young gods. A not unknown novelist told dialect stories of purely territorial interest; a lady recited with astounding spirit; another fiddled, no less courageously; but the back rows of the gallery were quite out of hand when a black-avised gentleman took the stage, and had not opened his mouth before those back rows were rows of Satans reproving sin and clapping with unsophisticated gusto.

"Who's this?" asked Dollar, instantly aware of the change behind him; but even Lucy Edenborough would only answer, "Hush, doctor!" as she bent forward with shining eyes. And certainly a hairpin could not have dropped unheard before the dark performer relieved the tension by plunging into a scene from *Pickwick*.

It was the scene of Mr Jingle's monologue on the Rochester coach—and the immortal nonsense was inimitably given. Yet nobody could have been less like the emaciated prototype than this tall tanned man, with the short black moustache, and the flashing teeth that bit off every word with ineffable snap and point.

"Mother—tall lady, eating sandwiches—forgot the arch—crash—knock—children look round—mother's head off—sandwich in her hand—no mouth to put it in——" and his own grim one only added to the fun and swelled the roar.

He waited darkly for them to stop, the wilful absence of any amusement on his side enormously increasing that of the audience. But when it came to the episode of Donna Christina and the stomach-pump, with the culminating discovery of Don Bolaro Fizzgig in the main pipe of the public fountain, the guffaws of half the house eventually drew from the other half the supreme compliment of exasperated demands for silence. Mrs George Edenborough was one of the loudest offenders. George himself had to wipe his eyes. And the crime doctor had forgotten that there was such a thing as crime.

"That chap's a genius! " he exclaimed, when a double encore had been satisfied by further and smaller doses of Mr Jingle, artfully held in reserve. "But who is he, Mrs Edenborough?"

"Poor Mr Scarth!" crowed the bride, brimming over with triumphant fun.

But the doctor's mirth was at an end.

"That the fellow who can't manage a bit of a boy, when he can hold an audience like this in the hollow of his hand?"

And at first he looked as though he could not believe it, and then all at once as though he could. But by this time the Edenboroughs were urging Scarth's poverty in earnest, and Dollar could only say that he wanted to meet him more than ever.

The wish was not to be gratified without a further sidelight and a fresh surprise. As George and the doctor were repairing to the billiard-room, before the conclusion of the lengthy programme, they found a group of backs upon the threshold, and a ribald uproar in full swing within. One voice was in the ascendant, and it was sadly indistinct; but it was also the voice of the vanquished, belching querulous futilities. The cold steel thrusts of an auto-cratic Jingle cut it shorter and shorter. It ceased altogether, and the men in the doorway made way for Mr Scarth, as he hurried a dishevelled youth off the scene in the most approved constabulary manner.

"Does it often happen, George?" Dollar's arm had slipped through his former patient's as they slowly followed at their distance.

"Most nights, I'm afraid."

"And does Scarth always do what he likes with him—after-wards?"

"Always; he's the sort of fellow who can do what he likes with most people," declared the young man, missing the point. "You should have seen him at the last concert, when those fools behind us behaved even worse than tonight! It wasn't his turn, but he came out and put them right in about a second, and had us all laughing the next! It was just the same at school; everybody was afraid of Mostyn Scarth, boys and men alike; and so is Jack Laverick still—in spite of being of age and having the money-bags—as you saw for yourself just now."

"Yet he lets this sort of thing happen continually?"

"It's pretty difficult to prevent. A glass about does it, as I told you, and you can't be at a fellow's elbow all the time in a place like this. But some of Jack's old pals have had a go at him. Do you know what they've done? They've taken away his Old Etonian tie, and quite right too!"

"And there was nothing of all this last year?"

"So Lucy says. I wasn't here. Mrs Laverick was, by the way; she may have made the difference. But being his own master seems to have sent him to the dogs altogether. Scarth's the only person to pull him up, unless—unless you'd take him on, doctor! You—you've pulled harder cases out of the fire, you know!"

They had been sitting a few minutes in the lounge. Nobody was very near them; the young man's face was alight and his eyes shining. Dollar took him by the arm once more, and they went together to the lift.

"In any case I must make friends with your friend Scarth," said he. "Do you happen to know his number?"

Edenborough did—it was 144—but he seemed dubious as to another doctor's reception after the tragedy that might have happened in the adjoining room.

"Hadn't I better introduce you in the morning?" he suggested with much deference in the lift. "I—I hate repeating things—but I want you to like each other, and I heard Scarth say he was fed up with doctors!"

This one smiled.

"I don't wonder at it."

"Yet it wasn't Mostyn Scarth who gave Dr Alt away."

"No?"

Edenborough shook his head as they left the lift together. "No, doctor. It was the chemist here, a chap called Schickel; but for him, Jack Laverick would be a dead man; and but for him again, nobody need ever have heard of his narrow shave. He spotted the mistake, and then started all the gossip."

"I know," said the doctor, nodding.

"But it was a terrible mistake! Decigrams instead of milligrams, so I heard. Just a hundred times too much strychnine in each pill."

"You are quite right," said John Dollar quietly. "I have the prescription in my pocket."

"*You* have, doctor?"

"Don't be angry with me, my dear fellow! I told you I had heard one version of the whole thing. It was Alt's. He's an old friend—but you wouldn't have said a word about him if I had told you that at first—and I still don't want it generally known."

"You can trust me, doctor, after all you've done for me."

"Well, Alt once did more for me. I want to do something for him, that's all."

And his knuckles still ached from the young man's grip as they rapped smartly at the door of No. 144.

II

It was opened a few inches by Mostyn Scarth. His raiment was still at concert pitch, but his face even darker than it had been as the crime doctor saw it last.

"May I ask who you are and what you want?" he demanded—not at all in the manner of Mr Jingle—rather in the voice that most people would have raised.

"My name's Dollar and I'm a doctor."

The self-announcement, pat as a polysyllable, had a foreseen effect only minimised by the precautionary confidence of Dr Dollar's manner.

"Thanks very much. I've had about enough of doctors."

And the door was shutting when the intruder got in a word like a wedge.

"Exactly!"

Scarth frowned through a chink just wide enough to show both his eyes. It was the intruder's tone that held his hand.

"What does that mean?" he demanded with more control.

"That I want to see you about the other doctor—this German fellow," returned Dollar, against the grain. But the studious phrase admitted him.

"Well, don't raise your voice," said Scarth, lowering his own as he shut the door softly behind them. "I believe I saw you downstairs outside the bar. So I need only explain that I've just got my bright young man off to sleep, on the other side of those folding doors."

Dollar could not help wondering whether the other room was as good as Scarth's, which was much bigger and better appointed than his own. But he sat down at the oval table under the electrolier, and came abruptly to his point.

"About that prescription," he began, and straightway produced it from his pocket.

"Well, what about it?" the other queried, but only keenly, as he sat down at the table, too.

"Dr Alt is a very old friend of mine, Mr Scarth."

Mostyn Scarth exhibited the slight but immediate change of front due from gentleman to gentleman on the strength of such a statement. His grim eyes softened with a certain sympathy; but the accession left his gravity the more pronounced.

"He is not only a friend," continued Dollar, "but the cleverest and best man I know in my profession. I don't speak from mere loyalty; he was my own doctor before he was my friend. Mr Scarth, he saved more than my life when every head in Harley Street had been shaken over my case. All the baronets gave me up; but chance or fate brought me here, and this little unknown man performed the miracle they shirked, and made a new man of me off his own bat. I wanted him to come to London and make his fortune; but his work was here, he wouldn't leave it; and here I find him under this sorry cloud. Can you wonder at my wanting to step in and speak up for him, Mr Scarth?"

"On the contrary, I know exactly how you must feel, and am very glad you have spoken," rejoined Mostyn Scarth, cordially enough in all the circumstances of the case. "But the cloud is none of my making, Dr Dollar, though I naturally feel rather strongly about the matter. But for Schickel, the chemist, I might be seeing a coffin to England at this moment! He's the man who found out the mistake, and has since made all the mischief."

"Are you sure it was a mistake, Mr Scarth?" asked Dollar quietly.

"What else?" cried the other, in blank astonishment. "Even Schickel has never suggested that Dr Alt was trying to commit a murder!"

"Even Schickel!" repeated Dollar, with a sharp significance. "Are you suggesting that there's no love lost between him and Alt?"

"I was not, indeed!" Scarth seemed still more astonished. "No. That never occurred to me for a moment."

"Yet it's a small place, and you know what small places are. Would one man be likely to spread a thing like this against another if there were no bad blood between them?"

Scarth could not say. The thing happened to be true, and it made such a justifiable sensation. He was none the less frankly interested in the suggestion. It was as though he had a tantalising glimmer of the crime doctor's meaning. Their heads were closer together across the end of the table, their eyes joined in mutual probation.

"Can I trust you with my own idea, Mr Scarth?"

"That's for you to decide, Dr Dollar."

"I shall not breathe it to another soul—not even to Alt himself—till I am sure."

"You may trust me, doctor. I don't know what's coming, but I sha'n't give it away."

"Then I shall trust you even to the extent of contradicting what I just said. I *am* sure—between ourselves—that the prescription now in my hands is a clever forgery."

Scarth held out his hand for it. A less deliberate announcement might have given him a more satisfactory surprise; but he could not have looked more incredulous than he did, or subjected Dollar to a cooler scrutiny.

"A forgery with what object, Dr Dollar?"

"That I don't pretend to say. I merely state the fact—in confidence. You have your eyes upon a flagrant forgery."

Scarth raised them twinkling. "My dear Dr Dollar, I saw him write it out myself!"

"Are you quite sure?"

"Absolutely, doctor. This lad, Jack Laverick, is a pretty handful; without a doctor to frighten him from time to time, I couldn't cope with him at all. His people are in despair about him—but that's another matter. I was only going to say that I took him to Dr Alt myself, and this is the prescription they refused to make up. Schickel may have a spite against Alt, as you suggest, but if he's a forger I can only say he doesn't look the part."

"The only looks I go by," said the crime doctor, "are those of the little document in your hand."

"It's on Alt's paper."

"Anybody could get hold of that."

"But you suggest that Alt and Schickel have been on bad terms?"

"That's a better point, Mr Scarth, that's a much better point," said Dollar, smiling and then ceasing to smile as he produced a magnifying lens. "Allow me to switch on the electric standard, and do me the favour of examining that handwriting with this loop; it's not very strong, but the best I could get here at the photographer's shop."

"It's certainly not strong enough to show anything fishy, to my inexperience," said Scarth, on a sufficiently close inspection.

"Now look at this one."

Dollar had produced, a second prescription from the same pocket as before. At first sight they seemed identical.

"Is this another forgery?" inquired Scarth, with a first faint trace of irony.

"No. That's the correct prescription, rewritten by Alt, at my request, as he is positive he wrote it originally."

"I see now. There are two more noughts mixed up with the other hieroglyphs."

"They happen to make all the difference between life and death," said Dollar, gravely. "Yet they are not by any means the only difference here."

"I can see no other, I must confess." And Scarth raised stolid eyes to meet Dollar's steady gaze.

"The other difference is, Mr Scarth, that the prescription with the strychnine in deadly decigrams has been drawn backwards instead of being written forwards."

Scarth's stare ended in a smile.

"Do you mind saying all that again, Dr Dollar?"

"I'll elaborate it. The genuine prescription has been written in the ordinary way—*currente calamo*. But forgeries are not written in the ordinary way, much less with running pens; the best of them are written backwards, or rather they are *drawn upside down*. Try to copy writing *as* writing, and your own will automatically creep in and spoil it; draw it upside down and wrong way on, as a mere meaningless scroll, and your own formation of the letters doesn't influence you, because you are not forming letters at all. You are drawing from a copy, Mr Scarth."

"You mean that I'm deriving valuable information from a hand-writing expert," cried Scarth, with another laugh.

"There are no such experts," returned Dollar, a little coldly. "It's all a mere matter of observation, open to everybody with eyes to see. But this happens to be an old forger's trick; try it for yourself, as I have, and you'll be surprised to see how much there is in it."

"I must," said Scarth. "But I can't conceive how you can tell that it has been played in this case."

"No? Look at the start, 'Herr Laverick,' and at the finish, 'Dr Alt.' You would expect to see plenty of ink in the 'Herr' wouldn't you? Still plenty in the 'Laverick,' I think, but now less and less until the pen is filled again. In the correct prescription, written at my request to-day, you will find that this is so. In the forgery the progression is precisely the reverse; the *t* in 'Alt' is full of ink, but you will find less and less till the next dip in the middle of the word 'Mahlzeit' in the line above. The forger, of course, dips oftener than the man with the running pen."

Scarth bent in silence over the lens, his dark face screwed awry. Suddenly he pushed back his chair.

"It's wonderful!" he cried softly. "I see everything you say. Dr Dollar, you have converted me to your view. I should like you to allow me to convert the hotel."

"Not yet," said Dollar rising, "if at all as to the actual facts of the case. It's no use making bad worse, Mr Scarth, or taking a dirty trick too seriously. It isn't as though the forgery had been committed with a view to murdering your young Laverick."

"I never dreamt of thinking that it was!"

"You are quite right, Mr Scarth. It doesn't bear thinking about. Of course, any murderer ingenious enough to concoct such a thing would have been far too clever to drop out *two* noughts; he would have been content to change the milligrams into centigrams, and risk a recovery. No sane chemist would have dispensed the pills in decigrams. But we are getting off the facts, and I promised to meet Dr Alt on his last round. If I may tell him, in vague terms, that

you at least think there may have been some mistake, other than
the culpable one that has been laid at his door, I shall go away less
uneasy about my unwarrantable intrusion than I can assure you
I was in making it."

It was strange how the balance of personality had shifted during an interview which Scarth himself was now eager to extend.
He was no longer the mesmeric martinet who had tamed an
unruly audience at sight; the last of Mr Jingle's snap had long been
in abeyance. And yet there was just one more suggestion of that
immortal, in the rather dilapidated trunk from which the swarthy
exquisite now produced a bottle of whisky, very properly locked
up out of Laverick's reach. And weakness of will could not be
imputed to the young man who induced John Dollar to cement
their acquaintance with a thimbleful.

III

It was early morning in the same week; the crime doctor lay
brooding over the most complicated case that had yet come his
way. More precisely it was two cases, but so closely related that
it took a strong mind to consider them apart, a stronger will to
confine each to the solitary brain-cell that it deserved. Yet the case
of young Laverick was not only much the simpler of the two, but
infinitely the more congenial to John Dollar, and not the one most
on his nerves.

It was too simple altogether. A year ago the boy had been all
right, wild only as a tobogganer, lucky to have got off with a
few stitches in his ear. Dollar heard all about that business from
Dr Alt, and only too much about Jack Laverick's subsequent

record from other informants. It was worthy of the Welbeck Street confessional. His career at Oxford had come to a sudden ignominious end. He had forfeited his motoring licence for habitually driving to the public danger, and on the last occasion had barely escaped imprisonment for his condition at the wheel. He had caused his own mother to say advisedly that she would "sooner see him in his coffin than going on in this dreadful way"; in writing she had said it, for Scarth had shown the letter addressed to him as her "last and only hope" for Jack; and yet even Scarth was powerless to prevent that son of Belial from getting "flown with insolence and wine" more nights than not. Even last night it had happened, at the masked ball, on the eve of this morning's races! Whose fault would it be if he killed himself on the ice-run after all?

Dollar writhed as he thought upon this case; yet it was not the case that had brought him out from England, not the reason of his staying out longer than he had dreamt of doing when Alt's telegram arrived. It was not, indeed, about Jack Laverick that poor Alt had telegraphed at all. And yet between them what a job they could have made of the unfortunate youth!

It was Dollar's own case over again—yet he had not been called in—neither of them had!

Nevertheless, when all was said that could be said to himself, or even to Alt—who did not quite agree—Laverick's was much the less serious matter; and John Dollar had turned upon the other side, and was grappling afresh with the other case, when his door opened violently without a knock, and an agitated voice spoke his name.

"It's me—Edenborough," it continued in a hurried whisper. "I want you to get into some clothes and come up to the ice-run as quick as possible!"

"Why? What has happened?" asked the doctor, jumping out of bed as Edenborough drew the curtains.

"Nothing yet. I hope nothing will——"

"But something has!" interrupted the doctor. "What's the matter with your eye?"

"I'll tell you as you dress, only be as quick as you can. Did you forget it was the toboggan races this morning? They're having them at eight instead of nine, because of the sun, and it's ten to eight now. Couldn't you get into some knickerbockers and stick a sweater over all the rest? That's what I've done—wish I'd come to you first! They'll *want* a doctor if we don't make haste!"

"I wish you'd tell me about your eye," said Dollar, already in his stockings.

"My eye's all right," returned Edenborough, going to the glass. "No, by Jove, it's blacker than I thought, and my head's still singing like a kettle. I shouldn't have thought Laverick could hit so hard— drunk *or* sober."

"That madman?" cried Dollar, looking up from his laces. "I thought he turned in early for once?"

"He was up early, anyhow," said Edenborough, grimly; "but I'll tell you the whole thing as we go up to the run, and I don't much mind who hears me. He's a worse hat even than we thought. I caught him tampering with the toboggans at five o'clock this morning!"

"Which toboggans?"

"One of the lot they keep in a shed just under our window, at the back of the hotel. I was lying awake and I heard something. It was like a sort of filing, as if somebody was breaking in somewhere. I got up and looked out, and thought I saw a light. Lucy was fast asleep; she is still, by the way, and doesn't know a thing."

"I'm ready," said Dollar. "Go on when we get outside."

It was a very pale blue morning, not a scintilla of sunlight in the valley, neither shine nor shadow upon clambering forest or overhanging rocks. Somewhere behind their jagged peaks the sun must have risen, but as yet no snowy facet winked the news to Winterwald, and the softer summits lost all character against a sky only less white than themselves.

The village street presented no difficulties to Edenborough's gouties and the doctor's hobnails; but there were other people in it, and voices travel in a frost over silent snow. On the frozen path between the snowfields, beyond the village, nails were not enough, and the novice depending upon them stumbled and slid as the elaborated climax of Edenborough's experience induced even more speed.

"It was him all right—try the edge, doctor, it's less slippy. It was that little brute in his domino, as if he'd never been to bed at all, and me in my dressing-gown not properly awake. We should have looked a funny pair in——have my arm, doctor."

"Thanks, George."

"But his electric lamp was the only light. He didn't attempt to put it out. 'Just tuning up my toboggan,' he whispered. 'Come and have a look.' I didn't and don't believe it was his own toboggan; it was probably that Captain Strong's, he's his most dangerous rival; but, as I tell you, I was just going to look when the young brute hit me full in the face without a moment's warning. I went over like an ox, but I think the back of my head must have hit something. There was daylight in the place when I opened the only eye I could."

"Had he locked you in?"

"No; he was too fly for that; but I simply couldn't move till I heard voices coming, and then I only crawled behind a stack of garden chairs and things. It was Strong and another fellow—they did curse to find the whole place open! I nearly showed up and told my tale, only I wanted to tell you first."

"I'm glad you have, George."

"I knew your interest in the fellow—besides, I thought it was a case for you," said George Edenborough simply. "But it kept me prisoner till the last of the toboggans had been taken out—I only hope it hasn't made us too late!"

His next breath was a devout thanksgiving, as a fold in the glistening slopes showed the top of the ice-run, and a group of men in sweaters standing out against the fir-trees on the crest. They seemed to be standing very still. Some had their padded elbows lifted as though they were shading their eyes. But there was no sign of a toboggan starting, no sound of one in the invisible crevice of the run. And now man after man detached himself from the group, and came leaping down the subsidiary snow-track meant only for ascent.

But John Dollar and George Edenborough did not see all of this. A yet more ominous figure had appeared in their own path, had grown into Mostyn Scarth, and stood wildly beckoning to them both.

"It's Jack!" he shouted across the snow. "He's had a smash—self and toboggan—flaw in a runner. I'm afraid he's broken his leg."

"Only his leg!" cried Dollar, but not with the least accent of relief. The tone made Edenborough wince behind him, and Scarth in front look round. It was as though even the crime doctor thought Jack Laverick better dead.

He lay on a litter of overcoats, the hub of a wheel of men that broke of itself before the first doctor on the scene. He was not even insensible, neither was he uttering moan or groan; but his white lips were drawn away from his set teeth, and his left leg had an odd look of being no more a part of him than its envelope of knicker-bocker and stocking.

"It's a bu'st, doctor, I'm afraid," the boy ground out as Dollar knelt in the snow. "Hurting? A bit—but I can stick it."

Courage was the one quality he had not lost during the last year; nobody could have shown more during the slow and excruciating progress to the village, on a bobsleigh carried by four stumbling men; everybody was whispering about it. Everybody but the crime doctor, who headed the little procession with a face in keeping with the tone which had made Edenborough wince and Scarth look round.

The complex case of the night—this urgent one—both were forgotten for Dollar's own case of years ago. He was back again in another Winterwald, another world. It was no longer a land of Christmas-trees growing out of mountains of Christmas cake; the snow melted before his mind's eye; he was hugging the shadows in a street of toy-houses yielding resin to an August sun, between green slopes combed with dark pines, under a sky of intolerable blue. And he was in despair; all Harley Street could or would do nothing for him. And then—and then—some forgotten ache or pain had taken him to the little man—the great man—down this very turning to the left, in the little wooden house tucked away behind the shops.

How he remembered every landmark—the handrail down the slope—the little porch—the bare stairs, his own ladder between death and life—the stark surgery with its uncompromising appliances in full view! And now at last he was there with such another case as his own—with the minor case that he had yet burned to bring there—and there was Alt to receive them in the same white jacket and with the same simple countenance as of old!

They might have taken him on to the hotel, as Scarth indeed urged strongly; but the boy himself was against another yard, though otherwise a hero to the end.

"Chloroform?" he cried faintly. "Can't I have my beastly leg set without chloroform? You're not going to have it off, are you? I can stick anything short of that."

The two doctors retired for the further consideration of a point on which they themselves were not of one mind.

"It's the chance of our lives, and the one chance for him," urged Dollar vehemently. "It isn't as if it were such a dangerous operation, and I'll take sole responsibility."

"But I am not sure you have been right," demurred the other. "He has not even had concussion, a year ago. It has been only the ear."

"There's a lump behind it still. Everything dates from when it happened; there's some pressure somewhere that has made another being of him. It's a much simpler case than mine, and you cured *me*. Alt, if you had seen how his own mother wrote about him, you would be the very last man to hesitate!"

"It is better to have her consent."

"No—nobody's—the boy himself need never know. There's a young bride here who'll nurse him like an angel and hold her tongue till doomsday. She and her husband may be in the secret, but not another soul!"

And when Jack Laverick came out of chloroform, to feel a frosty tickling under the tabernacle of bedclothes in which his broken bone was as the Ark, the sensation was less uncomfortable than he expected. But that of a dull deep pain in the head drew his first complaint, as an item not in the estimate.

"What's my head all bandaged up for?" he demanded, fingering the turban on the pillow.

"Didn't you know it was broken, too?" said Lucy Edenborough gravely. "I expect your leg hurt so much more that you never noticed it."

IV

Ten days later Mostyn Scarth called at Doctor Alt's, to ask if he mightn't see Jack at last. He had behaved extremely well about the whole affair; others in his position might easily have made trouble. But there had been no concealment of the fact that injuries were not confined to the broken leg, and the mere seat of the additional mischief was enough for a man of sense. It is not the really strong who love to display their power. Scarth not only accepted the situation, but voluntarily conducted the correspondence which kept poor Mrs Laverick at half Europe's length over the critical period. He had merely stipulated to be the first to see the convalescent, and he took it as well as ever when Dollar shook his head once more.

"It's not our fault this time, Mr Scarth. You must blame the sex that is privileged to change its mind. Mrs Laverick has arrived without a word of warning. She is with her son at this moment, and you'll be glad to hear that she thinks she finds him an absolutely changed character—or, rather, what he was before he ever saw Winterwald a year ago. I may say that this seems more or less the patient's own impression about himself."

"Glad!" cried Scarth, who for the moment had seemed rather staggered. "I'm more than glad; I'm profoundly relieved! It doesn't matter now whether I see Jack or not. Do you mind giving him these magazines and papers, with my love? I am thankful that my responsibility's at an end."

"The same with me," returned the crime doctor. "I shall go back to my work in London with a better conscience than I had when I left it—with something accomplished—something undone that wanted undoing."

He smiled at Scarth across the flap of an unpretentious table, on which lay the literary offering in all its glory of green and yellow wrappers; and Scarth looked up without a trace of pique, but with an answering twinkle in his own dark eyes.

"Alt exalted—restored to favour—Jack reformed character—born again—forger forgotten—forging ahead, eh?"

It was his best Mr Jingle manner; indeed, a wonderfully ready and ruthless travesty of his own performance on the night of Dollar's arrival. And that kindred critic enjoyed it none the less for a second strain of irony, which he could not but take to himself.

"I have not forgotten anybody, Mr Scarth."

"But have you discovered who did the forgery?"

"I always knew."

"Have you tackled him?"

"Days ago!"

Scarth looked astounded. "And what's to happen to him, doctor?"

"I don't know." The doctor gave a characteristic shrug. "It's not my job; as it was I'd done all the detective business, which I loathe."

"I remember," cried Scarth. "I shall never forget the way you went through that prescription, as though you had been looking over the blighter's shoulder! Not an expert—modest fellow— pride that apes!"

And again Dollar had to laugh at the way Mr Jingle wagged his head, in spite of the same slightly caustic undercurrent as before.

"That was the easiest part of it," he answered, "although you make me blush to say so. The hard part was what reviewers of novels call the 'motivation.'"

"But you had that in Schickel's spite against Alt."

"It was never quite strong enough to please me."

"Then what was the motive, doctor?"

"Young Laverick's death."

"Nonsense!"

"I wish it were, Mr Scarth."

"But who is there in Winterwald who could wish to compass such a thing?"

"There were more than two thousand visitors over Christmas, I understand," was the only reply.

It would not do for Mostyn Scarth. He looked less than politely incredulous, if not less shocked and rather more indignant than he need have looked. But the whole idea was a reflection upon his care of the unhappy youth. And he said so in other words, which resembled those of Mr Jingle only in their stiff staccato brevity.

"Talk about 'motivation'!—I thank you, doctor, for that word— but I should thank you even more to show me the thing itself in your theory. And what a way to kill a fellow! What a roundabout, risky way!"

"It was such a good forgery," observed the doctor, "that even Alt himself could hardly swear that it was one."

"Is *he* your man?" asked Scarth, in a sudden whisper, leaning forward with lighted eyes.

The crime doctor smiled enigmatically. "It's perhaps just as lucky for him, Scarth, that at least he could have had nothing to do with the second attempt upon his patient's life."

"What second attempt?"

"The hand that forged the prescription, Scarth, with intent to poison young Laverick, was the one that also filed the flaw in his toboggan, in the hopes of breaking his neck."

"My dear doctor," exclaimed Mostyn Scarth, with a pained shake of the head, "this is stark, staring madness!"

"I only hope it was—in the would-be murderer," rejoined Dollar gravely. "But he had a lot of method: he even did his bit of filing—a burglar couldn't have done it better—in the domino Jack Laverick had just taken off!"

"How do you know he had taken it off? How do you know the whole job wasn't one of Jack's drunken tricks?"

"What whole job?"

"The one you're talking about—the alleged tampering with his toboggan," replied Scarth, impatiently.

"Oh! I only thought you meant something more." Dollar made a pause. "Don't you feel it rather hot in here, Scarth?"

"Do you know, I do!" confessed the visitor, as though it were Dollar's house and breeding had forbidden him to volunteer the remark. "It's the heat of this stove, with the window shut. Thanks so much, doctor!"

And he wiped his strong, brown, beautifully shaven face; it was one of those that require shaving more than once a day, yet it was always glossy from the razor; and he burnished it afresh with a silk handkerchief that would have passed through a packing-needle's eye.

"And what are you really doing about this—monster?" he resumed, as one who should accept the monster's existence for the sake of argument.

"Nothing, Scarth."

"Nothing? You intend to do nothing at all?"

Scarth had started, for the first time; but he started to his feet, while he was about it, as though in overpowering disgust.

"Not if he keeps out of England," replied the crime doctor, who had also risen. "I wonder if he's sane enough for that?"

Their four eyes met in a protracted scrutiny, without a flicker on either side.

"What I am wondering," said Scarth deliberately, "is whether this Frankenstein effort of yours exists outside your own imagination, Dr Dollar."

"Oh! he exists all right," declared the doctor. "But I am charitable enough to suppose him mad—in spite of his method *and* his motive."

"Did he tell you what that was?" asked Scarth with a sneer.

"No; but Jack did. He seems to have been in the man's power—under his influence—to an extraordinary degree. He had even left him a wicked sum in a will made since he came of age. I needn't tell you that he has now made another, revoking——"

"No, you need not!" cried Mostyn Scarth, turning livid at the last moment. "I've heard about enough of your mares' nests and mythical monsters. I wish you good morning, and a more credulous audience next time."

"That I can count upon," returned the doctor at the door. "There's no saying what they won't believe—at Scotland Yard!"

MURDER!

ARNOLD BENNETT

Arnold Bennett (1867–1931) was one of those authors – Hugh Walpole, who also dabbled in fictional crime, was another – who achieve fame during their lifetime, only for their posthumous reputation to fade. A literary feud with Virginia Woolf, together with a commercial attitude that led him to write too much too quickly, were partly to blame for Bennett's fall from critical favour. His name ultimately became better known through its association with an omelette created in his honour by the Savoy Hotel, a favourite haunt.

Happily, in recent years Bennett's work has benefited from re-evaluation, and a new generation of readers has come to appreciate the quality of his best work. Novels such as *Anna of the Five Towns* and *The Card* were set in his native Potteries, but he enjoyed travelling, and lived in Paris for several years. Bennett reviewed detective fiction, and touched on the crime genre in his own work, as in *The Grand Babylon Hotel* and *The Loot of the Cities*. The latter features Cecil Thorold, who is like A. J. Raffles a wealthy rogue – a millionaire who swindles the rich. Here we have an enjoyable example of a popular sub-genre, the seaside crime story.

* * * * *

1

Many great ones of the earth have justified murder as a social act, defensible and even laudable in certain instances. There is something to be said for murder, though perhaps not much. All of us, or nearly all of us, have at one time or another had the desire and the impulse to commit murder. At any rate, murder is not an uncommon affair. On an average, two people are murdered every week in England, and probably about two hundred every week in the United States. And forty per cent of the murderers are not brought to justice. These figures take no account of the undoubtedly numerous cases where murder has been done but never suspected. Murders and murderesses walk safely abroad among us, and it may happen to us to shake hands with them. A disturbing thought! But such is life, and such is homicide.

2

Two men, named respectively Lomax Harder and John Franting, were walking side by side one autumn afternoon on the Marine Parade of the seaside resort and port of Quangate on the Channel coast. Both were well dressed and had the air of moderate wealth, and both were about thirty-five years of age. At this point the resemblances between them ceased. Lomax Harder had refined features, an enormous forehead, fair hair and a delicate, almost apologetic manner. John Franting was low-browed, heavy chinned, scowling, defiant, indeed what is called a tough customer. Lomax Harder corresponded in appearance with the popular notion of a poet – save that he was carefully barbered. He was in fact a poet, and not unknown in the tiny, trifling, mad world where poetry is a matter of first-rate interest. John Franting corresponded in appearance with the popular notion of a gambler, an amateur boxer and, in spare time, a deluder of women. Popular notions sometimes fit the truth.

Lomax Harder, somewhat nervously buttoning his overcoat, said in a quiet but firm and insistent tone: 'Haven't you got anything to say?'

John Franting stopped suddenly in front of a shop whose facade bore the sign: 'Gontle – Gunsmith'.

'Not in words,' answered Franting. 'I'm going in here.' And he brusquely entered the small, shabby shop.

Lomax Harder hesitated half a second, and then followed his companion.

The shopman was a middle-aged gentleman wearing a black velvet coat.

'Good-afternoon,' he greeted Franting, with an expression and in a tone of urbane condescension which seemed to indicate that Franting was a wise as well as a fortunate man in that he knew of the excellence of Gontle's and had the wit to come into Gontle's.

For the name of Gontle was favourably and respectfully known wherever triggers are pressed. Not only along the whole length of the Channel coast but throughout England was Gontle's renowned. Sportsmen would travel to Quangate from the far north, and even from London, to buy guns. To say: 'I bought it at Gontle's,' or, 'Old Gontle recommended it,' was sufficient to silence any dispute concerning the merits of a firearm. Experts bowed the head before the unique reputation of Gontle. As for old Gontle, he was extremely and pardonably conceited. His conviction that no other gunsmith in the wide world could compare with him was absolute. He sold guns and rifles with the gesture of a monarch conferring an honour. He never argued; he stated; and the customer who contradicted him was as likely as not to be courteously and icily informed by Gontle of the geographical situation of the shop-door. Such shops exist in the English provinces, and nobody knows how they have achieved their renown. They could exist nowhere else.

'd-afternoon,' said Franting gruffly, and paused.

'What can I do for you?' asked Mr Gontle, as if saying: 'Now don't be afraid. This shop is tremendous, and I am tremendous; but I shall not eat you.'

'I want a revolver,' Franting snapped.

'Ah! A revolver!' commented Mr Gontle, as if saying: 'A gun or a rifle, yes! But a revolver – an arm without individuality, manufactured wholesale! ... However, I suppose I must deign to accommodate you.'

'I presume you know something about revolvers?' asked Mr Gontle, as he began to produce the weapons.

'A little.'

'Do you know the Webley Mark III?'

'Can't say that I do.'

'Ah! It is the best for all common purposes.' And Mr Gontle's glance said: 'Have the goodness not to tell me it isn't.'

Franting examined the Webley Mark III.

'You see,' said Mr Gontle, 'the point about it is that until the breach is properly closed it cannot be fired. So that it can't blow open and maim or kill the would-be murderer.' Mr Gontle smiled archly at one of his oldest jokes.

'What about suicides?' Franting grimly demanded.

'Ah!'

'You might show me just how to load it,' said Franting.

Mr Gontle, having found ammunition, complied with this reasonable request.

'The barrel's a bit scratched,' said Franting.

Mr Gontle inspected the scratch with pain. He would have denied the scratch, but could not.

'Here's another one,' said he, 'since you're so particular.' He simply had to put customers in their place.

'You might load it,' said Franting.

Mr Gontle loaded the second revolver.

'I'd like to try it,' said Franting.

'Certainly,' said Mr Gontle, and led Franting out of the shop by the back exit and down to a cellar where revolvers could be experimented with.

Lomax Harder was now alone in the shop. He hesitated a long time and then picked up the revolver rejected by Franting, fingered it, put it down, and picked it up again. The back-door of the shop opened suddenly, and startled, Harder dropped the revolver into his overcoat pocket: a thoughtless, quite unpremeditated act. He dared not remove the revolver. The revolver was as fast in his pocket as though the pocket had been sewn up.

'And cartridges?' asked Mr Gontle of Franting.

'Oh,' said Franting, 'I've only had one shot. Five'll be more than enough for the present. What does it weigh?'

'Let me see. Four-inch barrel? Yes. One pound four ounces.'

Franting paid for the revolver, receiving thirteen shillings in change from a five-pound note, and strode out of the shop, weapon in hand. He was gone before Lomax Harder decided upon a course of action.

'And for you, sir?' said Mr Gontle, addressing the poet.

Harder suddenly comprehended that Mr Gontle had mistaken him for a separate customer, who had happened to enter the shop a moment after the first one. Harder and Franting had said not a word to one another during the purchase, and Harder well knew that in the most exclusive shops it is the custom utterly to ignore a second customer until the first one has been dealt with.

'I want to see some foils.' Harder spoke stammeringly the only words that came into his head.

'Foils!' exclaimed Mr Gontle, shocked, as if to say: 'Is it conceivable that you should imagine that I, Gontle, gunsmith, sell such things as foils?'

After a little talk Harder apologised and departed – a thief.

'I'll call later and pay the fellow,' said Harder to his restive conscience. 'No. I can't do that. I'll send him some anonymous postal orders.'

He crossed the Parade and saw Franting, a small left-handed figure all alone far below on the deserted sands, pointing the revolver. He thought that his ear caught the sound of a discharge, but the distance was too great for him to be sure. He continued to watch, and at length Franting walked westward diagonally across the beach.

'He's going back to the Bellevue,' thought Harder, the Bellevue being the hotel from which he had met Franting coming out half an hour earlier. He strolled slowly towards the white hotel. But

Franting, who had evidently come up the face of the cliff in the penny lift, was before him. Harder, standing outside, saw Franting seated in the lounge. Then Franting rose and vanished down a long passage at the rear of the lounge. Harder entered the hotel rather guiltily. There was no hall-porter at the door, and not a soul in the lounge or in sight of the lounge. Harder went down the long passage.

3

At the end of the passage Lomax Harder found himself in a billiard-room – an extension built partly of brick and partly of wood on a sort of courtyard behind the main structure of the hotel. The roof, of iron and grimy glass, rose to a point in the middle. On two sides the high walls of the hotel obscured the light. Dusk was already closing in. A small fire burned feebly in the grate. A large radiator under the window was steel-cold, for though summer was finished, winter had not officially begun in the small economically-run hotel: so that the room was chilly; nevertheless, in deference to the English passion for fresh air and discomfort, the window was wide open.

Franting, in his overcoat and with an unlit cigarette between his lips, stood lowering with his back to the bit of fire. At sight of Harder he lifted his chin in a dangerous challenge.

'So you're still following me about,' he said resentfully to Harder.

'Yes,' said the latter, with his curious gentle primness of manner. 'I came down here specially to talk to you. I should have said all I had to say earlier, only you happened to be going out of the hotel just as I was coming in. You didn't seem to want to talk in the street; but there's some talking has to be done. I've a few things I must tell you.' Harder appeared to be perfectly calm, and he felt perfectly calm. He advanced from the door towards the billiard-table.

Franting raised his hand, displaying his square-ended, brutal fingers in the twilight.

'Now listen to me,' he said with cold, measured ferocity. 'You can't tell me anything I don't know. If there's some talking to be done I'll do it myself, and when I've finished you can get out. I know that my wife has taken a ticket for Copenhagen by the steamer from Harwich, and that she's been seeing to her passport, and packing. And of course I know that you have interests in Copenhagen and spend about half your precious time there. I'm not worrying to connect the two things. All that's got nothing to do with me. Emily has always seen a great deal of you, and I know that the last week or two she's been seeing you more than ever. Not that I mind that. I know that she objects to my treatment of her and my conduct generally. That's all right, but it's a matter that only concerns her and me. I mean that it's no concern of yours, for instance, or anybody else's. If she objects enough she can try and divorce me. I doubt if she'd succeed, but you can never be sure – with these new laws. Anyhow she's my wife till she does divorce me, and so she has the usual duties and responsibilities towards me – even though I was the worst husband in the world. That's how I look at it, in my old-fashioned way. I've just had a letter from her – she knew I was here, and I expect that explains how you knew I was here.'

'It does,' said Lomax Harder quietly.

Franting pulled a letter from his inner pocket and unfolded it. 'Yes,' he said, glancing at it, and read some sentences aloud:

'I have absolutely decided to leave you, and I won't hide from you that I know you know who is doing what he can to help me. I can't live with you any longer. You may be very fond of me, as you say, but I find your way of showing your fondness too humiliating and painful. I've said this to you before, and now I'm saying it for the last time.

And so on and so on.'

Franting tore the letter in two, dropped one half on the floor, twisted the other half into a spill, turned to the fire, and lit his cigarette.

'That's what I think of her letter,' he proceeded, the cigarette between his teeth. 'You're helping her, are you? Very well. I don't say you're in love with her, or she with you. I'll make no wild statements. But if you aren't in love with her I wonder why you're taking all this trouble over her. Do you go about the world helping ladies who say they're unhappy just for the pure sake of helping? Never mind. Emily isn't going to leave me. Get that into your head. I shan't let her leave me. She has money, and I haven't. I've been living on her, and it would be infernally awkward for me if she left me for good. That's a reason for keeping her, isn't it? But you may believe me or not – it isn't my reason. She's right enough when she says I'm very fond of her. That's a reason for keeping her too. But it isn't my reason. My reason is that a wife's a wife, and she can't break her word just because everything isn't lovely in the garden. I've heard it said I'm unmoral. I'm not all unmoral. And I feel particularly strongly about what's called the marriage tie.' He drew the revolver from his overcoat pocket, and held it up to view. 'You see this thing. You saw me buy it. Now you needn't be afraid. I'm not threatening you; and it's no part of my game to shoot you. I've nothing to do with your goings-on. What I have to do with is the goings-on of my wife. If she deserts me – for you or for anybody or for nobody – I shall follow her, whether it's to Copenhagen or Bangkok or the North Pole, and I shall kill her – with just this very revolver that you saw me buy. And now you can get out.'

Franting replaced the revolver, and began to consume the cigarette with fierce and larger puffs.

Lomax Harder looked at the grim, set, brutal, scowling, bitter face, and knew that Franting meant what he had said. Nothing would stop him from carrying out his threat. The fellow was not an argufier; he could not reason; but he had unmistakable grit and would never recoil from the fear of consequences. If Emily left him, Emily was a dead woman; nothing in the end could protect her from the execution of her husband's menace. On the other hand, nothing would persuade her to remain with her husband. She had decided to go, and she would go. And indeed the mere thought of this lady to whom he, Harder, was utterly devoted, staying with her husband and continuing to suffer the tortures and humiliations which she had been suffering for years – this thought revolted him. He could not think it.

He stepped forward along the side of the billiard-table, and simultaneously Franting stepped forward to meet him. Lomax Harder snatched the revolver which was in his pocket, aimed and pulled the trigger.

Franting collapsed, with the upper half of his body somehow balanced on the edge of the billiard-table. He was dead. The sound of the report echoed in Harder's ear like the sound of a violin string loudly twanged by a finger. He saw a little reddish hole in Franting's bronzed right temple.

'Well,' he thought, 'somebody had to die. And it's better him than Emily.' He felt that he had performed a righteous act. Also he felt a little sorry for Franting.

Then he was afraid. He was afraid for himself, because he wanted not to die, especially on the scaffold; but also for Emily Franting, who would be friendless and helpless without him; he could not bear to think of her alone in the world – the central point of a terrific scandal. He must get away instantly…

Not down the corridor back into the hotel-lounge! No! That would be fatal! The window. He glanced at the corpse. It was more odd, curious, than affrighting. He had made the corpse. Strange! He could not unmake it. He had accomplished the irrevocable. Impressive! He saw Franting's cigarette glowing on the linoleum in the deepening dusk, and picked it up and threw it into the fender.

Lace curtains hung across the whole width of the window. He drew one aside, and looked forth. The light was much stronger in the courtyard than within the room. He put his gloves on. He gave a last look at the corpse, straddled the window-sill, and was on the brick pavement of the courtyard. He saw that the curtain had fallen back into the perpendicular.

He gazed around. Nobody! Not a light in any window! He saw a green wooden gate, pushed it; it yielded; then a sort of entry-passage ... In a moment, after two half-turns, he was on the Marine Parade again. He was a fugitive. Should he fly to the right, to the left? Then he had an inspiration. An idea of genius for baffling pursuers. He would go into the hotel by the main-entrance. He went slowly and deliberately into the portico, where a middle-aged hall-porter was standing in the gloom.

'Good-evening, sir.'

'Good-evening. Have you got any rooms?'

'I think so, sir. The housekeeper is out, but she'll be back in a moment – if you'd like a seat. The manager's away in London.'

The hall-porter suddenly illuminated the lounge, and Lomax Harder, blinking, entered and sat down.

'I might have a cocktail while I'm waiting,' the murderer suggested with a bright and friendly smile. 'A Bronx.'

'Certainly, sir. The page is off duty. He sees to orders in the lounge, but I'll attend to you myself.'

'What a hotel!' thought the murderer, solitary in the chilly lounge, and gave a glance down the long passage. 'Is the whole place run by the hall-porter? But of course it's the dead season.'

Was it conceivable that nobody had heard the sound of the shot?

Harder had a strong impulse to run away. But no! To do so would be highly dangerous. He restrained himself.

'How much?' he asked of the hall-porter, who had arrived with surprising quickness, tray in hand and glass on tray.

'A shilling, sir.'

The murderer gave him eighteenpence, and drank off the cocktail.

'Thank you very much, sir.' The hall-porter took the glass.

'See here!' said the murderer. 'I'll look in again. I've got one or two little errands to do.'

And he went, slowly, into the obscurity of the Marine Parade.

4

Lomax Harder leant over the left arm of the sea-wall of the man-made port of Quangate. Not another soul was there. Night had fallen. The lighthouse at the extremity of the right arm was occulting. The lights – some red, some green, many white – of ships at sea passed in both directions in endless processions. Waves plashed gently against the vast masonry of the wall. The wind, blowing steadily from the north-west, was not cold. Harder, looking about – though he knew he was absolutely alone, took his revolver from his overcoat pocket and stealthily dropped it into the sea. Then he turned round and gazed across the small harbour at the mysterious amphitheatre of the lighted town, and heard public clocks and religious clocks striking the hour.

He was a murderer, but why should he not successfully escape detection? Other murderers had done so. He had all his wits. He was not excited. He was not morbid. His perspective of things was not askew. The hall-porter had not seen his first entrance into the hotel, nor his exit after the crime. Nobody had seen them. He had left nothing behind in the billiard-room. No fingermarks on the window-sill. (The putting-on of his gloves was in itself a clear demonstration that he had fully kept his presence of mind.) No footmarks on the hard, dry pavement of the courtyard.

Of course there was the possibility that some person unseen had seen him getting out of the window. Slight: but still a possibility! And there was also the possibility that someone who knew Franting by sight had noted him walking by Franting's side in the streets. If such a person informed the police and gave a description of him, enquiries might be made ... No! Nothing in it. His appearance offered nothing remarkable to the eye of a casual observer – except his forehead, of which he was rather proud, but which was hidden by his hat.

It was generally believed that criminals always did something silly. But so far he had done nothing silly, and he was convinced that, in regard to the crime, he never would do anything silly. He had none of the desire, supposed to be common among murderers, to revisit the scene of the crime or to look upon the corpse once more. Although he regretted the necessity for his act, he felt no slightest twinge of conscience. Somebody had to die, and surely it was better that a brute should die than the heavenly, enchanting, martyrised creature whom his act had rescued for ever from the brute! He was aware within himself of an ecstasy of devotion to Emily Franting – now a widow and free. She was a unique woman. Strange that a woman of such gifts should have come under the sway of so obvious a scoundrel as Franting. But she was very young at the time, and such freaks of sex had happened before and would happen again; they were a widespread phenomenon in the history of the relations of men and women.

He would have killed a hundred men if a hundred men had threatened her felicity. His heart was pure; he wanted nothing from Emily in exchange for what he had done in her defence. He was passionate in her defence. When he reflected upon the coarseness and cruelty of the gesture by which Franting had used Emily's letter to light his cigarette, Harder's cheeks grew hot with burning resentment.

A clock struck the quarter. Harder walked quickly to the harbour front, where there was a taxi-rank, and drove to the station … A sudden apprehension! The crime might have been discovered! Police might already be watching for suspicious-looking travellers! Absurd! Still, the apprehension remained despite its absurdity. The taxi-driver looked at him queerly. No! Imagination! He hesitated on the threshold of the station, then walked boldly in, and showed his return ticket to the ticket-inspector. No sign of a policeman. He got into the Pullman car, where five other passengers were sitting. The train started.

5

He nearly missed the boat-train at Liverpool Street because according to its custom the Quangate Flyer arrived twenty minutes late at Victoria. And at Victoria the foolish part of him, as distinguished from the common-sense part, suffered another spasm of fear. Would detectives, instructed by telegraph, be waiting for the train? No! An absurd idea! The boat-train from Liverpool Street was crowded with travellers, and the platform crowded with senders-off. He gathered from scraps of talk overheard that an international conference was about to take place in Copenhagen. And he had known nothing of it – not seen a word of it in the papers! Excusable perhaps; graver matters had held his attention.

Useless to look for Emily in the vast bustle of the compartments! She had her through ticket (which she had taken herself, in order to avoid possible complications), and she happened to be the only woman in the world who was never late and never in a hurry. She was certain to be on the train. But was she on the train? Something sinister might have come to pass. For instance, a telephone message to the flat that her husband had been found dead with a bullet in his brain.

The swift two-hour journey to Harwich was terrible for Lomax Harder. He remembered that he had left the unburnt part of the letter lying under the billiard-table. Forgetful! Silly! One of the silly things that criminals did! And on Parkeston Quay the confusion was enormous. He did not walk he was swept on to the great shaking steamer whose dark funnels rose amid wisps of steam into the starry sky. One advantage: detectives would have no chance in that multitudinous scene, unless indeed they held up the ship.

The ship roared a warning, and slid away from the quay, groped down the tortuous channel to the harbour mouth, and was in the North Sea; and England dwindled to naught but a string of lights. He searched every deck from stem to stern, and could not find Emily. She had not caught the train, or, if she had caught the train, she had not boarded the steamer because he had failed to appear. His misery was intense. Everything was going wrong. And on the arrival at Esbjerg would not detectives be lying in wait for the Copenhagen train?...

Then he descried her, and she him. She too had been searching. Only chance had kept them apart. Her joy at finding him was
ecstatic; tears came into his eyes at sight of it. He was everything
to her, absolutely everything. He clasped her right hand in both
his hands and gazed at her in the dim, diffused light blended of
stars, moon and electricity. No woman was ever like her: mature,
innocent, wise, trustful, honest. And the touching beauty of her
appealing, sad, happy face, and the pride of her carriage! A unique
jewel – snatched from the brutal grasp of that fellow – who had
ripped her solemn letter in two and used it as a spill for his cigarette! She related her movements; and he his. Then she said:
'Well?'

'I didn't go,' he answered. 'Thought it best not to. I'm convinced
it wouldn't have been any use.'

He had not intended to tell her this lie. Yet when it came to the
point, what else could he say? He had told one lie instead of twenty.
He was deceiving her, but for her sake. Even if the worst occurred,
she was for ever safe from that brutal grasp. And he had saved her.
As for the conceivable complications of the future, he refused to
confront them; he could live in the marvellous present. He felt
suddenly the amazing beauty of the night at sea, but beneath all
his other sensations was the obscure sensation of a weight at his
heart.

'I expect you were right,' she angelically acquiesced.

6

The superintendent of police (Quangate was the county town of
the western half of the county) and a detective-sergeant were in

the billiard-room of the Bellevue. Both wore mufti. The powerful green-shaded lamps usual in billiard-rooms shone down ruthlessly on the green table, and on the reclining body of John Franting, which had not moved and had not been moved.

A charwoman was just leaving these officers when a stout gentleman, who had successfully beguiled a policeman guarding the other end of the long corridor, squeezed past her, greeted the two officers and shut the door.

The superintendent, a thin man, with lips to match, and a moustache, stared hard at the arrival.

'I am staying with my friend Dr Furnival,' said the arrival cheerfully. 'You telephoned for him, and as he had to go out to one of those cases in which nature will not wait, I offered to come in his place. I've met you before, superintendent, at Scotland Yard.'

'Dr Austin Bond!' exclaimed the superintendent.

'He,' said the other.

They shook hands, Dr Bond genially, the superintendent half-consequential, half-deferential, as one who had his dignity to think about; also as one who resented an intrusion, but dared not show resentment.

The detective-sergeant reeled at the dazzling name of the great amateur detective, a genius who had solved the famous mysteries of 'The Yellow Hat', 'The Three Towns', 'The Three Feathers', 'The Gold Spoon', etc., etc., etc., whose devilish perspicacity had again and again made professional detectives both look and feel foolish, and whose notorious friendship with the loftiest heads of Scotland Yard compelled all police forces to treat him very politely indeed.

'Yes,' said Dr Austin Bond, after detailed examination. 'Been shot about ninety minutes, poor fellow! Who found him?'

'That woman who's just gone out. Some servant here. Came in to look after the fire.'

'How long since?'

'Oh! About an hour ago.'

'Found the bullet? I see it hit the brass on that cue-rack there.'

The detective-sergeant glanced at the superintendent, who, however, resolutely remained unastonished.

'Here's the bullet,' said the superintendent.

'Ah!' commented Dr Austin Bond, glinting through his spectacles at the bullet as it lay in the superintendent's hand. 'Decimal 38, I see. Flattened. It would be.'

'Sergeant,' said the superintendent, 'you can get help and have the body moved now Dr Bond has made his examination. Eh, doctor?'

'Certainly,' answered Dr Bond, at the fireplace. 'He was smoking a cigarette, I see.'

'Either he or his murderer.'

'You've got a clue?'

'Oh yes,' the superintendent answered, not without pride. 'Look here. Your torch, sergeant.'

The detective-sergeant produced a pocket electric-lamp, and the superintendent turned to the window-sill.

'I've got a stronger one than that,' said Dr Austin Bond, producing another torch.

The superintendent displayed fingerprints on the window-frame, footmarks on the sill, and a few strands of inferior blue cloth. Dr Austin Bond next produced a magnifying glass, and inspected the evidence at very short range.

'The murderer must have been a tall man – you can judge that from the angle of fire; he wore a blue suit, which he tore slightly on this splintered wood of the window-frame; one of his boots had a hole in the middle of the sole, and he'd only three fingers on his left hand. He must have come in by the window and gone out by the window, because the hall-porter is sure that nobody except the dead man entered the lounge by any door within an hour of the time when the murder must have been committed.'

The superintendent proudly gave many more details, and ended by saying that he had already given instructions to circulate a description.

'Curious,' said Dr Austin Bond, 'that a man like John Franting should let anyone enter the room by the window! Especially a shabby-looking man!'

'You knew the deceased personally then?'

'No! But I know he was John Franting.'

'How, doctor?'

'Luck.'

'Sergeant,' said the superintendent, piqued. 'Tell the constable to fetch the hall-porter.'

Dr Austin Bond walked to and fro, peering everywhere, and picked up a piece of paper that had lodged against the step of the platform which ran round two sides of the room for the raising of the spectators' benches. He glanced at the paper casually, and dropped it again.

'My man,' the superintendent addressed the hall-porter. 'How can you be sure that nobody came in here this afternoon?'

'Because I was in my cubicle all the time, sir.'

The hall-porter was lying. But he had to think of his own welfare. On the previous day he had been reprimanded for quitting his post against the rule. Taking advantage of the absence of the manager, he had sinned once again, and he lived in fear of dismissal if found out.

'With a full view of the lounge?'

'Yes, sir.'

'Might have been in there beforehand,' Dr Austin Bond suggested.

'No,' said the superintendent. 'The charwoman came in twice. Once just before Franting came in. She saw the fire wanted making up and she went for some coal and then returned later with the scuttle. But the look of Franting frightened her, and she turned back with her coal.'

'Yes,' said the hall-porter. 'I saw that.'

Another lie.

At a sign from the superintendent he withdrew.

'I should like to have a word with that charwoman,' said Dr Austin Bond.

The superintendent hesitated. Why should the great amateur meddle with what did not concern him? Nobody had asked his help. But the superintendent thought of the amateur's relations with Scotland Yard, and sent for the charwoman.

'Did you clean the window here today?' Dr Austin Bond interrogated her.

'Yes, please, sir.'

'Show me your left hand.' The slattern obeyed. 'How did you lose your little finger?'

'In a mangle accident, sir.'

'Just come to the window, will you, and put your hands on it. But take off your left boot first.'

The slattern began to weep.

'It's quite all right, my good creature,' Dr Austin Bond reassured her. 'Your skirt is torn at the hem, isn't it?'

When the slattern was released from her ordeal and had gone, carrying one boot in her grimy hand, Dr Austin Bond said genially to the superintendent: 'Just a fluke. I happened to notice she'd only three fingers on her left hand when she passed me in the corridor. Sorry I've destroyed your evidence. But I felt sure almost from the first that the murderer hadn't either entered or decamped by the window.'

'How?'

'Because I think he's still here in the room.'

The two police officers gazed about them as if exploring the room for the murderer.

'I think he's there.'

Dr Austin Bond pointed to the corpse.

'And where did he hide the revolver after he'd killed himself?' demanded the thin-lipped superintendent icily, when he had somewhat recovered his aplomb.

'I'd thought of that, too,' said Dr Austin Bond, beaming. 'It is always a very wise course to leave a dead body absolutely untouched until a professional man has seen it. But *looking* at the body can do no harm. You see the left-hand pocket of the overcoat. Notice how it bulges. Something unusual in it. Something that has the shape of a – Just feel inside it, will you?'

The superintendent, obeying, drew a revolver from the overcoat pocket of the dead man.

'Ah! Yes!' said Dr Austin Bond. 'A Webley Mark III. Quite new. You might take out the ammunition.' The superintendent dismantled the weapon. 'Yes, yes! Three chambers empty. Wonder how he used the other two! Now, where's that bullet? You see? He fired. His arm dropped, and the revolver happened to fall into the pocket.'

'Fired with his left hand, did he?' asked the superintendent, foolishly ironic.

'Certainly. A dozen years ago Franting was perhaps the finest amateur lightweight boxer in England. And one reason for it was that he bewildered his opponents by being left-handed. His lefts were much more fatal than his rights. I saw him box several times.'

Whereupon Dr Austin Bond strolled to the step of the platform near the door and picked up the fragment of very thin paper that was lying there.

'This,' said he, 'must have been blown from the hearth to here by the draught from the window when the door was opened. It's part of a letter. You can see the burnt remains of the other part in the corner of the fender. He probably lighted the cigarette with it. Out of bravado! His last bravado! Read this.'

The superintendent read:

'...repeat that I realise how fond you are of me, but you have killed my affection for you, and I shall leave our home tomorrow. This is absolutely final. E.'

Dr Austin Bond, having for the nth time satisfactorily demonstrated in his own unique, rapid way that police officers were a set of numskulls, bade the superintendent a most courteous good-evening, nodded amicably to the detective-sergeant, and left in triumph.

7

'I must get some mourning and go back to the flat,' said Emily Franting.

She was sitting one morning in the lobby of the Palads Hotel, Copenhagen. Lomax Harder had just called on her with an English newspaper containing an account of the inquest at which the jury had returned a verdict of suicide upon the body of her late husband. Her eyes filled with tears.

'Time will put her right,' thought Lomax Harder, tenderly watching her. 'I was bound to do what I did. And I can keep a secret for ever.'

THE MURDER ON THE GOLF LINKS

M. McDonnell Bodkin

Matthias McDonnell Bodkin (1850–1933) was an Irishman of many parts: barrister (and later a judge who wrote a book of legal reminiscences), journalist, and politician. He spent three years as a Member of Parliament, as an anti-Parnellite Irish nationalist. He had one thing in common with many men and women of distinction who wrote detective stories as a sideline – today, he is remembered more for his fiction than his public service.

Bodkin's claim to fame in the genre is that he created the first detective family. Having introduced Paul Beck ('the rule of thumb detective'), he came up with a female sleuth, Dora Myrl, who marries Paul. In due course, their son (also called Paul) turned to crime solving in *Paul Beck; a Chip off the Old Block*. This is a holiday and sporting mystery with, as one golf fan put it, 'a twist to match any blind dogleg on your own golf course'.

* * * * *

"Don't go in, don't! don't! please don't!"

The disobedient ball, regardless of her entreaties, crept slowly up the smooth green slope, paused irresolute on the ridge, and then trickled softly down into the hole; a wonderful "put."

Miss Mag Hazel knocked her ball impatiently away from the very edge. "Lost again on the last green," she cried petulantly. "You have abominable luck, Mr Beck."

Mr Beck smiled complacently. "Never denied it, Miss Hazel. Better be born lucky than clever is what I always say."

"But you are clever, too," said the girl, repentantly. "I hear everyone say how clever you are."

"That's where my luck comes in."

He slung the girl's golf bag over a broad shoulder, and caught his own up in a big hand. "Come," he said, "you will be late for dinner, and every man in the hotel will curse me as the cause."

They were the last on the links. The western sky was a sea of crimson and gold, in which floated a huge black cloud, shaped like a sea monster with the blazing sun in its jaws. The placid surface of the sea gave back the beauty of the sky, and in the clear, still air familiar objects took on a new beauty. Their way lay over the crisp velvet of the seaside turf, embroidered with wild flowers, to the Thornvale Hotel in the valley a mile away.

"How beautiful!" the girl whispered half to herself, and caught her breath with a queer little sigh.

Mr Beck looked down and saw that the blue eyes were very bright with tears. She met his look and smiled a wan little smile.

"Lovely scenery always makes me sad," she explained feebly. Then after a second she added impulsively: "Mr Beck, you and I are good friends, aren't we?"

"I hope so," said Mr Beck, gravely. "I can speak for myself anyway."

"Oh, I'm miserable! I must tell it to someone. I'm a miserable girl!"

"If I can help you in any way," said Mr Beck, stoutly, "you may count on me."

"I know I oughtn't to talk about such things, but I must, I cannot stop myself; then perhaps you could say a word to father; you and he are such good friends."

Mr Beck knew there was a confession coming. In some curious way Mr Beck attracted the most unlikely confidences. All sorts and conditions of people felt constrained to tell him secrets.

"It's this way," Miss Hazel went on. "Sit down there on that bank and listen. I'll be in lots of time for dinner, and anyhow I don't care. Father wants me to marry Mr Samuel Hawkins, a horrible name and a horrible man. I didn't mind much at the time he first spoke of it. I was very young, you see; I lived in a French convent school until father came back from India, and then we lived in a cottage near a golf links. Oh! such a quiet golf links, and Mr Hawkins came down to see us, and he first taught me how to play. I liked him because there was no one else. So when he asked me to marry him, and father wished it so much, I half promised—that is, I really did promise, and we were engaged, and he gave me a diamond ring, which I have here—in my purse."

Mr Beck smiled benignly. The girl was very young and pretty and innocent—little more than a child, who had been playing at a make-believe engagement.

"How long is it since you changed your mind?" he asked.

"Well, I never really made it up to marry Mr Hawkins. I only just agreed to become engaged. But about a week or ten days ago I found I could not go on with it."

"I see; that was about the time, was it not, that the young electrical engineer, Mr Ryan, arrived?"

She flushed hotly.

"Oh! it's not that at all—how hateful you are! Mr Ryan is nothing to me, nothing. Besides, he was most rude; called me a flirt, and said I led him on and never told him I was engaged. Now we don't even speak, and I'm so miserable. What shall I do?"

"Don't fret," said Mr Beck, cheerily; "it will come all right."

"Oh! but it cannot come all right. Father will be bitterly disappointed if I don't marry Mr Hawkins. He's awfully rich, carries diamonds about loose in his waistcoat pocket. He has fifty thousand pounds' worth of diamonds getting brightened up in Amsterdam; that's where they put a polish on them, you know. He showed father the receipt for them mixed up with bank-notes in his pocket-book. His friend, Mr Bolton, who is in the same business, says Mr Hawkins is a millionaire."

"And Mr Ryan has only his brains and his profession," said Mr Beck, cynically.

"Now you are just horrid. I don't care twopence about Mr Hawkins' diamonds or his millions. But I love father better than anyone else."

"Except?" suggested Mr Beck, maliciously.

"There is no exception—not one. You come second-best yourself."

"Oh, do I? Then I will see if I cannot find some diamonds and cut out Mr Hawkins. Meantime, let us get on to our dinner. You need not be in any hurry to break your heart. You are not going to marry Mr Hawkins to-morrow or the day after. Something may happen to stop the marriage altogether. Come along."

Something did happen. What that awful something was neither Miss Hazel nor Mr Beck dreamt of at the time.

It was the fussy half hour before dinner when they arrived at the veranda of the big Thornvale Hotel that had grown out of the Thornvale golf links. As Miss Mag Hazel passed through the throng every eye paid its tribute of admiration; she was by reason of her golf and good looks the acknowledged queen of the place.

A tall, handsome young fellow near the porch gave a pitiful look as she passed, the humble, appealing look in the eyes of a dog who has offended his master.

"How handsome he is; what beautiful black eyes he has!" her heart whispered, but her face was unconscious of his existence.

She evaded a small, dark man with a big hooked nose who came forward eagerly to claim her. "Don't speak to me, Mr Hawkins, don't look at me. I have not five minutes to dress for dinner."

A tall, thin man with a grey, drooping moustache stood close by her left in the central hall. To him she said: "I will be down in a minute, dad. I want you to take me in to dinner, mind. You are worth the whole lot of them put together."

Colonel Hazel's sallow cheek flushed with delight, for he loved his daughter with a love that was the best part of his life.

Big, good-humoured, smiling Tom Bolton, as the girl went in to dinner on her father's arm, whispered a word in the ear of his friend, Sam Hawkins, and the millionaire diamond merchant cast a scowling glance at handsome Ned Ryan, who gave him frown for frown with interest thereto.

At Thornvale Hotel the company lived, moved, and had their being in golf. They played golf all day on the links, and talked golf all the evening at the hotel. All the varied forms of golf lunacy were in evidence there. There was the fat elderly lady who went round "for her figure," tapping the ball before her on the smooth ground, and throwing it or carrying it over the bunkers. There was the man who was always grumbling about his "blanked" luck, and who never played what he was pleased to think was his "true game."

There was the man who sang comic songs on the green, and the man whose nerves were strained like fiddle-strings and tingled at every stir or whisper, whom the flight of a butterfly put off his stroke. There was a veteran of eighty-five, who still played a steady game. He had once been a scratch man, and though the free, loose vigour of his "swing" was lost, his eye and arm had not forgotten the lesson of years. His favourite opponent was a boy of twelve, who swung loose and free as if he were a figure of indiarubber with no bones in his arms.

Mr Hawkins and Mr Bolton were a perfect match with a level handicap of twelve; each believed that he could just beat the other, and the excitement of their incessant contests was intense.

But Miss Mag Hazel reigned undisputed queen of the links. None of the ladies, and only one or two of the men, could even "give her a game." Lissom as an ash sapling, every muscle in her body, from her shoulder to her ankle, took part in the graceful swing which, without effort, drove the ball further than a strong man could smite it by brute force. Her wrist was like a fine steel spring, as sensitive and as true.

Heretofore only one player disputed her supremacy—Mr Beck, the famous detective, who was idling a month in the quiet hotel after an exciting and successful criminal hunt half way round the world. Mr Beck was, as he always proclaimed, a lucky player. If he never made a brilliant stroke, he never made a bad one, and kept wonderfully clear of the bunkers. The brilliant players found he had an irritating trick of plodding on steadily, and coming out a hole ahead at the end of the round.

He and Mag Hazel played constantly together until young Ned Ryan came on the scene. Ryan was a brilliant young fellow with muscles of whipcord and whalebone, whose drive was like a shot from a catapult. But he played a sporting game, and very often drove into the bunker which was meant to catch the second shot of a second-class player. Mag Hazel found it easier to hold her own against his brilliance than against the plodding pertinacity of Mr Beck.

It may be that the impressionable young Irishman could not quite play his game when she was his opponent. He found it hard to obey the golfer's first commandment: "Keep your eye on the ball." He tried to play two games at the same time, and golf will have no divided allegiance.

The end of a happy fortnight came suddenly. It was a violent scene when, in a grassy bunker wide of the course, into which he had deliberately pulled his ball, he asked her to marry him, and learnt that she was engaged to the millionaire diamond merchant, Mr Hawkins. Poor Ned Ryan, with Irish impetuosity, raved and stormed at her cruelty in leading him to love her, swore his life was barren for evermore, and even muttered some very mysterious, meaningless threats against the more fortunate Mr Hawkins.

Tender-hearted Mag had been very meek and penitent while he raved and stormed, but he was not to be appeased by her meekness, and flung away from her in a rage.

Then it was her turn to be implacable when he became penitent. All that evening he hovered round her like a blundering moth round a lamp, but she ignored him as completely as the lamp the moth and shed the light of her smiles on Mr Beck.

So those two foolish young people played the old game in the old, foolish fashion, and tormented themselves and each other. The two men concerned in the matter, Mr Ryan and Mr Hawkins, scowled at each other on the golf links and at the bridge table, to the intense amusement of the company, who understood how little golf or cards had to do with the quarrel.

At last Ned Ryan had an open row with Mr Hawkins on the golf links, and told him, quite unnecessarily, he was no gentleman.

Then suddenly this light comedy deepened into sombre tragedy. The late breakfasters at the hotel were still at table when the thrilling, shocking news came to them that Mr Hawkins had been found murdered on the links.

Perhaps it is more convenient to tell the dismal story in the order in which it was told in evidence at the coroner's inquest.

Mr Hawkins and Mr Bolton had arranged a round in the early morning before breakfast, when they would have the links to themselves. They had a glass of milk and a biscuit, and started off in good spirits, each boasting he was certain to win.

They started some time between half-past six and seven, and about an hour afterwards Mr Bolton returned hastily, saying that he had forgotten an important letter he had to send by that morning's post, and that he had left Mr Hawkins grumbling at having to finish his round alone. Mr Bolton then went up to his own room, and five minutes later came back with a letter, which he carefully posted with his own hand just as the box was being cleared.

At half–past seven Colonel Hazel, strolling across the links, specially noticed there were no players to be seen. Ned Ryan went out at a quarter to eight o'clock to have a round by himself, having first asked Mr Bolton to join him. He had, as he stated, almost completed his round, when in the great, sandy bunker that guarded the seventeenth green he found Mr Hawkins stone dead.

He instantly gave the alarm, and Mr Beck and Mr Bolton were among the first on the scene. The detective, placid and imperturbable as ever, poked and pried about the body and the bunker where it lay. Mr Bolton was plainly broken-hearted at the sudden death of his life-long friend.

Beyond all doubt and question the man was murdered. There was a deep dint of some heavy, blunt weapon on the back of his head, fracturing the skull. But death had not been instantaneous. The victim had turned upon his assassin, for there were two other marks on his face—one an ugly, livid bruise on his cheek, and the other a deep, horrible gash on the temple from the same blunt-edged weapon. The last wound must have been instantly fatal. The weapon slew as it struck.

It was plain that robbery was not the motive of the crime. His heavy purse with a score of sovereigns and his pocket-book full of bank-notes were in his pockets, his fine diamond pin in his scarf, and his handsome watch in his fob.

The watch had been struck and smashed, and, as so often happens in such cases, it timed the murder to a moment. It had stopped at half-past eight. It was five minutes after nine when Mr Ryan had given the alarm.

While all the others looked on in open-eyed horror, incapable of thought or action, Mr Beck's quick eyes found a corner of the bunker where the sand had been disturbed recently. Rooting with his hands as a dog digs at a rabbit burrow with his paws, he dug out a heavy niblick. The handle was snapped in two, and the sand that clung damply round the iron face left a dark crimson stain on the fingers that touched it.

No one then could doubt that the murderous weapon had been found.

Mr Beck examined it a moment, and a frown gathered on his placid face. "This is Mr Ryan's niblick," he said slowly.

The words sent a quiver of excitement through the crowd. All eyes turned instinctively to the face of the young Irishman, who flushed in sudden anger.

"It's a lie," he shouted, "my niblick is here." He turned to his bag which lay on the sward beside him. "My God! it's gone. I never noticed it until this moment."

"Yes, that is mine," he added, as Mr Beck held out the blood-stained iron for inspection. "But I swear I never missed it till this moment."

Not a word more was said.

The crowd broke up into groups, each man whispering suspicions under his breath. The whisperers recalled the recent quarrel between the men, and in every trifling circumstance clear proof of guilt was found. Only Mr Bolton stood out staunchly for the young Irishman, and professed his faith in his innocence.

Like a man in a dream Ned Ryan returned alone to the hotel, where an hour later he was arrested. On being searched after arrest a five-pound note with Hawkins' name on the back of it was found in his pocket, and his explanation that he had won it at golf provoked incredulous smiles and shrugs amongst the gossipers. Two days later a coroner's jury found a verdict of wilful murder against the young engineer.

There was a second sensation, in its way almost as exciting as the first, when it was found that the murdered man had willed the whole of his huge fortune unconditionally to Miss Margaret Hazel.

But the girl declared vehemently she would never touch a penny of it, never, until the real murderer was discovered. She had a stormy interview with Mr Beck, whom she passionately charged with attempts to fix the guilt on an innocent man. She made no secret now of her love for the young Irishman, to the horror of the respectable and proper people at the hotel, who looked forward with cheerful assurance to her lover's execution.

But the distracted girl cared for none of those things. She poured the vials of her wrath on Mr Beck.

"You pretended to be my friend," she said, "and then you did all in your power to hang the innocent man I love."

Mr Beck was soothing and imperturbable. "Nothing of the kind, my dear young lady. It is always my pleasant duty to save the innocent and hang the guilty."

"Then why did you find out that niblick?"

"The more things that are found," said Mr Beck, "the better for the innocent and the worse for the guilty."

"Oh! I'm not talking about that," she cried, with a bewildering change of front. "But here you are pottering about doing nothing instead of trying to save him. I will give you every penny poor Mr Hawkins left me if you save him."

Mr Beck smiled benignly at this magnificent offer. "Won't you two want something to live on?" he asked, "when I have saved him, and before he makes his fortune."

She let the question go by. "Then you will, you promise me you will!" she cried eagerly.

"I will try to assist the course of justice," he said, with formal gravity, but his eyes twinkled, and she took comfort therefrom.

"That's not what I want at all."

"You believe Mr Ryan is innocent?" asked Mr Beck.

"Of course I do. What a question!"

"If he is innocent I will try to save him—if not—"

"There is no 'if not.' Oh! I'm quite satisfied, and I thank you with all my heart."

She caught up the big, strong hand and kissed it, and then collapsed on the sofa for a good cry, while Mr Beck stole discreetly from the room and set out for a solitary stroll on the golf links, every yard of which he questioned with shrewd eyes.

He made one small discovery on the corner of the second green. He found a ball which had belonged to the murdered man. There was no doubt about the ownership. Mr Hawkins had a small gold seal with his initial cut in it. This he used to heat with a match to brand his ball. The tiny black letters, "S.H.," were burnt through the white skin of the new "Professional" ball, which Mr Beck found on the corner of the second green. He put the ball in his pocket and said nothing about his find.

But about another curious discovery of his he was quite voluble that evening at dinner. He found, he said, a peculiar-looking waistcoat button in the bunker that guarded the second green. It seemed to him to have been torn violently from the garment, for a shred of the cloth still clung to it.

"If I had found it in the bunker where the murder was committed," said Mr Beck, "I would have regarded it as a very important piece of evidence. Anyhow it may help. I will examine young Ryan's waistcoats to see if it fits any of them."

Then for a few days nothing happened, and excitement smouldered. People had no heart to play golf over the scene of the murder. The parties gradually dispersed and scattered homewards. Colonel Hazel, who had been completely broken up by the tragedy, was amongst the first to go.

Mag gave her address to Mr Beck, with strict injunctions to wire the moment he had good news. "Remember, I trust you," were the last words she said as they parted at the hotel door.

Mr Bolton and Mr Beck were almost the two last to leave. The diamond merchant was disconsolate over the death of his old friend and comrade, and the detective did all in his power to comfort him.

One morning Mr Bolton had a telegram which, as he explained to Mr Beck, called him away on urgent business. He left that afternoon, and Mr Beck went with him as far as Liverpool, when they parted, each on his respective business.

*   *   *   *   *

The next scene in the tragedy was staged in Holland.

Two men sat alone together in a first-class railway carriage that slid smoothly through a level landscape intersected with canals. They had put aside their papers, and talked and smoked. One of the men was plainly a German by his dress and manner—the other a Frenchman.

The Frenchman had tried vainly to stagger through a conversation in German and the German in French until they had found a common ground in English which both spoke well though with a strong foreign accent.

There had been an account of a big diamond robbery in the papers, and their talk drifted on to crimes and criminals of all countries—a topic with which the Frenchman seemed strangely familiar. He did most of the talking. The German sat back in his corner and grunted out a word or two of assent, to all appearance deeply interested in the talk. Now and again a silver flask passed between the two men, who grew momentarily more intimate.

"Herr Raphael," said the Frenchman, "I am glad to have met you. You have made the journey very pleasant for me. You are a man I feel I can trust. I am not, as I told you, Victor Grandeau, a French journalist. I am plain Mr Paul Beck, an English detective, at your service."

With a single motion the shiny, sleek, black wig and the black moustache disappeared into a small handbag at his side. The whole character, and even the features of the face, seemed to change as suddenly, and the broad, bland, smiling face of our old friend Mr Beck presented itself to the eyes of the astonished German, who shrank back in his corner of the seat in astonishment at the sudden revelation. But Mr Beck quietly ignored his astonishment.

"As you seem interested in this kind of thing," he said, "I will tell you the story of one of the most curious cases I have ever had to deal with. You are the very first to hear the story. Indeed, it is so new that it hasn't yet got the right ending to it. Perhaps you have heard of the Thornvale murder in England? No! Then I'll begin at the beginning."

He began at the beginning and told the story clearly and vividly as it was told at the inquest. The German listened with most flattering interest and surprise.

"When I found that golf ball," Mr Beck went on, "it gave me an idea. Do you know anything of golf?"

"I play a little," the other confessed.

"Then you will understand that from the place where I found his ball I knew that the murdered man—I told you his name was Hawkins—Samuel Hawkins—never got as far as the second green. If he had, his ball would not have been lying where I found it. He would have holed it out and gone on.

"It was plain, therefore, he must have been murdered just after he played that shot—murdered somewhere between the tee and the green of the second hole. I went back to the deep bunker I told you of that guarded the second green, and I found there traces of a struggle.

"They had been cunningly obliterated, but to a detective's eye they were plain enough. The sand was smoothed over the footprints, but here and there the long grass and wild flowers had been torn away by a desperate grasp. I even found a faint bloodstain on one of the stones. Then, of course, I guessed what had happened. The man had been murdered in the bunker of the second green and carried under cover of the ridge to the bunker of the seven-teenth. That, you see, disposed of the alibi of Mr Bolton, who had left him early in the game."

"Oh, no!" interrupted the German, with eager interest in the story, "you told me that Mr Bolton was at the hotel from half-past seven, and the watch of the murdered man showed the murder had been committed at half-past eight."

Mr Beck looked at the German with manifest admiration. "Forgive me for mentioning it. You would have made a first-class detective if you hadn't gone into another line of business. I should have told you that the evidence of the watch had been faked."

"Faked!" queried the other, with a blank look on his face.

"Oh! I see. Being a German, of course you don't understand our slang phrases. I examined the watch, and I found that though the glass had been violently broken, the dial was not even scratched. The spring had been snapped, not by the blow but by overwind-ing. It was pretty plain to me the murderer had done the trick. He first put the hands on to half-past eight and then broke the spring, and so made his alibi. He got the watch to perjure itself. Neat, wasn't it?"

The German merely grunted. He was plainly impressed by the devilish ingenuity of the murderer.

"Besides," Mr Beck went on placidly, "to make quite sure, I laid a trap for Mr Bolton which worked like a charm. The night of the murder I went into his room and tore one of the buttons out of his waistcoat. The next day I mentioned at dinner that I had found a button in the second bunker where, if I guessed rightly, he and only he knew the murder was really committed. It was a lie, of course. But it caught the truth. That same evening Mr Bolton burnt the waistcoat. It was a light cotton affair that burnt like paper. The glass buttons he cut off with a knife and buried. That looked bad, didn't it?"

"Very bad," the German agreed. He was more deeply interested than ever. "Did you arrest the man, then?"

"Not then."

"But why?"

"I wanted to make quite sure of my proofs. I wanted to lay my hands on the receipts for the diamonds which I believed he had stolen. I told you of those, didn't I?"

"Oh, yes, you told me of those. Did you search for them?"

"Yes, but I couldn't find them. I searched Mr Bolton's room, and searched his clothes carefully, but I couldn't find a trace of the papers."

Again the German grunted. He seemed somehow pleased at the failure. Possibly the quiet confidence of this cock-sure detective annoyed him.

"But," Mr Beck went on, placid as ever, "I tried a guess. You may remember, Herr Raphael, that when Mr Bolton came back from the golf links he posted a letter immediately. I had a notion that he stuck the receipts in the envelope and posted it addressed to himself at some post-office to be left till called for. Wasn't a bad guess, was it?"

"A very good guess."

"Then I did a little bit of forgery."

"You what?"

"Did a little bit of forgery. I forged the name of Mr Bolton's partner to a telegram to say that five thousand pounds were urgently needed. That, I knew, was likely to make Mr Bolton gather up the receipts and start for Amsterdam. We went to Liverpool together and I changed to an elderly lady. I saw him as an able-bodied seaman pick up his own letter at the Liverpool Post-Office. I came over with him in the boat to Rotterdam. As a French journalist I saw him as a stout German get into this very carriage and—here I am!"

It was a very lame ending to an exciting story. The stout German plainly thought so. He had listened with flattering eagerness almost to the end; now he leant back in the corner of his seat suppressing a yawn.

"It is a very amusing story," he said slowly. "But, my friend, you must be thirsty with much talking. I in my bag have a flask of excellent schnapps, you shall of it taste."

A small black bag rested on the seat beside him. He laid his hand on the fastening.

"It is no use," Mr Beck interrupted, "no use, Mr Bolton. I have taken the revolver out of the bag and have it with my own in my pocket. The game is up, I think. I have put my cards on the table. What do you say?"

Suddenly Mr Bolton broke into a loud, harsh laugh that ended in a sob. "You are a fiend, Beck," he shouted, "a fiend incarnate. What do you mean to do?"

"To take you back with me to London. I have a man in the next carriage to look after you. No use worrying about extradition. You have a return ticket, I suppose; so have I. There will be a train leaving as we arrive. Meanwhile, if you don't mind—" He took a neat pair of handcuffs from his pocket and held them out with an ingratiating smile.

Mr Bolton drew back a little. For a moment it seemed as if he would spring at the detective's throat. But the steady, fearless eyes held him. He put his hands out submissively and the steel bracelets clicked on his wrists.

They had only to cross the platform to reach the return train that was just starting. But Mr Beck found time to plunge into the telegraph office and scribble three words to Mag Hazel's address:

"All right.—BECK."

THE FINGER OF STONE

G. K. Chesterton

Gilbert Keith Chesterton (1874–1936) was another excessively accomplished all-rounder whose other achievements now seem less significant than the creation of a fictional detective. He was a theologian, critic, journalist and much else besides. He converted to Catholicism, and some campaigners have put him forward as a candidate for sainthood, prompting a fierce debate as to whether or not he was guilty of anti-Semitism.

There is much less room for argument about his importance in the history of detective fiction. In the first quarter of the twentieth century, Father Brown was second only to Sherlock Holmes in the pantheon of notable British detectives, although his fate a hundred years later was to be transformed into the unlikely hero of a lightweight daytime television series. Chesterton's influence on the genre was recognised when, in 1930, Anthony Berkeley invited him to become President of the Detection Club. He enjoyed walking, and a tramp across the Yorkshire moors with a priest called Father O'Connor was the prelude to his creation of Father Brown. Here, a walking tour in France supplies the context for the story.

* * * * *

THREE young men on a walking-tour came to a halt outside the little town of Carillon, in the south of France; which is doubtless described in the guide books as famous for its fine old Byzantine monastery, now the seat of a university; and for having been the scene of the labours of Boyg. At that name, at least, the reader will be reasonably thrilled; for he must have seen it in any number of newspapers and novels. Boyg and the Bible are periodically reconciled at religious conferences; Boyg broadens and slightly bewilders the minds of numberless heroes of long psychological stories, which begin in the nursery and nearly end in the madhouse. The journalist, writing rapidly his recurrent reference to the treatment meted out to pioneers like Galileo, pauses in the effort to think of another example, and always rounds off the sentence either with Bruno or with Boyg. But the mildly orthodox are equally fascinated, and feel a glow of agnosticism while they continue to say that, since the discoveries of Boyg, the doctrine of the Homoousian or of the human conscience does not stand where it did; wherever that was. It is needless to say that Boyg was a great discoverer, for the public has long regarded him with the warmest reverence and gratitude on that ground. It is also unnecessary to say what he discovered; for the public will never display the faintest curiosity about that. It is vaguely understood that it was something about fossils, or the long period required for petrifaction; and that it generally implied those anarchic or anonymous forces of evolution supposed to be hostile to religion. But certainly none of the discoveries he made while he was alive was so sensational, in the newspaper sense, as the discovery that was made about him when he was dead. And this, the more private and personal matter, is what concerns us here.

The three tourists had just agreed to separate for an hour, and meet again for luncheon at the little café opposite; and the different ways in which they occupied their time and indulged their

tastes will serve for a sufficient working summary of their person-
alities. Arthur Armitage was a dark and grave young man, with
a great deal of money, which he spent on a conscientious and
continuous course of self-culture, especially in the matter of art
and architecture; and his earnest aquiline profile was already set
towards the Byzantine monastery, for the exhaustive examination
of which he had already prepared himself, as if he were going to
pass an examination rather than to make one. The man next him,
though himself an artist, betrayed no such artistic ardour. He was
a painter who wasted most of his time as a poet; but Armitage,
who was always picking up geniuses, had become in some sense his
patron in both departments. His name was Gabriel Gale; a long,
loose, rather listless man with yellow hair; but a man not easy for
any patron to patronize.

He generally did as he liked in an abstracted fashion; and what
he very often liked to do was nothing. On this occasion he showed
a lamentable disposition to drift towards the café first; and having
drunk a glass or two of wine, he drifted not into the town but out
of it, roaming about the steep bare slope above, with a rolling eye
on the rolling clouds; and talking to himself until he found somebody else to talk to, which happened when he put his foot through
the glass roof of a studio just below him on the steep incline. As it
was an artist's studio, however, their quarrel fortunately ended in
an argument about the future of realistic art; and when he turned
up to lunch, that was the extent of his acquaintance with the
quaint and historic town of Carillon.

The name of the third man was Garth; he was shorter and
uglier and somewhat older than the others, but with a much

livelier eye in his hatchet face; he stepped much more briskly, and in the matter of a knowledge of the world, the other two were babies under his charge. He was a very able medical practitioner, with a hobby of more fundamental scientific inquiry; and for him the whole town, university and studio, monastery and café, was only the temple of the presiding genius of Boyg. But in this case the practical instinct of Dr. Garth would seem to have guided him rightly; for he discovered things considerably more startling than anything the antiquarian found in the Romanesque arches or the poet in the rolling clouds. And it is his adventures, in that single hour before lunch, upon which this tale must turn.

The café tables stood on the pavement under a row of trees opposite the old round gate in the wall, through which could be seen the white gleam of the road up which they had just been walking. But the steep hills were so high round the town that they rose clear above the wall, in a more enormous wall of smooth and slanting rock, bare except for occasional clumps of cactus. There was no crack in that sloping wilderness of stone except the rather shallow and stony bed of a little stream. Lower down, where the stream reached the level of the valley, rose the dark domes of the basilica of the old monastery; and from this a curious stairway of rude stones ran some way up the hill beside the water-course, and stopped at a small and solitary building looking little more than a shed made of stones. Some little way higher the gleam of the glass roof of the studio, with which Gale had collided in his unconscious wanderings, marked the last spot of human habitation in all those rocky wastes that rose about the little town.

Armitage and Gale were already seated at the table when Dr. Garth walked up briskly and sat down somewhat abruptly.

"Have you fellows heard the news?" he asked.

He spoke somewhat sharply, for he was faintly annoyed by the attitudes of the antiquarian and the artist, who were deep in their own dreamier and less practical tastes and topics. Armitage was saying at the moment:

"Yes, I suppose I've seen to-day some of the very oldest sculpture of the veritable Dark Ages. And it's not stiff like some Byzantine work; there's a touch of the true grotesque you generally get in Gothic."

"Well, I've seen to-day some of the newest sculpture of the Modern Ages," replied Gale, "and I fancy they are the veritable Dark Ages. Quite enough of the true grotesque up in that studio, I can tell you."

"Have you heard the news, I say?" rapped out the doctor. "Boyg is dead."

Gale stopped in a sentence about Gothic architecture, and said seriously, with a sort of hazy reverence:

"*Requiescat in pace*. Who was Boyg?"

"Well, really," replied the doctor, "I did think every baby had heard of Boyg."

"Well, I dare say you've never heard of Paradou," answered Gale. "Each of us lives in his little cosmos with its classes and degrees. Probably you haven't heard of the most advanced sculptor, or perhaps of the latest lacrosse expert or champion chess player."

It was characteristic of the two men, that while Gale went on talking in the air about an abstract subject, till he had finished his own train of thought, Armitage had a sufficient proper sense of the presence of something more urgent to relapse into silence. Nevertheless, he unconsciously looked down at his notes; at the name of the advanced sculptor he looked up.

"Who is Paradou?" he asked.

"Why, the man I've been talking to this morning," replied Gale. "His sculpture's advanced enough for anybody. He's no end of a chap; talks more than I do, and talks very well. Thinks too; I should think he could do everything except sculpt. There his theories get in his way. As I told him, this notion of the new realism——"

"Perhaps we might drop realism and attend to reality," said Dr. Garth grimly. "I tell you Boyg is dead. And that's not the worst either."

Armitage looked up from his notes with something of the vagueness of his friend the poet. "If I remember right," he said, "Professor Boyg's discovery was concerned with fossils."

"Professor Boyg's discovery involved the extension of the period required for petrifaction as distinct from fossilization," replied the doctor stiffly, "and thereby relegated biological origins to a period which permits the chronology necessary to the hypothesis of natural selection. It may affect you as humorous to interject the observation 'loud cheers,' but I assure you the scientific world, which happens to be competent to judge, was really moved with amazement as well as admiration."

"In fact it was petrified to hear it couldn't be petrified," suggested the poet.

"I have really no time for your flippancy," said Garth. "I am up against a great ugly fact."

Armitage interposed in the benevolent manner of a chairman. "We must really let Garth speak; come, doctor, what is it all about? Begin at the beginning."

"Very well," said the doctor, in his staccato way. "I'll begin at the beginning. I came to this town with a letter of introduction to Boyg himself; and as I particularly wanted to visit the geological museum, which his own munificence provided for this town, I went there first. I found all the windows of the Boyg Museum were broken; and the stones thrown by the rioters were actually lying about the room within a foot or two of the glass cases, one of which was smashed."

"Donations to the geological museum, no doubt," remarked Gale. "A munificent patron happens to pass by, and just heaves in a valuable exhibit through the window. I don't see why that shouldn't be done in what you call the world of science; I'm sure it's done all right in the world of art. Old Paradou's busts and bas-reliefs are just great rocks chucked at the public and——"

"Paradou may go to—Paradise, shall we say?" said Garth, with pardonable impatience. "Will nothing make you understand that something has really happened that isn't any of your ideas and isms? It wasn't only the geological museum; it was the same everywhere. I passed by the house Boyg first lived in, where they very properly put up a medallion; and the medallion was all splashed with mud. I crossed the market-place, where they put up a statue to him just recently. It was still hung with wreaths of laurel by his pupils and the party that appreciates him; but they were half torn away, as if there had been a struggle, and stones had evidently been thrown, for a piece of the hand was chipped off."

"Paradou's statue, no doubt," observed Gale. "No wonder they threw things at it."

"I think not," replied the doctor, in the same hard voice. "It wasn't because it was Paradou's statue, but because it was Boyg's statue. It was the same business as the museum and the medallion. No, there's been something like a French Revolution here on the subject; the French are like that. You remember the riot in the Breton village where Renan was born, against having a statue of him. You know, I suppose, that Boyg was a Norwegian by birth, and only settled here because the geological formation, and the supposed mineral properties of that stream there, offered the best field for his investigations. Well, besides the fits the parsons were in at his theories in general, it seems he bumped into some barbarous local superstition as well; about it being a sacred stream that froze snakes into ammonites at a wink; a common myth, of course, for the same was told about St. Hilda at Whitby. But there are peculiar conditions that made it pretty hot in this place. The theological students fight with the medical students, one for Rome and the other for Reason; and they say there's a sort of raving lunatic of a Peter the Hermit, who lives in that hermitage on the hill over there, and every now and then comes out waving his arms and setting the place on fire."

"I heard something about that," remarked Armitage. "The priest who showed me over the monastery; I think he was the head man there—anyhow, he was a most learned and eloquent gentleman—told me about a holy man on the hill who was almost canonized already."

"One is tempted to wish he were martyred already; but the martyrdom, if any, was not his," said Garth darkly. "Allow me to continue my story in order. I had crossed the market-place to find Professor Boyg's private house, which stood at the corner of it. I found the shutters up and the house apparently empty, except for one old servant, who refused at first to tell me anything; indeed, I found a good deal of rustic reluctance on both sides to tell a foreigner anything. But when I had managed to make the nature of my introduction quite plain to him, he finally broke down; and told me his master was dead."

There was a pause, and then Gale, who seemed for the first time somewhat impressed, asked abstractedly:

"Where is his tomb? Your tale is really rather strange and dramatic, and obviously it must go on to his tomb. Your pilgrimage ought to end in finding a magnificent monument of marble and gold, like the tomb of Napoleon, and then finding that even the grave had been desecrated."

"He has no tomb," replied Garth sternly, "though he will have many monuments. I hope to see the day when he will have a statue in every town, he whose statue is now insulted in his own town. But he will have no tomb."

"And why not?" asked the staring Armitage.

"His body cannot be found," answered the doctor; "no trace of him can be found anywhere."

"Then how do you know he is dead?" asked the other.

There was an instant of silence, and then the doctor spoke out in a voice fuller and stronger than before:

"Why, as to that," he said, "I think he is dead because I am sure he is murdered."

Armitage shut his note book, but continued to look down steadily at the table. "Go on with your story," he said.

"Boyg's old servant," resumed the doctor, "who is a queer, silent, yellow-faced old card, was at last induced to tell me of the existence of Boyg's assistant, of whom I think he was rather jealous. The Professor's scientific helper and right-hand man is a man of the name of Bertrand, and a very able man, too, eminently worthy of the great man's confidence, and intensely devoted to his cause. He is carrying on Boyg's work so far as it can be carried on; and about Boyg's death or disappearance he knows the little that can be known. It was when I finally ran him to earth in a little house full of Boyg's books and instruments, at the bottom of the hill just beyond the town, that I first began to realize the nature of this sinister and mysterious business. Bertrand is a quiet man, though he has a little of the pardonable vanity which is not uncommon in assistants. One would sometimes fancy the great discovery was almost as much his as his master's; but that does no harm, since it only makes him fight for his master's fame almost as if it were his. But in fact he is not only concerned about the discovery; or rather, he is not only concerned about that discovery. I had not looked for long at the dark bright eyes and keen face of that quiet young man before I realized that there was something else that he is trying to discover. As a matter of fact, he is no longer merely a scientific assistant, or even a scientific student. Unless I am much mistaken, he is playing the part of an amateur detective.

"Your artistic training, my friends, may be an excellent thing for discovering a poet, or even a sculptor; but you will forgive me for thinking a scientific training rather better for discovering a murderer. Bertrand has gone to work in a very workmanlike way, I consider, and I can tell you in outline what he has discovered so far. Boyg was last seen by Bertrand descending the hillside by the water-course, having just come away from the studio of Gale's friend the sculptor, where he was sitting for an hour every morning. I may say here, rather for the sake of logical method than because it is needed by the logical argument, that the sculptor at any rate had no quarrel with Boyg, but was, on the contrary, an ardent admirer of him as an advanced and revolutionary character."

"I know," said Gale, seeming to take his head suddenly out of the clouds. "Paradou says realistic art must be founded on the modern energy of science; but the fallacy of that——"

"Let me finish with the facts first before you retire into your theories," said the doctor firmly. "Bertrand saw Boyg sit down on the bare hillside for a smoke; and you can see from here how bare a hillside it is; a man walking for hours on it would still be as visible as a fly crawling on a ceiling. Bertrand says he was called away to the crisis of an experiment in the laboratory; when he looked again he could not see his master, and he has never seen him from that day to this.

"At the foot of the hill, and at the bottom of the flight of steps which runs up to the hermitage, is the entrance to the great monastic buildings on the very edge of the town. The very first thing you come to on that side is the great quadrangle, which is enclosed by cloisters, and by the rooms or cells of the clerical or semi-clerical students. I need not trouble you with the tale of the political compromise by which this part of the institution has remained clerical, while the scientific and other schools beyond it are now entirely secular. But it is important to fix in your mind the fact itself: that the monastic part is on the very edge of the town, and the other part bars its way, so to speak, to the inside of the town. Boyg could not possibly have gone past that secular barrier, dead or alive, without being under the eyes of crowds who were more excited about him than about anything else in the world. For the whole place was in a fuss, and even a riot for him as well as against him. Something happened to him on the hillside, or anyhow before he came to the internal barrier. My friend the amateur detective set to work to examine the hillside, or all of it that could seriously count; an enormous undertaking, but he did it as if with a microscope. Well, he found that rocky field, when examined closely, very much what it looks even from here. There are no caves or even holes, there are no chasms or even cracks in that surface of blank stone for miles and miles. A rat could not be hidden in those few tufts of prickly pear. He could not find a hiding-place; but for all that, he found a hint. The hint was nothing more than a faded scrap of paper, damp and draggled from the shallow bed of the brook, but faintly decipherable on it were words in the writing of the Master. They were but part of a sentence, but they included the words, 'will call on you tomorrow to tell you something you ought to know.'

"My friend Bertrand sat down and thought it out. The letter had been in the water, so it had not been thrown away in the town, for the highly scientific reason that the river does not flow uphill. There only remained on the higher ground the sculptor's studio and the hermitage. But Boyg would not write to the sculptor to warn him that he was going to call, since he went to his studio every morning. Presumably the person he was going to call on was the hermit; and a guess might well be made about the nature of what he had to say. Bertrand knew better than anybody that Boyg had just brought his great discovery to a crushing completeness, with fresh facts and ratifications; and it seems likely enough that he went to announce it to his most fanatical opponent, to warn him to give up the struggle."

Gale, who was gazing up into the sky with his eye on a bird, again abruptly intervened.

"In these attacks on Boyg," he said, "were there any attacks on his private character?"

"Even these madmen couldn't attack that," replied Garth with some heat. "He was the best sort of Scandinavian, as simple as a child, and I really believe as innocent. But they hated him for all that; and you can see for yourself that their hatred begins to appear on the horizon of our inquiry. He went to tell the truth in the hour of triumph; and he never reappeared to the light of the sun."

Armitage's far-away gaze was fixed on the solitary cell half-way up the hill. "You don't mean seriously," he said, "that the man they talk about as a saint, the friend of my friend the abbot, or whatever he is, is neither more nor less than an assassin?"

"You talked to your friend the abbot about Romanesque sculpture," replied Garth. "If you had talked to him about fossils, you might have seen another side to his character. These Latin priests are often polished enough, but you bet they're pointed as well. As for the other man on the hill, he's allowed by his superiors to live what they call the eremitical life; but he's jolly well allowed to do other things, too. On great occasions he's allowed to come down here and preach, and I can tell you there is Bedlam let loose when he does. I might be ready to excuse the man as a sort of a maniac; but I haven't the slightest difficulty in believing that he is a homicidal maniac."

"Did your friend Bertrand take any legal steps on his suspicions?" asked Armitage, after a pause.

"Ah, that's where the mystery begins," replied the doctor.

After a moment of frowning silence, he resumed. "Yes, he did make a formal charge to the police, and the Juge d'Instruction examined a good many people and so on, and said the charge had broken down. It broke down over the difficulty of disposing of the body; the chief difficulty in most murders. Now the hermit, who is called Hyacinth, I believe, was summoned in due course; but he had no difficulty in showing that his hermitage was as bare and as hard as the hill-side. It seemed as if nobody could possibly have concealed a corpse in those stone walls, or dug a grave in that rocky floor. Then it was the turn of the abbot, as you call him, Father Bernard of the Catholic College. And he managed to convince the magistrate that the same was true of the cells surrounding the college quadrangle, and all the other rooms under his control. They were all like empty boxes, with barely a stick or two of furniture; less than usual, in fact, for some of the sticks had been broken up for the bonfire demonstration I told you of.

Anyhow, that was the line of defence, and I dare say it was well conducted, for Bernard is a very able man, and knows about many other things besides Romanesque architecture; and Hyacinth, fanatic as he is, is famous as a persuasive orator. Anyhow, it was successful, the case broke down; but I am sure my friend Bertrand is only biding his time, and means to bring it up again. These difficulties about the concealment of a corpse—Hullo! why here he is in person."

He broke off in surprise as a young man walking rapidly down the street paused a moment, and then approached the café table at which they sat. He was dressed with all the funereal French respectability: his black stove-pipe hat, his high and stiff black neck-cloth resembling a stock, and the curious corners of dark beard at the edges of his chin, gave him an antiquated air like a character out of Gaboriau. But if he was out of Gaboriau, he was nobody less than Lecocq; the dark eyes in his pale face might indeed be called the eyes of a born detective. At this moment, the pale face was paler than usual with excitement, and as he stopped a moment behind the doctor's chair, he said to him in a low voice:

"I have found out."

Dr. Garth sprang to his feet, his eyes brilliant with curiosity; then, recovering his conventional manner, he presented M. Bertrand to his friends, saying to the former, "You may speak freely with us, I think; we have no interest except an interest in the truth."

"I have found the truth," said the Frenchman, with compressed lips. "I know now what these murderous monks have done with the body of Boyg."

"Are we to be allowed to hear it?" asked Armitage gravely.

"Everyone will hear it in three days' time," replied the pale Frenchman. "As the authorities refuse to reopen the question, we are holding a public meeting in the market-place to demand that they do so. The assassins will be there, doubtless, and I shall not only denounce but convict them to their faces. Be there yourself, monsieur, on Thursday at half-past two, and you will learn how one of the world's greatest men was done to death by his enemies. For the moment I will only say one word. As the great Edgar Poe said in your own language, 'Truth is not always in a well.' I believe it is sometimes too obvious to be seen."

Gabriel Gale, who had rather the appearance of having gone to sleep, seemed to rouse himself with an unusual animation.

"That's true," he said, "and that's the truth about the whole business."

Armitage turned to him with an expression of quiet amusement.

"Surely you're not playing the detective, Gale," he said. "I never pictured such a thing as your coming out of fairyland to assist Scotland Yard."

"Perhaps Gale thinks he can find the body," suggested Dr. Garth laughing.

Gale lifted himself slowly and loosely from his seat, and answered in his dazed fashion:

"Why, yes, in a way," he said; "in fact, I'm pretty sure I can find the body. In fact, in a manner of speaking, I've found it."

* * * * *

Those with any intimations of the personality of Mr. Arthur Armitage will not need to be told that he kept a diary; and endeavoured to note down his impressions of foreign travel with atmospheric sympathy and the *mot juste*. But the pen dropped from his hand, so to speak, or at least wandered over the page in a mazy desperation, in the attempt to describe the great mob meeting, or rather the meeting of two mobs, which took place in the picturesque market-place in which he had wandered alone a few days before, criticising the style of the statue, or admiring the sky-line of the basilica. He had read and written about democracy all his life; and when first he met it, it swallowed him like an earthquake. One actual and appalling difference divided this French mob in a provincial market from all the English mobs he had ever seen in Hyde Park or Trafalgar Square. These Frenchmen had not come there to get rid of their feelings, but to get rid of their enemies. Something would be done as a result of this sort of public meeting; it might be murder, but it would be something.

And although, or rather because, it had this militant ferocity, it had also a sort of military discipline. The clusters of men voluntarily deployed into cordons, and in some rough fashion followed the command of leaders. Father Bernard was there, with a face of bronze, like the mask of a Roman emperor, eagerly obeyed by his crowd of crusading devotees, and beside him the wild preacher, Hyacinth, who looked himself like a dead man brought out of the grave, with a face built out of bones, and cavernous eye-sockets deep and dark enough to hide the eyes. On the other side were the grim pallor of Bertrand and the rat-like activity of the red-haired Dr. Garth; their own anti-clerical mob was roaring behind them, and their eyes were alight with triumph. Before

Armitage could collect himself sufficiently to make proper notes of any of these things, Bertrand had sprung upon a chair placed near the pedestal of the statue, and announced almost without words, by one dramatic gesture, that he had come to avenge the dead.

Then the words came, and they came thick and fast, telling and terrible; but Armitage heard them as in a dream till they reached the point for which he was waiting; the point that would awaken any dreamer. He heard the prose poems of laudation, the hymn to Boyg the hero, the tale of his tragedy so far as he knew it already. He heard the official decision about the impossibility of the clerics concealing the corpse, as he had heard it already. And then he and the whole crowd leapt together at something they did not know before; or rather, as in all such riddles, something they did know and did not understand.

"They plead that their cells are bare and their lives simple," Bertrand was saying, "and it is true that these slaves of superstition are cut off from the natural joys of men. But they have their joys; oh, believe me, they have their festivities. If they cannot rejoice in love, they can rejoice in hatred. And everybody seems to have forgotten that on the very day the Master vanished, the theological students in their own quadrangle burnt him in effigy. In effigy."

A thrill that was hardly a whisper, but was wilder than a cry, went through the whole crowd; and men had taken in the whole meaning before they could keep pace with the words that followed.

"Did they burn Bruno in effigy? Did they burn Dolet in effigy?" Bertrand was saying, with a white, fanatical face. "Those martyrs of the truth were burned alive for the good of their Church and for the glory of their God. Oh, yes, progress has improved them; and they did not burn Boyg alive. But they burned him dead; and that is how they obliterated the traces of the way they had done him to death. I have said that truth is not always hidden in a well, but rather high on a tower. And while I have searched every crevice and cactus bush for the bones of my master, it was in truth in public, under the open sky, before a roaring crowd in the quadrangle, that his body vanished from the sight of men."

When the last cheer and howl of a whole hell of such noises had died away, Father Bernard succeeded in making his voice heard.

"It is enough to say in answer to this maniac charge that the atheists who bring it against us cannot induce their own atheistic Government to support them. But as the charge is against Father Hyacinth rather than against me, I will ask him to reply to it."

There was another tornado of conflicting noises when the eremitical preacher opened his mouth; but his very tones had a certain power of piercing, and quelling it. There was something strange in such a voice coming out of such a skull-and-cross-bones of a countenance; for it was unmistakably the musical and moving voice that had stirred so many congregations and pilgrimages. Only in this crisis it had an awful accent of reality, which was beyond any arts of oratory. But before the tumult had yet died away Armitage, moved by some odd nervous instinct, had turned abruptly to Garth and said, "What's become of Gale? He said he was going to be here. Didn't he talk some nonsense about bringing the body himself?"

Dr. Garth shrugged his shoulders. "I imagine he's talking some other nonsense at the top of the hill somewhere else. You mustn't ask poets to remember all the nonsense they talk."

"My friends," Father Hyacinth was saying, in quiet but penetrating tones. "I have no answer to give to this charge. I have no proofs with which to refute it. If a man can be sent to the guillotine on such evidence, to the guillotine I will go. Do you fancy I do not know that innocent men have been guillotined? M. Bertrand spoke of the burning of Bruno, as if it is only the enemies of the Church that have been burned. Does any Frenchman forget that Joan of Arc was burned; and was she guilty? The first Christians were tortured for being cannibals, a charge as probable as the charge against me. Do you imagine because you kill men now by modern machinery and modern law, that we do not know that you are as likely to kill unjustly as Herod or Heliogabalus? Do you think we do not know that the powers of the world are what they always were, that your lawyers who oppress the poor for hire will shed innocent blood for gold? If I were here to bandy such lawyer's talk, I could use it against you more reasonably than you against me. For what reason am I supposed to have imperilled my soul by such a monstrous crime? For a theory about a theory; for a hypothesis about a hypothesis, for some thin fantastic notion that a discovery about fossils threatened the everlasting truth. I could point to others who had better reasons for murder than that. I could point to a man who by the death of Boyg has inherited the whole power and position of Boyg. I could point to one who is truly the heir and the man whom the crime benefits; who is known to claim much of the discovery as his own; who has been not so much the assistant as the rival of the dead. He alone has given evidence that Boyg was seen on the hill at all on that fatal day. He alone inherits by the death anything solid, from the largest ambitions in the scientific world, to the smallest magnifying glass in his collection. The man lives, and I could stretch out my hand and touch him."

Hundreds of faces were turned upon Bertrand with a frightful expression of inhuman eagerness; the turn of the debate had been too dramatic to raise a cry. Bertrand's very lips were pale, but they smiled as they formed the words:

"And what did I do with the body?"

"God grant you did nothing with it, dead or alive," answered the other. "I do not charge you; but if ever you are charged as I am unjustly, you may need a God on that day. Though I were ten times guillotined, God could testify to my innocence; if it were by bidding me walk these streets, like St. Denis, with my head in my hand. I have no other proof. I can call no other witness. He can deliver me if He will."

There was a sudden silence, which was somehow stronger than a pause; and in it Armitage could be heard saying sharply, and almost querulously:

"Why, here's Gale again, after all. Have you dropped from the sky?"

Gale was indeed sauntering in a clear space round the corner of the statue with all the appearance of having just arrived at a crowded At Home; and Bertrand was quick to seize the chance of an anti-climax to the hermit's oratory.

"This," he cried, "is a gentleman who thinks he can find the body himself. Have you brought it with you, monsieur?"

The joke about the poet as detective had already been passed round among many people, and the suggestion received a new kind of applause. Somebody called out in a high, piping voice, "He's got it in his pocket"; and another, in deep sepulchral tones, "His waistcoat pocket."

Mr. Gale certainly had his hands in his pockets, whether or no he had anything else in them; and it was with great nonchalance that he replied:

"Well, in that sense, I suppose I haven't got it. But you have."

The next moment he had astonished his friends, who were not used to seeing him so alert, by leaping on the chair, and himself addressing the crowd in clear tones, and in excellent French:

"Well, my friends," he said, "the first thing I have to do is to associate myself with everything said by my honourable friend, if he will allow me to call him so, about the merits and high moral qualities of the late Professor Boyg. Boyg, at any rate, is in every way worthy of all the honour you can pay to him. Whatever else is doubtful, whatever else we differ about, we can all salute in him that search for truth which is the most disinterested of all our duties to God. I agree with my friend Dr. Garth that he deserves to have a statue, not only in his own town, but in every town in the world."

The anti-clericals began to cheer warmly, while their opponents watched in silence, wondering where this last eccentric development might lead. The poet seemed to realize their mystification, and smiled as he continued:

"Perhaps you wonder why I should say that so emphatically. Well, I suppose you all have your own reasons for recognizing this genuine love of truth in the late Professor. But I say it because I happen to know something that perhaps you don't know, which makes me specially certain about his honesty."

"And what is that?" asked Father Bernard, in the pause that followed.

"Because," said Gale, "he was going to see Father Hyacinth to own himself wrong."

Bertrand made a swift movement forward that seemed almost to threaten an assault: but Garth arrested it, and Gale went on, without noticing it.

"Professor Boyg had discovered that his theory was wrong after all. That was the sensational discovery he had made in those last days and with those last experiments. I suspected it when I compared the current tale with his reputation as a simple and kindly man. I did not believe he would have gone merely to triumph over his worst enemy; it was far more probable that he thought it a point of honour to acknowledge his mistake. For, without professing to know much about these things, I am sure it was a mistake. Things do not, after all, need all those thousand years to petrify in that particular fashion. Under certain conditions, which chemists could explain better than I, they do not need more than one year, or even one day. Something in the properties of the local water, applied or intensified by special methods, can really in a few hours turn an animal organism into a fossil. The scientific experiment has been made; and the proof is before you."

He made a gesture with his hand, and went on, with something more like excitement:

"M. Bertrand is right in saying that truth is not in a well, but on a tower. It is on a pedestal. You have looked at it every day. There is the body of Boyg!"

And he pointed to the statue in the middle of the market-place, wreathed with laurel and defaced with stones, as it had stood so long in that quiet square, and looked down at so many casual passers-by.

"Somebody suggested just now," he went on, glancing over a sea of gaping faces, "that I carried the statue in my waistcoat pocket. Well, I don't carry all of it, of course, but this is a part of it," and he took out a small object like a stick of grey chalk; "this is a finger of it knocked off by a stone. I picked it up by the pedestal. If anybody who understands these things likes to look at it, he will agree that the consistency is precisely the same as the admitted fossils in the geological museum."

He held it out to them, but the whole mob stood still as if it also was a mob of men turned to stone.

"Perhaps you think I'm mad," he said pleasantly. "Well, I'm not exactly mad, but I have an odd sort of sympathy with madmen. I can manage them better than most people can, because I can fancy somehow the wild way their minds will work. I understand the man who did this. I know he did, because I talked to him for half the morning; and it's exactly the sort of thing he would do. And when first I heard talk of fossil shells and petrified insects and so on, I did the same thing that such men always do. I exaggerated it into a sort of extravagant vision, a vision of fossil forests, and fossil cattle, and fossil elephants and camels; and so, naturally, to another thought: a coincidence that somehow turned me cold. A Fossil Man.

"It was then that I looked up at the statue; and knew it was not a statue. It was a corpse petrified by the curious chemistry of your strange mountain-stream. I call it a fossil as a loose popular term; of course I know enough geology to know it is not the correct term. But I was not exactly concerned with a problem of geology. I was concerned with what some prefer to call criminology and I prefer to call crime. If that extraordinary erection was the corpse, who and where was the criminal? Who was the assassin who had set up the dead man to be at once obvious and invisible; and had, so to speak, hidden him in the broad daylight? Well, you have all heard the arguments about the stream and the scrap of paper, and up to a point I have entirely followed them. Everyone agreed that the secret was somewhere hidden on that bare hill where there was nothing but the glass-roofed studio and the lonely hermitage; and suspicion centred entirely upon the hermitage. For the man in the studio was a fervent friend of the man who was murdered, and one of those rejoicing most heartily at what he had discovered. But perhaps you have rather forgotten what he really had discovered. His real discovery was of the sort that infuriates friends and not foes. The man who has the courage to say he is wrong has to face the worst hatred; the hatred of those who think he is right. Boyg's final discovery, like our final discovery, rather reverses the relations of those two little houses on the hill. Even if Father Hyacinth had been a fiend instead of a saint, he had no possible motive to prevent his enemy from offering him a public apology. It was a believer in Boygism who struck down Boyg. It was his follower who became his pursuer and persecutor; who at least turned in unreasonable fury upon him. It was Paradou the sculptor who snatched up a chisel and struck his philosophical teacher, at the end of some furious argument about the theory which the artist had valued only as a wild inspiration, being quite indifferent to the tame question of its truth. I don't think he meant to kill Boyg; I doubt whether anybody could possibly prove he did; and even if he did, I rather doubt whether he can be held responsible for that or for anything else. But though Paradou may be a lunatic, he is also a logician; and there is one more interesting logical step in this story.

"I met Paradou myself this morning; owing to my good luck in putting my leg through his skylight. He also has his theories and controversies; and this morning he was very controversial. As I say, I had a long argument with him, all about realism in sculpture. I know many people will tell you that nothing has ever come out of arguments; and I tell you that everything has always come out of arguments; and anyhow, if you want to know what has come out of this, you've got to understand this argument. Everybody was always jeering at poor old Paradou as a sculptor and saying he turned men into monsters; that his figures had flat heads like snakes, or sagging knees like elephants, or humps like human camels. And he was always shouting back at them, 'Yes, and eyes like blindworms when it comes to seeing your own hideous selves! This is what you *do* look like, you ugly brutes! These are the crooked, clownish, lumpish attitudes in which you really do stand; only a lot of lying fashionable portrait-painters have persuaded you that you look like Graces and Greek gods.' He was at it hammer and tongs with me this morning; and I dare say I was lucky he didn't finish that argument with a chisel. But anyhow the argument wasn't started then. It all came upon him with a rush, when he had committed his real though probably unintentional killing. As he stood staring at the corpse, there arose out of the very abyss of his disappointment the vision of a strange vengeance or reparation. He began to see the vast outlines of a joke as gigantic as the Great Pyramid. He would set up that grim granite jest in the market-place, to grin for ever at his critics and detractors. The dead man himself had just been explaining to him the process by which the water of that place would rapidly petrify organic substances. The notes and documents of his proof lay scattered about the studio where he had fallen. His own proof should be applied to his own body, for a purpose of which he had never dreamed. If the sculptor simply lifted the body in the ungainly attitude in which it had actually fallen, if he froze or fixed it in the stream, or set it upon the public pedestal, it would be the very thing about which he had so bitterly debated; a real man, in a real posture, held up to the scorn of men.

"That insane genius promised himself a lonely laughter, and a secret superiority to all his enemies, in hearing the critics discuss it as the crazy creation of a crank sculptor. He looked forward to the groups that would stand before the statue, and prove the anatomy to be wrong, and clearly demonstrate the posture to be impossible. And he would listen, and laugh inwardly like a true lunatic, knowing that they were proving the utter unreality of a real man. That being his dream, he had no difficulty in carrying it out. He had no need to hide the body; he had it brought down from his studio, not secretly but publicly and even pompously, the finished work of a great sculptor escorted by the devotees of a great discoverer.

But indeed, Boyg was something more than a man who made a discovery; and there is, in comparison, a sort of cant even in the talk of a man having the courage to discover it. What other man would have had the courage to undiscover it? That monument that hides a strange sin, hides a much stranger and much rarer virtue. Yes, you do well to hail it as a true scientific trophy. That is the statue of Boyg the Undiscoverer. That cold chimera of the rock is not only the abortion born of some horrible chemical change; it is the outcome of a nobler experiment, which attests for ever the honour and probity of science. You may well praise him as a man of science; for he, at least, in an affair of science, acted like a man. You may well set up statues to him as a hero of science; for he was more of a hero in being wrong than he could ever have been in being right. And though the stars have seen rise, from the soils and substance of our native star, no such monstrosity as that man of stone, heaven may look down with more wonder at the man than at the monster. And we of all schools and of all philosophies can pass it like a funeral procession taking leave of an illustrious grave and, like soldiers, salute it as we pass."

THE VANISHING OF MRS FRASER

Basil Thomson

Sir Basil Thomson (1861–1939) had a colourful career. Educated at Eton and Oxford, he entered the Colonial Service, and became a magistrate in Fiji before returning to England and starting to write. He decided to train as a barrister, but soon turned to prison governorship instead, working in Dartmoor and Wormwood Scrubs. As if that were not enough, he joined Scotland Yard and became head of the CID, as well as becoming involved in counter-espionage and interrogating Mata Hari. But after the First World War, he was pushed out of office, and then humiliated by a sex scandal which may or may not have been orchestrated by his enemies.

In 1925, he published *Mr Pepper, Investigator*, from which this story is taken. The plot is a variation on a familiar theme, turning up in a different guise, for instance, in a popular film of 1950. *PC Richardson's First Case* appeared in 1933, and Richardson's meteoric rise through the ranks of the police is recorded in a series of books. His work, although almost completely forgotten today, earned praise from Dorothy L. Sayers, and merits rediscovery.

* * * * *

If I had ever had any doubts about the almost uncanny cleverness of Mr. Pepper they were dispelled by the way in which he managed the case of Mrs. Fraser. True, his first theory had to be abandoned; but it was he who brought the mystery under his searchlight and probed it to the bottom.

On arriving at the office one day, I found him frowning over a typewritten sheet which purported to be a translation from a paragraph from one of the Paris newspapers. The covering letter, I remember, ran as follows:

> DEAR PEP,—This is something you need to take care of. I would mail you the original but I think you don't read the lingo.
>
> Yours cordially,
> WINSTON E. SLACK.

It was the first intimation I had had that Mr. Pepper was called "Pep" by his intimates.

The cutting related to the alleged disappearance of a Scottish lady, Mrs. Fraser, in Paris, under circumstances which were highly suspicious, if they were true. Supplemented by information that came to me at a later stage, the story was as follows:

Mrs. Fraser and her daughter Mary had been passing the winter in Naples. They left in April and travelled through to Paris without stopping. At the Midi Station a porter trundled a vast trunk to the cab rank and called up a cabman with a pallid, broad face framed in a bushy red beard, who refused to accept the trunk. If it did not sow the seeds of disease in him, he said, it would certainly kill his horse. Mary Fraser, who was the linguist of the two, reasoned with him, and in the end persuaded him to accept the two, trunk and all, for ten francs. They drove to that little family hotel in the Rue Cambon, the Hotel des Etrangers, much frequented by English people with slender means. There followed a fresh dispute with

Redbeard, who said that the trunk had strained the springs of his cab, and that sixteen francs was the least that he would take. Mary Fraser, being firm, came to a compromise for twelve; the cabman went off hurling his frank opinion of the English at the concierge, and Mary entered the hotel to find her mother collapsing on a seat in the hall. It fell to Mary to enter their names in the hotel register. She chanced to notice that the name just above theirs was "Dupont," executed with an elaborate flourish to indicate, I suppose, that the writer was a person of consideration.

The front room in the entre-sol was assigned to them. It was an old-fashioned room with a wooden bedstead, a peeling flowered wall-paper, and a threadbare carpet, but all was clean. Mary had to help her mother up the stairs and lay her on the bed. Her strength seemed to have given way. The porter staggered up the stairs with the trunk and dumped it on the floor: Mrs. Fraser groaned with pain at the noise. To her daughter's anxious questions, she answered faintly that she was feeling very ill: that she supposed it was fatigue; that she might sleep. But she was flushed and swollen, and Miss Fraser determined to send for a doctor, and went down to the manageress.

A doctor? Yes, the Manageress knew a very good doctor—Duphot was his name. All her English visitors when they were ill sent for him and spoke well of him afterwards: she could get him to the hotel in five minutes. Presently Dr. Duphot made his appearance. He was the typical French doctor, as round as ball, wearing a black beard cut like a spade. Mary explained the case as well as she could. The doctor listened without speaking, and then made a systematic examination of the sick woman. At last he stood up and addressed Mary Fraser:

"Mademoiselle, there is no cause for anxiety. I shall telephone for the necessary remedies. In the meantime, stay here with Madame. I shall return in a few moments."

Mrs. Fraser had sunk back exhausted. She was breathing quickly and seemed to be half-delirious. The doctor tarried, and at last Mary, unable any longer to bear the strain, went out to the head of the stairs to call him. She did not go down because from her position she could see his back and shoulders in the telephone-box. He seemed to be speaking emphatically; and the Manageress was hovering about outside, listening. Why all this fuss about her mother unless she were very ill indeed? Mary could bear the suspense no longer: she was on her way down when the doctor left the box and met her on the stairs.

"You should not have left your mother, Mademoiselle!" he said gravely, leading the way back into the sickroom. "Now listen; there is no cause for anxiety, but it will save time if you go yourself to fetch the drug I require. My colleague, whose address is on this card, will give it to you. As soon as you receive it, come back. I have ordered a cab for you. You can quite safely leave your mother in my care. It is only for a few minutes: you will soon be back."

There seemed nothing to do but to obey. Mary ran down to the cab and drove off. The sun had set: it began to grow dark as the cab threaded its way through a maze of narrow streets. The distance seemed interminable. At last they crossed the Seine and plunged into another maze. Mary became uneasy and questioned the driver, who answered shortly that the house was now quite near. But it was dark when at last they pulled up at the door of a large block of flats. In spite of the distance they had come, Miss Fraser was surprised at the lowness of the fare. She climbed the interminable stairs to the fifth floor, and touched the bell. The door flew open and a florid woman in a decorated dressing-gown received her as the expected guest. She took her into a tiny sitting-room and bade her feel at home. The doctor was expected every moment: he had gone out on the very business of Mrs. Fraser's illness. And then she branched out into the wonders of Paris. Did Mademoiselle know Paris? Was she under the charm of this capital of the world, so different from London with its gloom and its fogs? She would buy dresses? No? Ah, there was the telephone. Such an infliction, these telephones. She bustled off into the next room and through the communicating door Mary Fraser heard half the conversation and understood about a sixth of it. "Up till what hour?" "Eleven?" "Good"—and the conversation ceased. She waited many minutes: her hostess did not return. A clock struck a half-hour. The clock in the room marked eight: her wristwatch 9.30. Heavens, had she been all that time? She would wait no longer. She distrusted this glib, plausible woman. A terror lest she had fallen into a trap began to take hold of her. She crept softly out into the hall to let herself out by the front door. It was locked. She was trapped.

In her terror she shouted "Madame"! The door of the telephone room was next to that of the sitting-room. She knocked and, getting no answer, turned the handle. That, too, was locked. She beat upon it with her hands.

The door flew open and there stood Madame, flaming with indignation. What was this? Why all this noise? Locked in? Impossible! No one but their two selves was in the flat. She had not locked the front door and therefore, if it was locked, it was

Mademoiselle herself. If she chose to leave just when the doctor was due—he had telephoned that he was coming—well, she was free to go. Mary saw her fumbling in her pocket for the key, and she was first to the door to pull on it. Madame tried it herself and cried, "Tiens! It is indeed locked, but how?" Could she herself have turned the key in absence of mind? What an extraordinary thing! And so saying, she released the catch and threw it open. Before she could close it again Mary was through the gap and racing down the stairs, hearing imploring cries of "Mademoiselle!" growing fainter behind her.

Safe in the street she was not free from her troubles. It had begun to rain and not a vehicle, not even a foot passenger, was to be seen. She hurried from street to street all silent and deserted. At the last she saw the lights of a vehicle which stopped and discharged passengers. She ran and reached it breathless just as the horse began to move. It was a cab and a cab ready for a fare. She gave the name of her hotel and settled down for the interminable drive. But it was not interminable. Two streets, a bridge, the Place de la Concorde, the Rue Cambon, and in five minutes she was at her hotel. It was closed. She rang and a night porter—one she did not know—appeared and asked her politely what she wanted. She replied that she wanted to return to her room. The man admitted her and asked for her name. Fraser? Was she registered? "Yes," she said. "Produce the register and I will show you." But the name of Fraser was not in the register, nor the name of "Dupont," the gentleman who wrote his name with a flourish, nor any other name that she had seen on the page.

"This is the Hotel des Etrangers, isn't it?"

"Yes, Mademoiselle, but you must have mistaken your hotel."

She looked round the hall. It was the same. She asserted that she had been given No. 4 on the first floor.

"No, Mademoiselle," said the man, consulting the room list. "There is no one in No. 4."

"Then send for the Manageress." But this, it seemed, was not to be thought of. When Madame had once retired for the night it would cost him his place if he disturbed her. Mademoiselle had better try to find her own hotel: it must be one of the others in that street. But Mademoiselle was firm. If he would not call the Manageress she would, if she had to force her way into every room in the house. He went off unwillingly to do the deed that might cost him his place and presently Madame, in a dressing-gown and curling pins, appeared. It was the same woman, stern, uncompromising and cold.

"You wish, Mademoiselle...?"

"Madame, you know me. I want to go to my mother." The woman looked puzzled.

"Please explain yourself, Mademoiselle. I have never seen you before." Mary explained; the register was consulted; the woman persisted that she knew nothing of her story. No doctor had been summoned to the hotel that evening. None of the guests had complained of illness. But, as Mademoiselle appeared to be lost and the hour was late, she would let her sleep there. In the morning she could go to the British Consulate!

And so Mary was assigned a room on the second floor and when all was quiet she took her candle and crept softly down to No. 4 to find her mother. The number was on the door; she was in the room, but it was not the same room. There were no roses on an old wall-paper, but a blue art wall-paper, devoid of pattern: no wooden bedstead, but a brass bedstead of the modern kind: no worn carpet, but a staring new floor covering. The washhandstand was of mahogany with a white marble top. The crockery was different, and so were the chairs. It was not the same room. She was worn out. In her own room she sobbed herself to sleep.

They brought her coffee in the morning, and when she went downstairs to pay for it she found that there was no charge. The Manageress, repenting of her rudeness overnight, was polite and even sympathetic.

At ten o'clock she related her story to the British Vice-Consul, whose only comment was to ask her for the address of her relations in England. It was clear that he did not believe her, but she gave him the address of her uncle in Kensington. He introduced her to a colleague, a pleasant man of middle-age, who took her out to lunch with his wife. She gathered that he was the Consulate doctor, and that he was probing her hallucination to its source. His wife, to whom she told her story, was the first person who believed her, and perhaps it was this sensible lady who procured her another interview with the Vice-Consul and an offer to accompany her to the hotel. He explained his mission to the Manageress, who consented to a questioning of the hotel servants on one condition—that the Police Commissary of the district should be present.

This functionary arrived presently with his clerk and a semi-official enquiry was opened. Mary told her story and the Commissary remarked judicially that two witnesses ought to be called—the red-bearded cabman and Dr. Duphot. The clerk went to the telephone while the Manageress was answering the Vice-Consul's questions. She reasserted that she had never seen Mary Fraser before she arrived late in the evening, that no doctor had been summoned and no lady had complained of illness. The Vice-Consul scrutinized the hotel register and then the cabman was announced. He, too, had never seen Mary, had carried no large trunk, had driven no one to the hotel on the previous day. Yes, he had driven foreigners, of course, but never to this hotel for several weeks. And then the doctor—the same man with his square cut beard. He had never seen Mademoiselle in his life—nor had he been called to the hotel yesterday, or indeed for more than three weeks. His evidence was strictly professional and the more convincing on that account. The Vice-Consul asked to see the room, to question the concierge, and when all was done he took leave ceremoniously and escorted Mary to the Consulate.

She, poor girl, saw from his manner that he was now convinced beyond hope of redemption that she was mentally unstable, but at the Consulate she had no time for brooding: her uncle had arrived from London. Mr. Anderson, of Mincing Lane and Vicarage Gate, was not a sympathetic person. He had quarrelled with his sister, Mrs. Fraser, many years before and he had come over in response to the Consul's telegram unwillingly—from what he called a sense of duty, which was really, though he did not know it, the insistence of his wife. After a brief interview with the Vice-Consul he announced that they were leaving by the train at four, and that they must leave for the Gare du Nord immediately.

It was a melancholy journey. Mr. Anderson made no reference to his sister, and if he spoke at all it was about the weather. Mary replied in monosyllables. Her aunt's warm-hearted welcome made up for much, but she, too, said nothing about her mother, nor about Paris or their travels. It was very late and all trooped off to bed. Mary did not sleep.

The details of the story reached me at a later date. All that we had at first was the paragraph in the French newspaper which had published a garbled version of gossip from the Consulate clerks. Mr. Pepper was pondering noisily: I did not like to interrupt him, although to me the case seemed simple enough. Miss Fraser, I thought, must be one of those neurotic young women who imagine things. She must have lost first her memory, then her luggage and then herself. The hotel she pitched on as the site for her hallucination about the loss of her mother refused to admit her, and somewhere her mother must be searching for her and for all we knew might already have found her. Mr. Pepper fetched a book from the laboratory—an American book about Secret Societies—and while he was turning over the pages with his thick fingers I ventured to ask whether he had formed any theory. He made no answer until he had found the passage he was looking for, and then he said, "I want to hear what you think, Mr. Meddleston-Jones." I told him. He gave a short laugh.

"The young woman was telling the truth."

"Then you think it was a murder?—that she murdered her mother?"

"Not at all." There was a triumphant note in his voice that convinced me that he had solved the problem. I was puzzled and expectant.

"You noticed," he went on, "that the daughter described how she was spirited away to the other side of Paris and detained there for hours."

"To get her out of the way?"

"And that when she returned she found the room entirely changed—new wall-paper, new furniture, a new carpet."

"You mean that they re-furnished the room while she was away? But why, unless someone had murdered her."

"And that these two ladies had come from Naples?"

"Yes, but I don't see the connection——"

"Evidently you've never heard of the Mafia." Light was beginning to dawn on me.

"You mean, Mr. Pepper, that she was kidnapped by the Mafia."

"I mean that this lady, Mrs. Fraser, had been dabbling in Naples with politics, as so many of your English women do; that the Mafia took her measure and hunted her out of the place; that she knew too much. First they tried to poison her on the train—a waiter in the restaurant car dropped a pinch of powder into her food, but she was a Scotchwoman and it wasn't strong enough—and then they went to work in Paris in their usual way. They terrorized the hotel management, the cabman and the others; got the daughter out of the way, terrorized the furniture man and changed the room——"

"But the doctor?"

"Oh, he wasn't a doctor at all. He was the head of the Mafia outfit in Paris. I think I could lay my finger on him in five minutes."

"And Mrs. Fraser is dead?"

"Probably not dead yet: she is being held to ransom while they are going through her papers. If she can't pay they will drop her into the Seine in a sack, probably to-morrow or on Thursday."

"Do you know that Mrs. Fraser is the sort of woman who would dabble in Neapolitan politics, Mr. Pepper?"

"They all do, or if they don't the Mafia think they do, which comes to the same thing."

"But this is frightful. What are you going to do about it?"

"I am going to get that Mafia outfit before they get me. That's what I am going to do. I may want you to run over to Paris some day this week. You speak French, I know." He had risen and was putting on his coat. I took the hint and made for the Club with my head full of the impending fate of that poor lady held to ransom in the attic of a filthy Italian lodging-house, with death hanging over her head.

The only man in the smoking-room was Jimmy Boyd, whose practice at the Bar was growing so fast that one scarcely saw him in these days. He laid down his evening paper and seemed inclined to talk.

"Someone told me that you were mixed up with that Yankee detective fellow, Pepper," he said. "What's all this nonsense about a Mrs. Fraser and the Mafia?" He pointed to a paragraph and gave it me to read. These reporters are extraordinarily indiscreet. Nothing escapes them. The paragraph was an English version of the French newspaper account, but it went on to say that Mr. Pepper, "the world-famous American detective," was engaged upon the case and that sensational developments were expected; that there was now reason to believe that Mrs. Fraser had been the victim of a widespread secret conspiracy, from which, unless it was unmasked by Mr. Pepper, no English traveller would be safe.

"What I want to know," said Boyd, "is the identity of Mrs. Fraser. It is a common name. In my dancing days I used to know a mother and daughter of that name. They lived in Hampstead when they were not travelling abroad. They were charming people. I wouldn't have anything happen to them for worlds."

I had to confess that I did not know them, and could not say where they lived.

"This Pepper fellow who is always getting his name into the newspapers——" At this moment a club waiter came up and, addressing Boyd, said, "You are wanted on the telephone, sir." He left me for a few minutes and returned in some excitement.

"A most extraordinary thing, Meddleston-Jones. Do you know who called me on the telephone? Miss Fraser herself. She wants me to go to her in Kensington at once. Have you had lunch?" I had not. "Because I want you to go with me. She asked me whether I knew anyone who could help her and begged that I would bring him with me."

I had no thought of lunch, nor had he. While we were bowling along to Vicarage Gate he told me about Miss Fraser's journey and her position in her uncle's house—disbelieved by everyone and treated as a person suffering from delusions. All this she had contrived to tell him on the telephone after two unsuccessful attempts to find him earlier in the day.

Miss Fraser was at luncheon when we arrived, but she came out of the dining-room at once. She was a handsome, slender girl of about twenty-five, a little nervous and overwrought, but perfectly collected. I hung back when she showed us into her uncle's den, something in her manner and Boyd's having warned me that they had better be left alone together. In earlier days, I fancy that there must have been a dawning romance between them.

Presently I was called in to hear the whole story from her lips. I don't know what Boyd had been saying about me, but she treated me as if I were a master of detective science—as if I were the Master himself. It was very flattering to my self-esteem. I was certain after hearing and seeing her that Mr. Pepper had been right: she was telling me the actual truth, but when Boyd said suddenly, "I believe that Mr. Meddleston-Jones is prepared to cross by the next boat if you ask him," I was taken aback. How could I do this without consulting Mr. Pepper?

"You see," said Boyd, "I don't speak French, and I've an important case on to-morrow or I'd come with you. According to the papers you, or this Pepper fellow, have got a theory and you can run it to ground while the scent is fresh. I see that you took notes of the names while Miss Fraser was telling her story. Will you go?"

I looked at my watch. There was just time to catch the four o'clock train. My chief himself had talked about sending me to Paris. Why should I not surprise him? Leaving Jimmy Boyd with Miss Fraser, who really seemed quite grateful to me, I went back to the Club to cash a cheque and to scribble a note to Mr. Pepper telling him that business had taken me to Paris for a day or two and that I would keep my eyes open while I was there. I gave him my Paris address in case he should wish to communicate with me.

I pondered deeply over the case on my way over: somehow Mr. Pepper's theory, fantastic though it was, that the daughter was purposely got rid of while the mother was being spirited away and the aspect of the room was changed, did seem to fit the facts. For what other reason could the page in the register have been tampered with? Mrs. Fraser was poor; if the photograph shown to me by her daughter did not lie, she was unattractive, but the people who thought it worth while to take all this trouble to kidnap her and cover up their tracks were Southerners actuated by motives quite different from those of reasoning beings like ourselves—motives which Mr. Pepper seemed to understand and I did not.

I drove from the Nord Station to the Hotel des Etrangers in the Rue Cambon. I was received by the Manageress, who, to do her justice, did not at all look like a person who would be intimidated into doing what she did not want to do by an Italian with a pistol. I felt that if terrorizing were resorted to in our relations it would be exercised by her without having recourse to any pistol. She did not seem to take to me.

She assigned me a room on the second floor at the back which lent itself to the comedy I intended to play on the morrow. At about nine in the morning I sought her out at the receipt of custom and complained about my room. I was, she was surprised to hear, a literary person, travelling for my health, and I had been medically recommended always to choose a front room on the first floor in every hotel I stayed at. Expense was no object. The lady was sorry but firm. She could not turn the people out of their rooms to meet my wishes: the front rooms of every floor were engaged. I was equally firm. I liked the hotel, but not its back bedrooms. I was writing my experiences for the English papers and if I had been comfortable, I should have liked to mention the Hotel des Etrangers in my article. As it was—

"You write, Monsieur? Tiens! There is certainly a room, but it is newly decorated, and smells of paint. Would Monsieur like to see it?"

I will not try to describe my emotions when I saw the room in which the drama or tragedy of Mrs. Fraser had been enacted. Miss Fraser's account of it was photographic in its accuracy. My luggage was moved down and I was at last able to lock the door against interruption. My first business was to search the room from top to bottom in order to discover who had supplied the new furniture in a desperate hurry. The furniture itself disclosed no maker's name, but when I turned back the carpet I was lucky enough to find half a torn billhead:

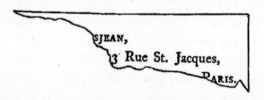

My conjectures about the case had now taken a more concrete form. There might be other more cogent reasons for getting rid of Mrs. Fraser than the suspicions of a secret society, and a news paragraph from Naples had given me a new line to work upon. If I was successful it was Mr. Pepper's wonderful intuition that had furnished me with the first clue and no credit attaches to me, his humble fellow-worker.

With the scrap of paper in my pocket-book I set out on foot for the Rue St. Jacques and visited in turn No. 3, 13, 23, none of which was a shop bearing any name ending in SJEAN, but No. 33 bore the name "Grosjean" in gilt letters over the shop window, and M. Grosjean dealt in wallpapers, paints and bathroom furniture. I walked in boldly and asked the young man for patterns of wallpapers. He showed me hundreds, but found me hard to please. Not one was of the shade of dark blue that I was looking for. I demanded an interview with the manager, who was vapouring about the office at the back. He emerged a little unwillingly, I thought.

"I have not seen all your patterns, Monsieur."

"Yes, Monsieur; we have no others."

"Forgive me, but the pattern I have set my heart on is that which you used in papering the front first-floor bedroom of an hotel in the Rue Cambon last Thursday. You remember, you did it in two hours at the special desire of the authorities?"

The curious change in his features warmed my heart. He was quite a nice-looking French paperhanger when he first came in; he was an unpleasant paperhanger to look upon when I had done with him. Alarm, consternation, suppressed fury possessed his expressive features in turn, and when words failed him and he was reduced to inarticulate hissing, I said suavely, "Used it all up, did you? Well, I am sorry. Good morning."

I took a cab for my next visit, feeling sure that my paperhanger was busy with his telephone.

The policeman on duty in the police station of the Arrondissement was polite but perfectly firm in insisting that I should divulge my business before I had a private interview with his Commissary.

He found me equally firm and when I paltered with the truth and said that I represented the *Times* newspaper in London he departed from his desk to take counsel. Presently he returned and beckoned to me. The Commissary was suspicious and short with me. I said, "Monsieur the Commissary, is it an offence to tamper with an hotel register?"

"If you have a complaint to make, Monsieur, I am listening."

"I assume, Monsieur, that it is an offence. I am come to denounce the Manageress of the Hotel des Etrangers, in the Rue Cambon, of erasing the names of two English ladies named Fraser from her register."

His face was not pretty to look upon. He appeared to be biting his lips to keep the words in. I thought for a moment that he was going to shout for his myrmidons to drop me down an oubliette.

"No matter, Monsieur," I said lightly. "I am quite satisfied," and then as I was going out I dropped these words over my shoulder:

"For a newspaper like the *Times* I am more than satisfied. 'Bubonic Plague in Paris. The Eve of the Great Exhibition.' It will be a great sensation, Monsieur. Good day!"

I returned to my hotel, for now, I felt sure, I had nothing to do but to wait. I think that the telephone had been busy; the Manageress' eyes scorched my face once but did not linger on it. I knew what she was feeling, for I had myself allowed my eyes to rest upon the puff-adder at the Zoo. But I was as easy and unconcerned as that unamiable reptile. Having left my card with the Police Commissary I told the porter that I expected a visitor and went into the salon to wait. Nor was I kept waiting long. The Manageress herself announced my visitor—M. Henri Bonchamps, of the Ministry of the Interior; a very diplomatic gentleman in silk hat and frock coat, brimming over with nervous amiability.

"Mr. Meddleston-Jones? Ah! Monsieur, I am enchanted to make your acquaintance." He looked at the retreating form of the Manageress and assured himself that the door was shut behind her. I put a chair for him and he sat down. "I call upon you at the desire of the Minister himself. His Excellency would have come in person, but unfortunately he has been summoned to the Elysée and he felt that the business was not one that brooked delay. His Excellency has been shocked at learning only this morning that some of his subordinates have been guilty of proceedings that he condemns in the strongest manner. It appears that a poor lady, a compatriot of yours, Monsieur, arrived in Paris with her daughter a day or two ago. She complained of illness, a doctor was called in; he discovered her to be suffering from bubonic plague contracted, no doubt, in Naples, whence she had come. The doctor notified the police and thus far no exception can be taken. But at this point their zeal ran away with them. They ought, of course to have informed the lady's daughter and the British Consul, but instead of this they began an elaborate course of concealment. The daughter was sent away on some pretext and during her absence the poor lady was removed to a hospital, where, unfortunately, she died the same night. They then appear to have deliberately deceived the daughter by pretending that the incident had not occurred. This was entirely indefensible and the Minister is taking very serious measures with all the officials and others concerned.

"You are, no doubt, a relation of the poor lady, Monsieur,—a relation closely connected with the press in England. In tendering His Excellency's apologies, I am desired to say that the lady was reverently interred in the Père La Chaise cemetery. I have with me the certificate and the title to the grave which His Excellency begs you to accept on behalf of the lady's family. If there is anything else that you think should be done, Monsieur, you have only to suggest it. There is one request, one hope, I should say, that His Excellency desires to express. He does hope, he does most earnestly hope, that if possible no mention should be made in any newspaper of this most unfortunate occurrence. A mention of bubonic plague, for example, on the very eve of a Great Exhibition, would be deplored by us all—deplored even by your own compatriots in Paris. May I reassure His Excellency on this point?"

The gentleman had discharged his task with delicacy and skill, but I was not at all convinced that the Minister's indignation and regret had not made its appearance at the moment when he thought he had been found out. I had the documentary evidence, the case was cleared up; I had only to tell the Consul and return to London.

My first visit was to Vicarage Gate, where I broke the news to the aunt and left her to tell Miss Fraser. She was very strongly against any publicity and on this occasion I resolved to tell Mr. Pepper something less than the truth. I felt that in all innocence he might happen to mention the case in the hearing of his press agent and these journalists are so dreadfully indiscreet.

I presented myself at the office without saying a word.

"Well," said Mr. Pepper, "what was Paris like?"

"Cool and a little showery," I replied.

"Ah!"—a pause—"did you hear anything about the Fraser case?"

"Yes," I said, "you were right, Mr. Pepper, as you generally are, I believe that the furniture in the room was changed while Miss Fraser was out."

"Under threats from the Mafia?" He was begining to crow.

"Under a threat of some sort emanating from Naples, Mr. Pepper—at least, that is what I think. But the poor lady is dead—so the police believe—and the British Consul desires that for the present everything should be left to him. Any publicity at this point would ruin everything."

"Ah, well. They will never get the guilty people. You'll see."

"I think you are right in that too, Mr. Pepper."

A MYSTERY OF THE SAND-HILLS

R. AUSTIN FREEMAN

Richard Austin Freeman (1862–1943) was, like Arthur Conan Doyle, a doctor who turned to writing to supplement his income, and found success beyond his dreams. Freeman never matched Conan Doyle for creation of atmosphere, and his principal detective, Dr John Thorndyke, was a much less charismatic figure than Holmes. But what he lacked in literary flair, he made up for with meticulous craftsmanship, and his admirers included T. S. Eliot and Raymond Chandler.

Freeman's 'inverted stories' were a notable innovation; he showed the criminal at work, before describing how he was tracked down. This method of storytelling has stood the test of time: the American TV series *Columbo*, for instance, used it splendidly. And Freeman's depiction of scientific methods of detection, as practised by Thorndyke in this story, remains a model for writers seeking to combine mystification with authenticity.

* * * * *

I HAVE occasionally wondered how often Mystery and Romance present themselves to us ordinary men of affairs only to be passed by without recognition. More often, I suspect, than most of us imagine. The uncanny tendency of my talented friend John Thorndyke to become involved in strange, mysterious and abnormal circumstances has almost become a joke against him. But yet, on reflection, I am disposed to think that his experiences have not differed essentially from those of other men, but that his extraordinary powers of observation and rapid inference have enabled him to detect abnormal elements in what, to ordinary men, appeared to be quite commonplace occurrences. Certainly this was so in the singular Roscoff case, in which, if I had been alone, I should assuredly have seen nothing to merit more than a passing attention.

It happened that on a certain summer morning—it was the fourteenth of August, to be exact—we were discussing this very subject as we walked across the golf-links from Sandwich towards the sea. I was spending a holiday in the old town with my wife, in order that she might paint the ancient streets, and we had induced Thorndyke to come down and stay with us for a few days. This was his last morning, and we had come forth betimes to stroll across the sand-hills to Shellness.

It was a solitary place in those days. When we came off the sand-hills on to the smooth, sandy beach, there was not a soul in sight, and our own footprints were the first to mark the firm strip of sand between high-water mark and the edge of the quiet surf.

We had walked a hundred yards or so when Thorndyke stopped and looked down at the dry sand above tide-marks and then along the wet beach.

"Would that be a shrimper?" he cogitated, referring to some impressions of bare feet in the sand. "If so, he couldn't have come from Pegwell, for the River Stour bars the way. But he came out of the sea and seems to have made straight for the sand-hills."

"Then he probably was a shrimper," said I, not deeply interested.

"Yet," said Thorndyke, "it was an odd time for a shrimper to be at work."

"What was an odd time?" I demanded. "When was he at work?"

"He came out of the sea at this place," Thorndyke replied, glancing at his watch, "at about half-past eleven last night, or from that to twelve."

"Good Lord, Thorndyke!" I exclaimed, "how on earth do you know that?"

"But it is obvious, Anstey," he replied. "It is now half-past nine, and it will be high-water at eleven, as we ascertained before we came out. Now, if you look at those footprints on the sand, you see that they stop short—or rather begin—about two-thirds of the distance from high-water mark to the edge of the surf. Since they are visible and distinct, they must have been made after last high-water. But since they do not extend to the water's edge, they must have been made when the tide was going out; and the place where they begin is the place where the edge of the surf was when the footprints were made. But that place is, as we see, about an hour below the high-water mark. Therefore, when the man came out of the sea, the tide had been going down for an hour, roughly. As it is high-water at eleven this morning, it was high-water at about ten-forty last night; and as the man came out of the sea about an hour after high-water, he must have come out at, or about, eleven-forty. Isn't that obvious?"

"Perfectly," I replied, laughing. "It is as simple as sucking eggs when you think it out. But how the deuce do you manage always to spot these obvious things at a glance? Most men would have just glanced at those footprints and passed them without a second thought."

"That," he replied, "is a mere matter of habit; the habit of trying to extract the significance of simple appearances. It has become almost automatic with me."

During our discussion we had been walking forward slowly, straying on to the edge of the sand-hills. Suddenly, in a hollow between the hills, my eye lighted upon a heap of clothes, apparently, to judge by their orderly disposal, those of a bather. Thorndyke also had observed them and we approached together and looked down on them curiously.

"Here is another problem for you," said I. "Find the bather. I don't see him anywhere."

"You won't find him here," said Thorndyke. "These clothes have been out all night. Do you see the little spider's web on the boots with a few dewdrops still clinging to it? There has been no dew forming for a good many hours. Let us have a look at the beach."

We strode out through the loose sand and stiff, reedy grass to the smooth beach, and here we could plainly see a line of prints of naked feet leading straight down to the sea, but ending abruptly about two-thirds of the way to the water's edge.

"This looks like your nocturnal shrimper," said I. "He seems to have gone into the sea here and come out at the other place. But if they are the same footprints, he must have forgotten to dress before he went home. It is a quaint affair."

"It is a most remarkable affair," Thorndyke agreed; "and if the footprints are not the same it will be still more inexplicable."

He produced from his pocket a small spring tape-measure with which he carefully took the lengths of two of the most distinct footprints and the length of the stride. Then we walked back along the beach to the other set of tracks, two of which he measured in the same manner.

"Apparently they are the same," he said, putting away his tape; "indeed, they could hardly be otherwise. But the mystery is, what has become of the man? He couldn't have gone away without his clothes, unless he is a lunatic, which his proceedings rather suggest. There is just the possibility that he went into the sea again and was drowned. Shall we walk along towards Shellness and see if we can find any further traces?"

We walked nearly half a mile along the beach, but the smooth surface of the sand was everywhere unbroken. At length we turned to retrace our steps; and at this moment I observed two men advancing across the sand-hills. By the time we had reached the mysterious heap of garments they were quite near, and, attracted no doubt by the intentness with which we were regarding the clothes, they altered their course to see what we were looking at. As they approached, I recognized one of them as a barrister named Hallett, a neighbour of mine in the Temple, whom I had already met in the town, and we exchanged greetings.

"What is the excitement?" he asked, looking at the heap of clothes and then glancing along the deserted beach; "and where is the owner of the togs? I don't see him anywhere."

"That is the problem," said I. "He seems to have disappeared."

"Gad!" exclaimed Hallett, "if he has gone home without his clothes, he'll create a sensation in the town! What?"

Here the other man, who carried a set of golf clubs, stooped over the clothes with a look of keen interest.

"I believe I recognize these things, Hallett; in fact, I am sure I do. That waistcoat, for instance. You must have noticed that waistcoat. I saw you playing with the chap a couple of days ago. Tall, clean-shaven, dark fellow. Temporary member, you know. What was his name? Popoff, or something like that?"

"Roscoff," said Hallett. "Yes, by Jove, I believe you are right. And now I come to think of it, he mentioned to me that he sometimes came up here for a swim. He said he particularly liked a paddle by moonlight, and I told him he was a fool to run the risk of bathing in a lonely place like this, especially at night."

"Well, that is what he seems to have done," said Thorndyke, "for these clothes have certainly been here all night, as you can see by that spider's web."

"Then he has come to grief, poor beggar!" said Hallett; "probably got carried away by the current. There is a devil of a tide here on the flood."

He started to walk towards the beach, and the other man, dropping his clubs, followed.

"Yes," said Hallett, "that is what has happened. You can see his footprints plainly enough going down to the sea; but there are no tracks coming back."

"There are some tracks of bare feet coming out of the sea farther up the beach," said I, "which seem to be his."

Hallett shook his head. "They can't be his," he said, "for it is obvious that he never did come back. Probably they are the tracks of some shrimper. The question is, what are we to do? Better take his things to the dormy-house and then let the police know what has happened."

We went back and began to gather up the clothes, each of us taking one or two articles.

"You were right, Morris," said Hallett, as he picked up the shirt. "Here's his name, 'P. Roscoff,' and I see it is on the vest and the shorts, too. And I recognize the stick now—not that that matters, as the clothes are marked."

On our way across the links to the dormy-house mutual introductions took place. Morris was a London solicitor, and both he and Hallett knew Thorndyke by name.

"The coroner will have an expert witness," Hallett remarked as we entered the house. "Rather a waste in a simple case like this. We had better put the things in here."

He opened the door of a small room furnished with a good-sized table and a set of lockers, into one of which he inserted a key.

"Before we lock them up," said Thorndyke, "I suggest that we make and sign a list of them and of the contents of the pockets to put with them."

"Very well," agreed Hallett. "You know the ropes in these cases. I'll write down the descriptions, if you will call them out."

Thorndyke looked over the collection and first enumerated the articles: a tweed jacket and trousers, light, knitted wool waistcoat, black and yellow stripes, blue cotton shirt, net vest and shorts, marked in ink "P. Roscoff," brown merino socks, brown shoes, tweed cap, and a walking-stick—a mottled Malacca cane with a horn crooked handle. When Hallett had written down this list, Thorndyke laid the clothes on the table and began to empty the pockets, one at a time, dictating the descriptions of the articles to Hallett while Morris took them from him and laid them on a sheet of newspaper. In the jacket pockets were a hand-kerchief, marked "P. R."; a lettercase containing a few stamps, one or two hotel bills and local tradesmen's receipts, and some visiting-cards inscribed "Mr. Peter Roscoff, Bell Hotel, Sand-wich"; a leather cigarette-case, a 3B pencil fitted with a point-protector, and a fragment of what Thorndyke decided to be vine charcoal.

"That lot is not very illuminating," remarked Morris, peering into the pockets of the letter-case. "No letter or anything indi-cating his permanent address. However, that isn't our concern." He laid aside the letter-case, and picking up a pocket-knife that Thorndyke had just taken from the trousers pocket, examined it curiously. "Queer knife, that," he remarked. "Steel blade—mighty sharp, too—nail file and an ivory blade. Silly arrangement, it seems. A paper-knife is more convenient carried loose, and you don't want a handle to it."

"Perhaps it was meant for a fruit-knife," suggested Hallett, add-ing it to the list and glancing at a little heap of silver coins that Thorndyke had just laid down. "I wonder," he added, "what has made that money turn so black. Looks as if he had been taking some medicine containing sulphur. What do you think, doctor?"

"It is quite a probable explanation," replied Thorndyke, "though we haven't the means of testing it. But you notice that this vesta-box from the other pocket is quite bright, which is rather against your theory."

He held out a little silver box bearing the engraved monogram "P.R.," the burnished surface of which contrasted strongly with the dull brownish-black of the coins. Hallett looked at it with an affirmative grunt, and having entered it in his list and added a bunch of keys and a watch from the waistcoat pocket, laid down his pen.

"That's the lot, is it?" said he, rising and beginning to gather up the clothes. "My word! Look at the sand on the table! Isn't it astonishing how saturated with sand one's clothes become after a day on the links here? When I undress at night, the bath-room floor is like the bottom of a bird-cage. Shall I put the things in the locker now?"

"I think," said Thorndyke, "that, as I may have to give evidence, I should like to look them over before you put them away."

Hallett grinned. "There's going to be some expert evidence after all," he said. "Well, fire away, and let me know when you have finished. I am going to smoke a cigarette outside."

With this, he and Morris sauntered out, and I thought it best to go with them, though I was a little curious as to my colleague's object in examining these derelicts. However, my curiosity was not entirely balked, for my friends went no farther than the little garden that surrounded the house, and from the place where we stood I was able to look in through the window and observe Thorndyke's proceedings.

Very methodical they were. First he laid on the table a sheet of newspaper and on this deposited the jacket, which he examined carefully all over, picking some small object off the inside near the front, and giving special attention to a thick smear of paint which I had noticed on the left cuff. Then, with his spring tape he measured the sleeves and other principal dimensions. Finally, holding the jacket upside down, he beat it gently with his stick, causing a shower of sand to fall on the paper. He then laid the jacket aside, and, taking from his pocket one or two seed-envelopes (which I believe he always carried), very carefully shot the sand from the paper into one of them and wrote a few words on it—presumably the source of the sand— and similarly disposing of the small object that he had picked off the surface.

This rather odd procedure was repeated with the other garments—a fresh sheet of newspaper being used for each—and with the socks, shoes, and cap. The latter he examined minutely, especially as to the inside, from which he picked out two or three small objects, which I could not see, but assumed to be hairs. Even the walking-stick was inspected and measured, and the articles from the pockets scrutinized afresh, particularly the curious pocket-knife, the ivory blade of which he examined on both sides through his lens.

Hallett and Morris glanced in at him from time to time with indulgent smiles, and the former remarked:

"I like the hopeful enthusiasm of the real pukka expert, and the way he refuses to admit the existence of the ordinary and commonplace. I wonder what he has found out from those things. But here he is. Well, doctor, what's the verdict? Was it temporary insanity or misadventure?"

Thorndyke shook his head. "The inquiry is adjourned pending the production of fresh evidence," he replied, adding: "I have folded the clothes up and put all the effects together in a paper parcel, excepting the stick."

When Hallett had deposited the derelicts in the locker, he came out and looked across the links with an air of indecision.

"I suppose," said he, "we ought to notify the police. I'll do that. When do you think the body is likely to wash up, and where?"

"It is impossible to say," replied Thorndyke. "The set of the current is towards the Thames, but the body might wash up anywhere along the coast. A case is recorded of a bather drowned off Brighton whose body came up six weeks later at Walton-on-the-Naze. But that was quite exceptional. I shall send the coroner and the Chief Constable a note with my address, and I should think you had better do the same. And that is all that we can do, until we get the summons for the inquest, if there ever is one."

To this we all agreed; and as the morning was now spent, we walked back together across the links to the town, where we encountered my wife returning homeward with her sketching kit. This Thorndyke and I took possession of, and having parted from Hallett and Morris opposite the Barbican, we made our way to our lodgings in quest of lunch. Naturally, the events of the morning were related to my wife and discussed by us all, but I noted that Thorndyke made no reference to his inspection of the clothes, and accordingly I said nothing about the matter before my wife; and no opportunity of opening the subject occurred until the evening, when I accompanied him to the station. Then, as we paced the platform while waiting for his train, I put my question:

"By the way, did you extract any information from those garments? I saw you going through them very thoroughly."

"I got a suggestion from them," he replied; "but it is such an odd one that I hardly like to mention it. Taking the appearances at their face value, the suggestion was that the clothes were not all those of the same man. There seemed to be traces of two men, one of whom appeared to belong to this district, while the other would seem to have been associated with the eastern coast of Thanet between Ramsgate and Margate, and by preference, on the scale of probabilities, to Dumpton or Broadstairs."

"How on earth did you arrive at the localities?" I asked.

"Principally," he replied, "by the peculiarities of the sand which fell from the garments and which was not the same in all of them. You see, Anstey," he continued, "sand is analogous to dust. Both consist of minute fragments detached from larger masses; and just as, by examining microscopically the dust of a room, you can ascertain the colour and material of the carpets, curtains, furniture coverings, and other textiles, detached particles of which form the dust of that room, so, by examining sand, you can judge of the character of the cliffs, rocks, and other large masses that occur in the locality, fragments of which become ground off by the surf and incorporated in the sand of the beach. Some of the sand from these clothes is very characteristic and will probably be still more so when I examine it under the microscope."

"But," I objected, "isn't there a fallacy in that line of reasoning? Might not one man have worn the different garments at different times and in different places?"

"That is certainly a possibility that has to be borne in mind," he replied. "But here comes my train. We shall have to adjourn this discussion until you come back to the mill."

As a matter of fact, the discussion was never resumed, for, by the time that I came back to "the mill," the affair had faded from my mind, and the accumulations of grist monopolized my attention; and it is probable that it would have passed into complete oblivion but for the circumstance of its being revived in a very singular manner, which was as follows.

One afternoon about the middle of October my old friend, Mr. Brodribb, a well-known solicitor, called to give me some verbal instructions. When we had finished our business, he said:

"I've got a client waiting outside, whom I am taking up to introduce to Thorndyke. You'd better come along with us."

"What is the nature of your client's case?" I asked.

"Hanged if I know," chuckled Brodribb. "He won't say. That's why I am taking him to our friend. I've never seen Thorndyke stumped yet, but I think this case will put the lid on him. Are you coming?"

"I am, most emphatically," said I, "if your client doesn't object."

"He's not going to be asked," said Brodribb. "He'll think you are part of the show. Here he is."

In my outer office we found a gentlemanly, middle-aged man to whom Brodribb introduced me, and whom he hustled down the stairs and up King's Bench Walk to Thorndyke's chambers. There we found my colleague earnestly studying a will with the aid of a watchmaker's eye-glass, and Brodribb opened the proceedings without ceremony.

"I've brought a client of mine, Mr. Capes, to see you, Thorndyke. He has a little problem that he wants you to solve."

Thorndyke bowed to the client and then asked:

"What is the nature of the problem?"

"Ah!" said Brodribb, with a mischievous twinkle, "that's what you've got to find out. Mr. Capes is a somewhat reticent gentleman."

Thorndyke cast a quick look at the client and from him to the solicitor. It was not the first time that old Brodribb's high spirits had overflowed in the form of a "leg-pull," though Thorndyke had no more whole-hearted admirer than the shrewd, facetious old lawyer.

Mr. Capes smiled a deprecating smile. "It isn't quite so bad as that," he said. "But I really can't give you much information. It isn't mine to give. I am afraid of telling some one else's secrets, if I say very much."

"Of course you mustn't do that," said Thorndyke. "But I suppose you can indicate in general terms the nature of your difficulty and the kind of help you want from us."

"I think I can," Mr. Capes replied. "At any rate, I will try. My difficulty is that a certain person with whom I wish to communicate has disappeared in what appears to me to be a rather remarkable manner. When I last heard from him, he was staying at a certain seaside resort and he stated in his letter that he was returning on the following day to his rooms in London. A few days later, I called at his rooms and found that he had not yet returned. But his luggage, which he had sent on independently, had arrived on the day which he had mentioned. So it is evident that he must have left his seaside lodgings. But from that day to this I have had no communication from him, and he has never returned to his rooms nor written to his landlady."

"About how long ago was this?" Thorndyke asked.

"It is just about two months since I heard from him."

"You don't wish to give the name of the seaside resort where he was staying?"

"I think I had better not," answered Mr. Capes. "There are circumstances—they don't concern me, but they do concern him very much—which seem to make it necessary for me to say as little as possible."

"And there is nothing further that you can tell us?"

"I am afraid not, excepting that, if I could get into communication with him, I could tell him of something very much to his advantage and which might prevent him from doing something which it would be much better that he should not do."

Thorndyke cogitated profoundly while Brodribb watched him with undisguised enjoyment. Presently my colleague looked up and addressed our secretive client.

"Did you ever play the game of 'Clumps,' Mr. Capes? It is a somewhat legal form of game in which one player asks questions of the others, who are required to answer 'yes' or 'no' in the proper witness-box style."

"I know the game," said Capes, looking a little puzzled, "but——"

"Shall we try a round or two?" asked Thorndyke, with an unmoved countenance. "You don't wish to make any statements, but if I ask you certain specific questions, will you answer 'yes' or 'no'?"

Mr. Capes reflected awhile. At length he said:

"I am afraid I can't commit myself to a promise. Still, if you like to ask a question or two, I will answer them if I can."

"Very well," said Thorndyke, "then, as a start, supposing I suggest that the date of the letter that you received was the thirteenth of August? What do you say? Yes or no?"

Mr. Capes sat bolt upright and stared at Thorndyke open-mouthed.

"How on earth did you guess that?" he exclaimed in an astonished tone. "It's most extraordinary! But you are right. It was dated the thirteenth."

"Then," said Thorndyke, "as we have fixed the time we will have a try at the place. What do you say if I suggest that the seaside resort was in the neighbourhood of Broadstairs?"

Mr. Capes was positively thunderstruck. As he sat gazing at Thorndyke he looked like amazement personified.

"But," he exclaimed, "you can't be guessing! You know! You know that he was at Broadstairs. And yet, how could you? I haven't even hinted at who he is."

"I have a certain man in my mind," said Thorndyke, "who may have disappeared from Broadstairs. Shall I suggest a few personal characteristics?"

Mr. Capes nodded eagerly and Thorndyke continued:

"If I suggest, for instance, that he was an artist—a painter in oil"—Capes nodded again—"that he was somewhat fastidious as to his pigments?"

"Yes," said Capes. "Unnecessarily so in my opinion, and I am an artist myself. What else?"

"That he worked with his palette in his right hand and held his brush with his left?"

"Yes, yes," exclaimed Capes, half-rising from his chair; "and what was he like?"

"By gum," murmured Brodribb, "we haven't stumped him after all."

Evidently we had not, for he proceeded:

"As to his physical characteristics, I suggest that he was a short-ish man—about five feet seven—rather stout, fair hair, slightly bald and wearing a rather large and ragged moustache."

Mr. Capes was astounded—and so was I, for that matter—and for some moments there was a silence, broken only by old Brodribb, who sat chuckling softly and rubbing his hands. At length Mr. Capes said:

"You have described him exactly, but I needn't tell you that. What I do not understand at all is how you knew that I was refer-ring to this particular man, seeing that I mentioned no name. By the way, sir, may I ask when you saw him last?"

"I have no reason to suppose," replied Thorndyke, "that I have ever seen him at all;" an answer that reduced Mr. Capes to a state of stupefaction and brought our old friend Brodribb to the verge of apoplexy. "This man," Thorndyke continued, "is a purely hypothetical individual whom I have described from certain traces left by him. I have reason to believe that he left Broadstairs on the fourteenth of August and I have certain opinions as to what became of him thereafter. But a few more details would be useful, and I shall continue my interrogation. Now this man sent his luggage on separately. That suggests a possible intention of breaking his journey to London. What do you say?"

"I don't know," replied Capes, "but I think it probable."

"I suggest that he broke his journey for the purpose of holding an interview with some other person."

"I cannot say," answered Capes: "but if he did break his journey it would probably be for that purpose."

"And supposing that interview to have taken place, would it be likely to be an amicable interview?"

"I am afraid not. I suspect that my—er—acquaintance might have made certain proposals which would have been unacceptable, but which he might have been able to enforce. However, that is only surmise," Capes added hastily. "I really know nothing more than I have told you, excepting the missing man's name, and that I would rather not mention."

"It is not material," said Thorndyke, "at least, not at present. If it should become essential, I will let you know."

"M—yes," said Mr. Capes. "But you were saying that you had certain opinions as to what has become of this person."

"Yes," Thorndyke replied; "speculative opinions. But they will have to be verified. If they turn out to be correct—or incorrect either—I will let you know in the course of a few days. Has Mr. Brodribb your address?"

"He has; but you had better have it, too."

He produced his card, and, after an ineffectual effort to extract a statement from Thorndyke, took his departure.

* * * * *

The third act of this singular drama opened in the same setting as the first, for the following Sunday morning found my colleague and me following the path from Sandwich to the sea. But we were not alone this time. At our side marched Major Robertson, the eminent dog-trainer, and behind him trotted one of his superlatively educated fox-hounds.

We came out on the shore at the same point as on the former occasion, and, turning towards Shellness, walked along the smooth sand with a careful eye on the not very distinctive landmarks. At length Thorndyke halted.

"This is the place," said he. "I fixed it in my mind by that distant tree, which coincides with the chimney of that cottage on the marshes. The clothes lay in that hollow between the two big sand-hills."

We advanced to the spot, but, as a hollow is useless as a landmark, Thorndyke ascended the nearest sand-hill and stuck his stick in the summit and tied his handkerchief to the handle.

"That," said he, "will serve as a centre which we can keep in sight, and if we describe a series of gradually widening concentric circles round it, we shall cover the whole ground completely."

"How far do you propose to go?" asked the major.

"We must be guided by the appearance of the ground," replied Thorndyke. "But the circumstances suggest that if there is anything buried, it can't be very far from where the clothes were laid. And it is pretty certain to be in a hollow."

The major nodded; and when he had attached a long leash to the dog's collar, we started, at first skirting the base of the sand-hill, and then, guided by our own footmarks in the loose sand, gradually increasing the distance from the high mound, above which Thorndyke's handkerchief fluttered in the light breeze. Thus we continued, walking slowly, keeping close to the previously made circle of footprints and watching the dog; who certainly did a vast amount of sniffing, but appeared to let his mind run unduly on the subject of rabbits.

In this way half an hour was consumed, and I was beginning to wonder whether we were going after all to draw a blank, when the dog's demeanour underwent a sudden change. At the moment we were crossing a range of high sand hills, covered with stiff, reedy grass and stunted gorse, and before us lay a deep hollow, naked of vegetation and presenting a bare, smooth surface of the characteristic greyish-yellow sand. On the side of the hill the dog checked, and, with upraised muzzle, began to sniff the air with a curiously suspicious expression, clearly unconnected with the rabbit question. On this, the major unfastened the leash, and the dog, left to his own devices, put his nose to the ground and began rapidly to cast to and fro, zig-zagging down the side of the hill and growing every moment more excited. In the same sinuous manner he proceeded across the hollow until he reached a spot near the middle; and here he came to a sudden stop and began to scratch up the sand with furious eagerness.

"It's a find, sure enough!" exclaimed the major, nearly as excited as his pupil; and, as he spoke, he ran down the hill-side, followed by me and Thorndyke, who, as he reached the bottom, drew from his "poacher's pocket" a large fern-trowel in a leather sheath. It was not a very efficient digging implement, but it threw up the loose sand faster than the scratchings of the dog.

It was easy ground to excavate. Working at the spot that the dog had located, Thorndyke had soon hollowed out a small cavity some eighteen inches deep. Into the bottom of this he thrust the pointed blade of the big trowel. Then he paused and looked round at the major and me, who were craning eagerly over the little pit.

"There is something there," said he. "Feel the handle of the trowel."

I grasped the wooden handle, and, working it gently up and down, was aware of a definite but somewhat soft resistance. The major verified my observation and then Thorndyke resumed his digging, widening the pit and working with increased caution. Ten minutes' more careful excavation brought into view a recognizable shape—a shoulder and upper arm; and following the lines of this, further diggings disclosed the form of a head and shoulders plainly discernible though still shrouded in sand. Finally, with the point of the trowel and a borrowed handkerchief—mine—the adhering sand was cleared away; and then, from the bottom of the deep, funnel-shaped hole, there looked up at us, with a most weird and horrible effect, the discoloured face of a man.

In that face, the passing weeks had wrought inevitable changes, on which I need not dwell. But the features were easily recognizable, and I could see at once that the man corresponded completely with Thorndyke's description. The cheeks were full; the hair on the temples was of a pale, yellowish brown; a straggling, fair moustache covered the mouth; and, when the sand had been sufficiently cleared away, I could see a small, tonsure-like bald patch near the back of the crown. But I could see something more than this. On the left temple, just behind the eyebrow, was a ragged, shapeless wound such as might have been made by a hammer.

"That turns into certainty what we have already surmised," said Thorndyke, gently pressing the scalp around the wound. "It must have killed him instantly. The skull is smashed in like an egg-shell. And this is undoubtedly the weapon," he added, drawing out of the sand beside the body a big, hexagon-headed screw-bolt, "very prudently buried with the body. And that is all that really concerns us. We can leave the police to finish the disinterment; but you notice, Anstey, that the corpse is nude with the exception of the vest and probably the pants. The shirt has disappeared. Which is exactly what we should have expected."

Slowly, but with the feeling of something accomplished, we took our way back to the town, having collected Thorndyke's stick on the way. Presently, the major left us, to look up a friend at the club house on the links. As soon as we were alone, I put in a demand for an elucidation.

"I see the general trend of your investigations," said I, "but I can't imagine how they yielded so much detail; as to the personal appearance of this man, for instance."

"The evidence in this case," he replied, "was analogous to circumstantial evidence. It depended on the cumulative effect of a number of facts, each separately inconclusive, but all pointing to the same conclusion. Shall I run over the data in their order and in accordance with their connections?"

I gave an emphatic affirmative, and he continued:

"We begin, naturally, with the first fact, which is, of course, the most interesting and important; the fact which arrests attention, which shows that something has to be explained and possibly suggests a line of inquiry. You remember that I measured the footprints in the sand for comparison with the other foot-prints. Then I had the dimensions of the feet of the presumed bather. But as soon as I looked at the shoes which purported to be those of that bather, I felt a conviction that his feet would never go into them.

"Now, that was a very striking fact—if it really was a fact—and it came on top of another fact hardly less striking. That bather had gone into the sea; and at a considerable distance he had unques-tionably come out again. There could be no possible doubt. In foot-measurements and length of stride the two sets of tracks were identical; and there were no other tracks. That man had come ashore and he had remained ashore. But yet he had not put on his clothes. He couldn't have gone away naked; but, obviously he was not there. As a criminal lawyer, you must admit that there was prima facie evidence of something very abnormal and probably criminal.

"On our way to the dormy-house, I carried the stick in the same hand as my own and noted that it was very little shorter. Therefore it was a tall man's stick. Apparently, then, the stick did not belong to the shoes, but to the man who had made the foot-prints. Then, when we came to the dormy-house, another striking fact presented itself. You remember that Hallett commented on the quantity of sand that fell from the clothes on to the table. I am astonished that he did not notice the very peculiar character of that sand. It was perfectly unlike the sand which would fall from his own clothes. The sand on the sand-hills is dune sand—wind-borne sand, or, as the legal term has it, aeolian sand; and it is perfectly characteristic. As it has been carried by the wind, it is necessarily fine. The grains are small; and as the action of the wind sorts them out, they are extremely uniform in size. Moreover, by being continually blown about and rubbed together, they become rounded by mutual attrition. And then dune sand is nearly pure sand, composed of grains of silica unmixed with other substances.

"Beach sand is quite different. Much of it is half-formed, freshly-broken-down silica and is often very coarse; and, as I pointed out at the time, it is mixed with all sorts of foreign substances derived from masses in the neighbourhood. This particular sand was loaded with black and white particles, of which the white were mostly chalk, and the black particles of coal. Now there is very little chalk in the Shellness sand, as there are no cliffs quite near, and chalk rapidly disappears from sand by reason of its softness; and there is no coal."

"Where does the coal come from?" I asked.

"Principally from the Goodwins," he replied. "It is derived from the cargoes of colliers whose wrecks are embedded in those sands, and from the bunkers of wrecked steamers. This coal sinks down through the seventy odd feet of sand and at last works out at the bottom, where it drifts slowly across the floor of the sea in a north-westerly direction until some easterly gale throws it up on the Thanet shore between Ramsgate and Foreness Point. Most of it comes up at Dumpton and Broadstairs, where you may see the poor people, in the winter, gathering coal pebbles to feed their fires.

"This sand, then, almost certainly came from the Thanet coast; but the missing man, Roscoff, had been staying in Sandwich, playing golf on the sand-hills. This was another striking discrepancy, and it made me decide to examine the clothes exhaustively, garment by garment. I did so; and this is what I found.

"The jacket, trousers, socks and shoes were those of a shortish, rather stout man, as shown by measurements, and the cap was his, since it was made of the same cloth as the jacket and trousers.

"The waistcoat, shirt, underclothes and stick were those of a tall man.

"The garments, socks and shoes of the short man were charged with Thanet beach sand, and contained no dune sand, excepting the cap, which might have fallen off on the sand-hills.

"The waistcoat was saturated with dune sand and contained no beach sand, and a little dune sand was obtained from the shirt and undergarments. That is to say, that the short man's clothes contained beach sand only, while the tall man's clothes contained only dune sand.

"The short man's clothes were all unmarked; the tall man's clothes were either marked or conspicuously recognizable, as the waistcoat and also the stick.

"The garments of the short man which had been left were those that could not have been worn by a tall man without attracting instant attention and the shoes could not have been put on at all; whereas the garments of the short man which had disappeared—the waistcoat, shirt and underclothes—were those that could have been worn by a tall man without attracting attention.

The obvious suggestion was that the tall man had gone off in the short man's shirt and waistcoat but otherwise in his own clothes.

"And now as to the personal characteristics of the short man. From the cap I obtained five hairs. They were all blonde, and two of them were of the peculiar, atrophic, 'point of exclamation' type that grow at the margin of a bald area. Therefore he was a fair man and partially bald. On the inside of the jacket, clinging to the rough tweed, I found a single long, thin, fair moustache hair, which suggested a long, soft moustache. The edge of the left cuff was thickly marked with oil-paint—not a single smear, but an accumulation such as a painter picks up when he reaches with his brush hand across a loaded palette. The suggestion—not very conclusive—was that he was an oil-painter and left-handed. But there was strong confirmation. There was an artist's pencil—3B— and a stump of vine charcoal such as an oil-painter might carry. The silver coins in his pocket were blackened with sulphide as they would be if a piece of artist's soft, vulcanized rubber has been in the pocket with them. And there was the pocket-knife. It contained a sharp steel pencil-blade, a charcoal file and an ivory palette-blade; and that palette-blade had been used by a left-handed man."

"How did you arrive at that?" I asked.

"By the bevels worn at the edges," he replied. "An old palette-knife used by a right-handed man shows a bevel of wear on the under side of the left-hand edge and the upper side of the right-hand edge; in the case of a left-handed man the wear shows on the under side of the right-hand edge and the upper side of the left-hand edge. This being an ivory blade, showed the wear very distinctly and proved conclusively that the user was left-handed; and as an ivory palette-knife is used only by fastidiously careful painters for such pigments as the cadmiums, which might be discoloured by a steel blade, one was justified in assuming that he was somewhat fastidious as to his pigments."

As I listened to Thorndyke's exposition I was profoundly impressed. His conclusions, which had sounded like mere speculative guesses, were, I now realized, based upon an analysis of the evidence as careful and as impartial as the summing up of a judge. And these conclusions he had drawn instantaneously from the appearances of things that had been before my eyes all the time and from which I had learned nothing.

"What do you suppose is the meaning of the affair?" I asked presently. "What was the motive of the murder?"

"We can only guess," he replied. "But, interpreting Capes' hints, I should suspect that our artist friend was a blackmailer; that he had come over here to squeeze Roscoff—perhaps not for the first time—and that his victim lured him out on the sand-hills for a private talk and then took the only effective means of ridding himself of his persecutor. That is my view of the case; but, of course, it is only surmise."

Surmise as it was, however, it turned out to be literally correct. At the inquest Capes had to tell all that he knew; which was uncommonly little, though no one was able to add to it. The murdered man, Joseph Bertrand, had fastened on Roscoff and made a regular income by blackmailing him. That much Capes knew; and he knew that the victim had been in prison and that that was the secret. But who Roscoff was and what was his real name—for Roscoff was apparently a *nom de guerre*—he had no idea. So he could not help the police. The murderer had got clear away and there was no hint as to where to look for him; and so far as I know, nothing has ever been heard of him since.

THE HAZEL ICE

H. C. Bailey

Henry Christopher Bailey (1878–1961), a major figure during the Golden Age of detective fiction, was one of the very few real-life crime writers mentioned in the novels of Agatha Christie; she also wrote a short story parodying his most famous detective, Reggie Fortune. Like Christie and Dorothy L. Sayers (who heaped praise on his short stories), Bailey was a founder-member of the Detection Club. Why, then, does he nowadays suffer from critical neglect? The answer lies in part in the fact that his fame rested heavily on his short stories rather than his novels, which were often less compelling. More seriously, his literary flourishes are mannered and utterly unfashionable.

And yet, Bailey's work has strikingly modern aspects, not least its emotional power. His hatred of cruelty – especially the mistreatment of children – is evident time and again. His plots are well worked, and (like this one) occasionally benefit from Alpine settings. Bailey and his family were fond of visiting the Swiss and Austrian Alps, and when he retired from work as a journalist for the *Daily Telegraph*, the Baileys moved to Llanfairfechan, where life in mountainous Snowdonia reminded them of happy holidays in Europe.

* * * * *

MRS. FORTUNE can be easily led to discuss the institution of marriage. She has then been heard to say, with a sad, impartial eye upon her husband, that the trials of being married to a small boy are not adequately explained in women's education.

They were eating ices under the trees of Interlaken when she mentioned this to an eminent expert of the Swiss police who put his eyebrows up to his shaven scalp and many tones of sympathic emotion and profound thought into his reply: "So? So!" Herr Stein's worship of Mrs. Fortune's Olympian beauty is ennobled by despair. He never knows when she means what she says.

To describe the case scientifically, Mrs. Fortune was eating an ice and Reggie Fortune was eating ices. Herr Stein drank coffee and smoked a cigar. A regrettable incident. The afternoon had no other flaw. The white shoulder of the Jungfrau shone clear. Under the trim trees it was delectably hot, but something of the freshness of the high pastures was in the genial air.

"I want a hazel ice," said Reggie Fortune.

"My dear child!" Mrs. Fortune's charming hands went up. She counted on her fingers.

"No. No. I've only had two. Peaches aren't an ice. And the others were only water ices. One of those nut things is clearly indicated. You know, we can't get them in England, Stein. A great country, but ices are one of the things it won't understand." He looked firmly at his wife. "I do want a hazel ice, Joan."

And then Adrian Trove arrived.

There was somebody at every table. None of them showed any desire to make room for the shabby, dusty man with a bandage round his head. He stood bent under his rucksack, his eyes bloodshot, his red face unshaven, drearily ashamed of himself in that clean company.

Mrs. Fortune has an incurable weakness for lame dogs. "There's a place here," she said gently. Reggie Fortune sighed and drew in a chair with his foot. Herr Stein sprang up and put it straight, smiled and bowed.

"Thanks awfully." Adrian Trove dropped into it. "Awful shame to bother you. I'm just down from Mürren. Going on to Kandersteg. There isn't a train. I just wanted some tea."

Herr Stein snapped his fingers at a waitress, who came and took the order. "You've been climbing?" Mrs. Fortune made conversation.

"Oh, just a bit. I'm no good really."

"That is very English." Herr Stein laughed and nodded to her. "You are all no good really. Then we find out what you have done."

"I haven't done anything," Adrian Trove growled.

Reggie was looking at him with some curiosity. "Have you had a fall, sir?"

"It's nothing. I was knocked over by a fall of stones."

"So." Herr Stein sympathized. "That is nasty luck. The best climbers, they cannot escape that." The tea came and Trove drank eagerly.

"Have you had a doctor look at your head?" said Reggie.

"No. Just tied it up. It's nothing."

"I should, you know. I'm a bit of a doctor myself. You oughtn't to run about till somebody's had a look at you."

"I'm all right, thanks." He gulped his tea. "I must get on. I had a man with me and I don't know what's happened to him."

"Ach, so," said Herr Stein.

"You must be anxious," Mrs. Fortune murmured.

"Yes, rather." He looked at her kind eyes. "You see, we were crossing from Mürren to Kandersteg and there was a fall of stones that laid me out. When I came to, I couldn't find Butler anywhere.

I went back to Mürren to get help. We've searched the whole place. Not a sign of him. So I thought he might have gone on down to Kandersteg."

"I hope you'll find him all right," said Mrs. Fortune.

"Thanks awfully. Thanks." He got on his feet stiffly.

"You know you'd better let me take you up in my car," said Reggie. "That'll be quicker than the train, won't it, Stein?"

Herr Stein laughed. "If you drive, oh yes. That is quicker than anything."

Trove made civil, stumbling objections, was talked down and led away under the trees to Mr. Fortune's hotel. "Now—what about letting me have a look at your head while Stein gets the car out?" But Trove was absolutely all right. Trove didn't want to stop, thanks. Mrs. Fortune vainly wished he would and Stein shrugged and Reggie went for the car.

It drew up at the door and Trove made for it. "Madame permits?" Stein bowed.

"You want to go with him?" said Mrs. Fortune.

"Yes. Perhaps." He ran for a coat and struggling into it reached the car as they started. "I show you the way, my dear Fortune."

"Thanks very much," Reggie smiled. Under his hand the big car had the abandon of a taxi of Paris. He was not thereby hampered in conversation with Mr. Adrian Trove: a very interesting conversation.

Mr. Trove was by trade a chemist, assistant to the eminent consulting chemist Dr. Hardy Butler. They had come to Switzerland on holiday together. They were to spend some time with that potentate of the chemical industry, Sir Samuel Ulyett, who was staying at the Bristol at Kandersteg. Dr. Butler was a veteran mountaineer. He proposed to train Adrian Trove and began with some easy passes. They went from Kandersteg over the Tschingel Glacier to Mürren, slept there and were on their way back by the Hohturli to Kandersteg when the stones fell and Butler vanished.

The car rushed through the pastures of the valley and climbed along a ledge above the river into forest. Far below a lake gleamed turquoise blue out of the trees. Herr Stein braced himself in his corner. Round corkscrew curves the car whirled on the outside edge up and up. The valley flattened out into a broad space between mountains and the purring speed rose high. "Achtung!" Herr Stein boomed. "There will be peoples, my friend." Strolling tourists scattered and fled. The big car cut figures round crawling station buses and stopped at an hotel very new and green and white. "So!" Herr Stein let stored breath out of him. "That was much quicker as the train, Mr. Trove, yes? And we are still alive." He patted Trove's shoulder. "That is wonderful."

Trove got out stiffly. "Thanks very much, Mr. Fortune. Excuse me, won't you? I want to find out——"

"Why, Adrian!" A girl came to him. "Where's Doctor Butler?"

Trove stopped and stared at her. She was a small plump creature, with a chin. Black hair struggled into curls above a dark face.

Her eyes grew big. "Adrian! What's happened?"

"Isn't he back?" said Trove.

"No, no. And you're hurt. Was there an accident?"

"It's nothing. Let's get in, Ruth. I must see your father." He hurried into the hotel, she at his heels.

Herr Stein leaned to Mr. Fortune. "We drink beer, my friend?" he suggested.

"Yes, I think so," Mr. Fortune said.

In the hall they found Trove standing before a little plump man, plainly (in every sense) the girl's father. "Eh lad, what's amiss?" He bent grey eyebrows. "What ha' you done with Butler?" And Trove stumbled through the tale which he had told Mr. Fortune.... "Eh, that's bad." Puckered eyes stared at Trove. "And you never saw what came to the old lad, the way you tell it?"

"He must have been carried away by the stones. When I came to, there wasn't a sign of him."

"But you've had men seeking t'other side, eh, and they found naught?"

"Nothing at all, sir. Not a trace."

"God, it's a queer thing, lad."

"I thought he must have lost me and come on here. He may have tried it and broken down. We must search up from this side, sir. I came round as quick as I could. A man ran me up in his car from Interlaken. We ought to get busy at once."

Mr. Fortune put down his beer and stood up. "I say, Trove, I'm afraid you may want me. Your friend's been lying out rather a long time."

Trove stared, not with good will. "Oh, thanks. Thanks very much. This is Sir Samuel Ulyett, Mr. Fortune."

"I'm a surgeon, sir," Reggie explained.

"I've heard of you," Ulyett said. "Will you be staying here?"

"I might be of some use, you know."

"I'll thank you kindly. If there's aught you can do. We've to find the old lad first. Eh, let's get about it." He bustled away to the office. The landlord was already in the hands of Herr Stein.

Sir Samuel's slow effort to explain himself subsided before the landlord's flow of words. But yes, an accident most distressing. He understood perfectly Sir Ulyett's anxieties. A search must be arranged at once, a thorough search, the whole Blumlisalp. Yes, everything should be done, Sir Ulyett might be sure. By great good fortune, here was Herr Stein of the greatest experience. He was already making the arrangements. With the dawn they would have men all over the mountains. Sir Ulyett must leave everything to him and—Herr Stein.

Ulyett looked at Stein as a sharp employer looks at a man asking for a job. "You know these mountains here?"

"Yes, I know them very well," Stein smiled. "But what I do not know, it is where your friend is lost. Let us ask the Mr. Trove. Pardon." He went out into the hall.

Trove was still there. He was telling his story all over again to a sunburnt man of his own age while the girl listened, pale and intent, Mr. Fortune with the patient interest of a connoisseur in narrative. It ended to exclamations. "Good God, Adrian, how ghastly for you! Poor old Butler! But I say—"

"Pardon." Stein came forward. "Mr. Trove, please. There is a map in the office. Could you show me where the stones fell?"

Trove looked blank. "I don't know. I told them at Mürren. We got up to the place again. At least I think it was the place. But we couldn't find anything. I feel an awful fool. You see, I wasn't taking any notice with Butler. He led and I followed. I'm no good at this mountain business."

"Oh I say, old chap!" the other man protested. "Pretty good work to get down again by yourself."

Trove stared at him. "Good God, I just followed my nose. Rolled down. Fell down. Oh, damned good work!" He laughed.

"But come," Stein was soothing, "let us look at the map, Mr. Trove; I can help you perhaps."

A large-scale map of the district hung on the office wall. He brought Trove to it. "See, there is Mürren and here Kandersteg. Now." Trove pored over it and Mr. Fortune watched his blank face and Stein demonstrated. "You come up here, yes? Then it is down again. There are many stones. On past some châlets. You remember? A stream in a gorge and rocks all twisted. And after—you would be near a glacier—then up over pasture—it becomes very steep—it is all stones. Perhaps you find wet. Then you see the great white mountain—beautiful view, wunderschön! Then——"

"Wait. Wait. It was above the scree. It was somewhere there. A sort of narrow passage in the rock. And a shower of stones came down. About there." Trove put his finger on the map.

"So." Stein smiled and rubbed his hands. "In the couloir, yes." He looked at Trove with his head on one side. "You were—how many hours from Mürren?"

"Oh, about six. Yes, my watch stopped at noon. It's broken. We started from Mürren at six in the morning. I got back there in the afternoon. We went off to search in the evening and slept in some châlet, got up to the passage place this morning soon after dawn. But he wasn't there, you know, he wasn't there!"

"Steady, old chap." The other man took hold of him.

"He is somewhere," said Stein. "We will be up there by the couloir at dawn to-morrow." He turned away to the landlord and talked brisk German.

Reggie came to Trove. "Now, my dear fellow, what about that head of yours?"

"By Jove, yes," the other man cried. "You ought to have that seen to, Adrian. It looks a nasty one."

"Oh damn it, I'm all right," Trove growled. "Don't fuss me, for God's sake." He thrust his way out.

The other man looked at Reggie. "Are you a doctor, sir?"

"Eh lad, he's Mr. Fortune," Ulyett said.

"What, the Mr. Fortune? I say!" He looked puzzled. "But anyway—Adrian ought to have a doctor."

"Yes, I think so," Mr. Fortune murmured.

"I say, I'll see what I can do with him. Poor old Adrian, this has rather knocked him over." He hurried away.

Mr. Fortune was left contemplating Ulyett with dreamy eyes. "Yes. Very distressin'," he murmured. "Well, I'll be here, you know." He sauntered off to a chair on the steps.

Stein made an end of his conference with the landlord and came marching out. Mr. Fortune arose and fell into step with him. "And what about it?" he said softly.

"I do not understand, my friend."

"The place on the map?"

"The place—that is all right. The simple Mr. Trove, who cannot be sure, he points out the very place where it might have happened as he says, the only place almost. That couloir, often there is a fall of stones there and even a good mountaineer might be caught. Yes, that is all right. But the rest——" He shrugged. "It is most curious. We shall see. If his friend is upon the mountain I will find him. I go to talk to the guides here."

"I was going to telephone to my chauffeur to bring up some kit. Yours too?"

"Please," Stein smiled. "Yes, telephone. And my regrets to Mrs. Fortune."

"It is a tryin' world," Mr. Fortune sighed.

Mr. Fortune sat in the lounge waiting for dinner when the girl came downstairs alone. She looked at him, hesitated, took the chair beside him. "You haven't seen Adrian?"

"No. No. The patient don't want to be a patient."

"Do you think he's badly hurt?"

Reggie spread out his hands.

"Of course he's had a horrible shock."

"Yes. That is indicated."

"He will come down to dinner. Father wanted him to go to bed. But David says there isn't much the matter really."

"Does he? David—that's Trove's friend?"

"Mr. Woodham, yes, well, he's really a friend of ours—of father's."

"I see. Have you been here long, Miss Ulyett?"

"Father and I, yes, a fortnight. And Mr. Woodham. Adrian only came the other day with Dr. Butler. That makes it more dreadful. They were old friends and it was all settled they were going to have a holiday together and father didn't even see him. Father was away when Dr. Butler came, he'd had to go over to Zürich. Oh, if he'd only been here it wouldn't have happened. Dr. Butler was very keen on climbing, you know. He said he'd snatch a day or two on the mountains and he took Adrian. And then—this!"

"I see. Yes. You don't climb, Miss Ulyett?"

"I? Oh no. I just walked a little way up the valley with them when they started. I——" Tears came into her eyes. "Just seeing them off, you know. Oh, I remember the hay in the morning air. And Adrian and Dr. Butler waving——" She hid her face. "I'm sorry. Then we came back."

"We?"

"Mr. Woodham and me. He wanted to go with them. But he had to go down to Brigue to see somebody. He only came back to-day—just before father. I——" The thunder of a Swiss dinner-gong overwhelmed her.

"I'm sorry," said Reggie, when he could hear himself speak.

"Oh, it's horrid waiting, Mr. Fortune." She clasped her hands, struggled for a moment with emotions and left him.

He became aware of the presence of Stein at his elbow. "I wonder," he said to the lifted eyebrows, and they went to dinner.

A moment later Ruth Ulyett came in with her father and after them Woodham and Trove, much stared at and uncomfortably conscious of it. Washed and shaven, Trove looked even more exhausted than in his squalor. He had made away with the bandage, but a patch of plaster hid one temple. Again Stein's eyebrows asked

Mr. Fortune a question. "Oh, my dear chap, how do I know," he protested.

Stein nodded. His hand swept the whole affair away. He took up the menu, he praised it, he commended a red wine of Neuchâtel as good for the nerves. Mr. Fortune was pained and delivered a lecture on wine and why it should be drunk, which became poetry (minor poetry) when Stein said humbly that an Englishman had told him the Cortaillod would be Burgundy if it could. Mr. Fortune sang the little joys of life. And the comfortable dinner lasted long.

Trove came to their table. "When do we start?" he muttered.

Two placid faces looked up at him. "The guides will start at one," Stein said. "It is not necessary for you, Mr. Trove. You—you cannot help them. And you are too tired. You should sleep."

Trove turned on his heel and went out. Ulyett and his daughter and Woodham made haste to follow.

The two finished their dinner at leisure. When they sat at coffee in the garden, Ulyett loomed up through the dark. "Making an early start, sir? That's good. Everything in train, eh? I'm much obliged to you, I am, surely. This is on me, you understand. Don't you think twice about spending. Do you want any money now?"

"I thank you." Stein waved him away. "I spend no money. The guides—the landlord will tell you, Sir Ulyett." He stood up. "Pardon, I go to sleep. We start early, yes. Your friend calls to us." He marched Reggie back to the hotel with a pompous gait. He puffed indignantly on the stairs. "Ach, my dear Fortune, that—that is why we do not always like Englishmen."

"Not a very nice man, no," said Reggie sadly. "You get 'em everywhere." He opened the door of his room. "Well—without prejudice—what about it?"

Stein spread himself in a big chair and undid his waistcoat. "My friend, I do not understand. It is possible all happened as Mr. Trove says and we trouble ourselves for nothing. Yes, it is possible. But I do not think so."

"For any particular reason?"

"No, for many particular reasons. If you ask, will I make a theory how it happened, I cannot, I have not begun to try. I am not sure in my mind that it happened at all. When we search to-morrow, I am ready to find that this Dr. Butler he is not by the couloir, he is not on the mountain at all. Perhaps he desired to vanish from Sir Ulyett—from the world—and he is gone quite safe."

"It could be," said Mr. Fortune slowly.

"You do not believe it? But we have had cases like that: deaths upon the mountain which were not deaths at all. We could prove nothing, but we knew. I do not believe it of this Dr. Butler yet. But I believe nothing. What is most hard to believe is what Mr. Trove says."

"Yes. Yes. He does make things difficult."

"Difficult! My God! Either he tells us not all the truth, or he is an imbecile."

"Behaviour not normal, no."

"My friend! He is knocked down, as he says, by stones, he is stunned, he is wounded on the head. But he will not show the wound to a doctor, no! His friend is swept away by the stones. He does not come down to the place where he is staying, where his other friends are, he goes back where nobody knows him. He sends men to search from there. He gives it up quick and goes back again to come round by train. So it is thirty-six hours after his friend is lost before his other friends can know of it. For he does not telephone, oh no. That is most wonderful. He gets down to Mürren, having lost Dr. Butler. But he sends no message to the friends at Kandersteg. He searches, he finds nothing, he goes back to Mürren and still he does not telephone. He thinks Butler may have come here; but he will not ask by telephone, no, he must drag round by train to see. Righteous God! It is as if he had not lived in this century. Had he never heard of the telephone? Ach, he may be an honest man, the Mr. Trove, but if he is, he is an idiot."

"There's an answer to all that, you know," said Reggie wearily.

"Then I shall be glad to hear it." Stein was annoyed.

"Well, you're using the professional fallacy."

"I beg your pardon?" said Stein.

"My dear fellow, I'm a policeman myself. We find a man caught in very abnormal circumstances and if he don't act normally we suspect him. It's the custom of the trade: but delusive. The one thing certain about Trove is he's had a shock. People suffering from shock won't be reasonable. He says, he's lost an old friend in a queer accident which nearly killed him too. Well, that ought to upset a fellow. Quite natural he should just drive on blundering, fumbling, groping blind after his friend. Quite human."

"So. You acquit the Mr. Trove?"

"My dear fellow, what's the charge?" Reggie smiled.

"God in heaven! Do I know?"

"It might be murder, but we haven't got a body. It might be manslaughter. Still you'd want a body. It might be assistin' an escape from justice. But we don't know Butler was running away. No. Preserve an open mind."

"And I do so," Stein cried. "I believe nothing. It is you who have not the open mind. You believe this story that he tells."

"I didn't say that. No. Acceptin' his story, Trove's quite natural. My trouble is that if you do accept it, it don't explain the rest."

Stein laughed. "In effect we know nothing. I confess to you, I thought perhaps the Mr. Trove was lying when he said he searched from Mürren. But it is true. I do not despise the telephone myself. I have talked to Mürren tonight. Some guides went with him and searched all up to the couloir that side. Nothing! They think either Trove took them to the wrong place or Butler did not fall. That also is very possible. Almost anything is possible." He put his head on one side and looked at Reggie.

"That Butler put up a sham accident? Butler set the stones falling on Trove?" Reggie said. "Yes. A skilled mountaineer and a novice. I suppose it could be worked."

"A climber with a fool, yes. Anything could be. And Butler was a good climber. But this pass is easy, it is nothing. If Butler wished to make away with the Mr. Trove, he could find a hundred better places. There is no reason to do it like this. But I see no reason for anything."

"No. We haven't got to the reasons yet. Why did they all come here, Stein?"

"Ach, my friend!" Stein laughed. "What do I know? Why do the English come to Switzerland?"

"My wife says I came to eat ices," said Reggie sadly. "Butler came to spend a holiday with his old friend Ulyett. But when he got to Kandersteg his old friend Ulyett had gone off for a day or two. That's why Butler went on the mountains."

"So. Let me understand, my friend. You think Sir Ulyett planned for them to go this expedition?"

"No. Oh no. I don't think anything. But his daughter says he'd run off to Zürich, so Butler being keen on mountains took Trove climbing."

"To Zürich? That is a very good alibi." Stein pulled his moustache. "I shall test it."

"Yes. Woodham's got an alibi too. He went to Brigue. Just after he'd seen Butler and Trove off. Neither Ulyett nor Woodham was here while the thing was happening. They only came back to-day."

"So. That is most interesting."

"Yes, I think so." Mr. Fortune smiled. "Lots of facts, aren't there?"

Stein groaned. "Facts? What is a fact? I have not found one that I believe in." He stood up. "Ach, let us sleep. Where they were, I will find that out. And if Butler is upon the mountain I will find him. But then—I do not know. I do not understand anything."

Mr. Fortune is aware of his limitations. He did not feel that he would be any use to a party of guides searching mountains. When Herr Stein tramped along the corridor at 1 a.m. he turned over and went to sleep again. His conscience was satisfied with him when he was drinking coffee at six. Upon a melancholy mule which a frowsy boy exhorted, he climbed slowly towards the glittering snows of the Blumlisalp, and with the sweet morning air mingled the pungent scents of mule and boy. Some hours of solemn progress brought them to a little dark lake laughing in the sunshine. A fir wood came down to its pleasant beaches on one side, from the other the mountains rose in bare slopes and cliff.

By a little inn the mule stopped with determination. "He go no more," the boy grinned. "We go up now." He pointed to the dark cliffs.

"My only aunt!" Reggie moaned.

The boy disposed of his mule and strode into the wood, and Reggie followed delicately. Walking is a pursuit which he considers obsolete. The path having got out of the wood went up steep, hot pastures. The frowsy boy took it in a swinging stride and Reggie's internal organs heaved and he melted. They came out on the edge of the cliff above the lake. There he dropped: to discover, when his sad sensations allowed him, the detestable boy gazing at him with surprise and contempt. The boy pointed up to the blue pitiless sky. "Oh, my aunt!" Reggie groaned.

He laboured on up endless slopes of rich grass enamelled with gentians and violas and anemones, populated with cheery choirs of grasshoppers and bland cows, and the abominable boy drew further and further away. He passed a cluster of châlets, he drank milk from the hands of a horrible cool girl who pitied him intolerably, he toiled on over stony ground in which the stars of edelweiss were thick-set and was again in rich pasture.

Then he began to see men like flies on the slopes above and heard faint calls. The boy turned. "Der Herr is found," he announced.

Reggie sat down. "You go on," he said. "Tell Herr Stein I'm here." He stretched himself out on the grass, arms and legs wide.

Stein came in long strides. "I have found him, Fortune. He is dead."

"Well, well," Reggie murmured. "Have you moved him?"

"No one has touched him. I wait for you. Come and see."

Reggie arose and climbed after him. A little party of men stood together bareheaded, looking up at the crags above, talking softly. Aloof from them Trove sat with his face hidden. It was a steep slope on which the grass grew rich but scattered with many stones.

"See. There above, that is the couloir." Stein pointed. "And we find him here." He looked at Reggie. "Yes. It is possible."

Reggie knelt by the dead man. He lay upon his face, almost hidden in the long grass, and about him was the vanilla scent of the red-brown mountain flower they call Faith-of-men.

Reggie turned the body over. The clothes bore dark stains of blood, there was blood dried upon the face and hair. His slow, careful hands moved here and there. He bent close....

Trove got on his feet and came to see what was being done and saw the dead man's face. "Oh, my God!" he cried.

"What, then?" said Stein quietly. "Is it not Dr. Butler?"

"What do you mean?" Trove stared with wild eyes. "Of course, it's Butler."

"So," said Stein with satisfaction.

"Oh, why do you keep him lying here? It's so ghastly! You can't do anything. You can't do anything, can you, Fortune?"

"I'm sorry," said Reggie, and rose and nodded to Stein. He spoke to the guides and the body was gathered up and borne away. Trove stood watching a moment, then hurried after, went ahead and plunged on down.

"So. He is in a hurry," said Stein.

"Perhaps he wants to tell Ulyett," Reggie suggested. "Or perhaps he wants to catch a train."

Stein stared at him. "You think——? Ach, no. But do not fear. I have men at Kandersteg by now."

"I dare say you're right," Reggie murmured, and began to wander about the mountain-side.

"You wonder how it happened?" Stein said.

"Yes. Yes. I'm no good on the mountains. Same like our Mr. Trove." He contemplated Stein in dreamy wonder. "How did it happen, Stein?"

"Come to the couloir." They climbed to that corridor in the ridge of rock and the other slope of the mountains opened before them. "See, there has been a new fall of stones. Those are all fresh. What Trove said, it is very possible. Here was more than enough to kill men, to sweep them away. Some of the stones have come to this side, some that. If Trove lay here if he was swept down towards Mürren, he would not see Butler. It is quite natural he should think Butler was carried down on the Mürren side. Also it is natural Butler should have been swept to the other."

"Yes. Yes. But Trove's search party ought to have looked both sides, oughtn't they?"

Stein shrugged. "He told them it happened on the Mürren side. When they could not find anything there, he was in a hurry to go back. They said so. Then he is a fool, yes. I always said that. But if he is a fool, it is all very possible, more possible as I thought."

Reggie turned back and, slowly wandering here and there, made a devious way down. "See. Here are new stones also." Stein rolled them over. "The grass is quite fresh beneath."

"Yes. I noticed that. Grass is a good deal beaten down, isn't it?"

"But it should be. The stones have rolled. The poor Butler has rolled down here. We found his rucksack here."

"Did you though?" Reggie looked at him. "Straps torn off?"

"No, nothing was torn. It was dragged off as he rolled. That also happens, my friend. Yes, it is all like a most natural accident." Still Reggie gazed at him and he burst out laughing. "Pardon, my dear friend. It is that you look so wondering, so sad. Like a child that is disappointed of something nice, with your round face so innocent."

"Yes. Yes. I have a sweet face," said Reggie. "Rolled rather a long way, didn't he?"

"What do I know?" Stein shrugged. "It could happen. It happened."

"Oh, yes. He did roll." Reggie smiled.

"You think something else?"

"Well, I was thinking it was quite a nice good accident. But they had no luck."

"How do you mean that?"

"All quite simple and accidental—and then Trove goes and has tea with Herr Stein, and there's the deuce to pay."

"We make trouble for nothing, yes?"

"I wonder," Reggie said. "Well, let's get on." He started down the slope and Herr Stein, accommodating his trained stride to Reggie's careful little steps, gave a lecture upon falls of stones, their habits and effects. Reggie said nothing to it. Reggie said nothing at all till they reached the châlets again. Then he called forth the maternal damsel, then he said, "Another little drink wouldn't do us any harm," and over his glass of milk surveyed Stein, who did not drink, benignly. "Yes. Very lucid and interesting. And what happens next?"

Stein shrugged. "Mr. Trove's story goes on the records. I write a report how I found the body. There is no more to do."

"And they all live happily ever after." Reggie smiled, said something pretty to the girl and went on.

Stein caught him up in two strides. "You are not fair with me, my friend. You are not frank. There is something in your mind you do not say."

"My dear fellow! Oh, my dear fellow! I told you. I said they had bad luck."

"Bad luck? Because Trove brought us here? What does it matter? We find nothing."

"I wouldn't say that. We haven't found enough. That's all. But Trove bumping into us wasn't the first bit of bad luck. The trouble began when the falling stones didn't kill poor Butler."

"Righteous God! But the man was dead, he had been long dead."

"Oh yes, a day or two. I think he died soon after the stones fell. Those wounds were made while he was still alive, probably by falling stones. But the wounds weren't enough to kill him."

"So. So. What then? He died lying out on the mountain at night." Stein shuddered dramatically. "B-r-r-r, the cold up there! You do not know the mountains, my dear Fortune. I promise you, it is enough to kill a man who is hurt. Or if he is not hurt, often. And he was not young, the poor Butler."

"Yes. Exposure. It could be. But why did he lie exposed? Why didn't he get on his legs again and come down, same like Trove? No just cause or impediment. No bones broken. No bad wound."

"What do you mean, then? What killed him?"

"I wonder. Do you have a medical examination in Switzerland when a man is found dead on the mountains?"

"But, of course. If there is any doubt."

"Well, I think you'd better doubt, Stein. But you needn't say so."

"My God, I say nothing. Only that I do not understand."

"Yes. And you needn't say that either."

"So. That is to tell me you suspect foul play, and by this man Trove. Ach, I remember, you hinted at that before. My dear Fortune, if you would only speak out."

Reggie smiled. "Well, speakin' broadly, I suspect them all. Trove, Ulyett, Woodham, person or persons unknown. Several obscure factors. Keep an open mind and look about. And I'll have a look at the body."

Stein rumbled and muttered. Stein had trouble in keeping his pace down to Reggie's dainty careful gait, and at last, "You forgive me, my friend? You are a little slow. I do better to go on."

"Don't mind me," Reggie smiled. "I don't suppose they've thought of doing me in yet."

"My God!" Stein said and turned about and surveyed the mountain-side, whereon nothing moved but cows. "I do not know whether you joke or not, Fortune."

"That was a joke, Stein."

"So!" Herr Stein was not pleased. "I go then. You cannot miss the path, I think. Not even you. But I send some one up from the inn." He swung into his stride.

Reggie went the slower without him, but rather for meditation than watching of steps, and when the mule boy climbed up, was found sitting above the lake contemplating nature with dreamy eyes. Thereafter he was led down, he was set upon the mule and that animal exhorted to a jolting speed.

Stein had a doctor waiting for him with the body, a bearded, bustling doctor, who was honoured to assist Mr. Fortune. "Oh, no, no. It's your opinion we want, doctor," Reggie smiled. The doctor rubbed his hands. He had heard, of course, the story of the accident—how the body was found—these disasters were very sad—in such cases, though the injuries were not grave, shock and exposure often caused death.

"Yes. We could certify death from exposure, couldn't we?" said Reggie. They moved to the body together.

The doctor worked upon it. "All points to that, Mr. Fortune."

Reggie opened the dead man's mouth. ...

It was long after when they made an end. "You're satisfied, doctor?" Reggie smiled.

The doctor wiped his face. "There is no doubt, Mr. Fortune. There is no doubt. But it is inhuman."

"Not a nice case, no. That's why every one had better think it's quite normal. Except Stein. Good-bye. I'll go and tell him."

He found Herr Stein drinking beer in the hotel garden. "How doth the little busy bee improve each shining hour!" he said sadly and went in.

Stein followed him to his room. "And now, my friend?"

"Well, you'll have to send some of your guides up that beastly mountain again."

"So. Why is that?"

"I want 'em to go up again and see if they can find any trace how that fall of stones started."

"Still you will not believe it was a natural accident?"

"No, not natural. Not accidental. Not originally. The accidents intervened: when Butler wasn't killed, that had to be put right; when Trove tumbled into you and me. That couldn't."

"I do not understand," Stein said. "But come, what did you make of the body? What was the cause of death? Are you sure now?"

"Oh, yes. Butler died of asphyxia."

"Asphyxia! How is that?"

"He was smothered by some woollen fabric pressed over his mouth while he lay unconscious."

"Is it possible!" Stein cried. "You can be sure?"

"Oh, yes. Yes. Both lungs much congested and one side of the heart. Fragments of wool in the mouth and nostrils. He made no resistance. The tongue is only a little bruised. Medical evidence quite clear. You see what happened. Somebody arranged a fall of stones to kill him. It only knocked him out. So somebody rolled him away down the slope and smothered him. Probably with a tweed coat." He stood up. "Well, we'd better get on, Stein. Mustn't be late for dinner." He began to shed clothes fast. "I say, my lad"— his face came out of the tail of his shirt as Stein withdrew—"I've booked the bath."

"So? So!" said Herr Stein, expressing the emotions of the human reason at the incomprehensible.

When Reggie came down he saw Stein in a corner with a glass of watered port and Sir Samuel Ulyett and avoided that distressing mixture. Stein was a little late for dinner. "Pardon," he smiled. "Will you guess what he said to me?"

"Oh, he was asking how you found the late Butler."

"And more, my friend. He asked me if the doctors were satisfied. That is very interesting. A death on the mountains like that—there is not one in a thousand where the doctors have anything to say."

"No. I've sometimes wondered about that. If I hadn't blown into this mess you'd have called it another mountain accident and buried him all cosy. I wonder how many of the others are this kind."

Stein shrugged. "What can one do? There is never any suspicion."

"No. No. These people could have banked on being safe. I'm afraid we're rather a nuisance, Stein."

"I think so, yes. Look, this Sir Ulyett, why should he think it anything but the ordinary accident? And he comes to ask me if I find foul play! Ach, I tell him nothing. I say the doctors will look at the dead man. But me—I look after Sir Ulyett." He nodded profusely.

"Yes, I dare say you're right. Have you looked into his alibi?"

"Have no fear. I look into all their alibis. First, Sir Ulyett. It is true he travelled to Zürich the day before Butler came—that is strange; he departs to be absent when his old friend comes—but he went. He told the landlord he must go to a chemical factory on business—he makes chemicals himself, you remember. And he did go. The next time he is seen, he is back at Kandersteg station the afternoon that Trove was having tea with us. So when the stones fell Sir Ulyett was in Zürich. Second, Mr. Woodham. It is true, he went to Brigue on the day Butler and Trove started. He told the landlord he had to see a friend passing through from Italy. He slept at Brigue that night and the next night. He came back to Kandersteg a little after Sir Ulyett. Those are very good alibis." Stein shrugged. "But a man may have his alibi and yet know too much. Pst! Do not look so solemn, my friend. They watch us from their table. Let us talk of it no more. They try to listen."

"Yes, I thought that." Reggie smiled. "Had you any more to say?"

"Soon perhaps." Herr Stein smiled back at him the smile of a Teutonic sphinx. "I am not idle, my dear friend. But now let us be gay." He began to tell Mr. Fortune all about London. He had been there once.

The gaiety of this conversation did not diminish the anxieties of the other table. They were a glum company. Trove said nothing at all and looked misery. The girl was either watching him, or, when he met her eyes, pretending she wasn't. Ulyett and Woodham talked in broken bits with effort and queer glances of uneasy understanding. The girl and Trove went out and left them still at table.

Reggie watched them dreamily, but they were not encouraged to come and talk. "Well, well"—he rose—"let's try the garden, Stein."

But a little man rose out of the office and intercepted Herr Stein. Reggie sauntered on, sat in a remote corner and lit a cigar and the voice of Trove came to him, husky and excited. "I say, Fortune. Could I speak to you?"

"I'm listening."

"I wanted to ask you. Do you think he suffered much?"

Reggie lay back and looked about him. There was a glimmer of a woman's dress in the gloom. "Did you?" he asked.

"No. Oh no. Not till I came to. But I mean, was it all over in a minute for him, like that?"

"I wasn't there, you know," said Reggie.

Trove swallowed. "I mean, you can tell how quickly he died, can't you?"

"I'm only a surgeon. Not God."

"You don't know? It's pretty ghastly, you see. I don't want to think of him lying there all night, alive; helpless, dying."

"I'm sorry," said Reggie.

Trove retired into the dark, and as he went Stein came. "We take our coffee here, yes?" He sat down. "I hope I do not interrupt."

"I'd finished. I don't know if he had. He wanted to know how Butler died."

"He also! My friend, they are very much afraid."

The high lamps which lit the garden were switched on and in the light Trove and the girl were seen with Woodham.

"So. They confer." Stein chuckled.

"Yes. What have you done with Ulyett?"

"He confers with the landlord." Stein began to hum the Preis-lied for the benefit of a waitress bringing their coffee. When she was gone he went on in a low voice. "They sit down and wait for him. Good. We can talk so. He confers with the landlord, yes. Will you guess what he has done? So soon as he heard that we had found Butler dead he went to Butler's room. He takes away to his own room a leather case. He spends some time in his room. Then he goes off quick to the telegraph office and sends a telegram. What do you say to that, my friend."

"Sounds all right."

"You think so, yes. The old friend takes charge of the dead man's papers and telegraphs to the family their sad bereavement. That is all right. That is most correct. But the telegram was not to the family. It was to a stockbroker. It was in code." He gave Reggie a slip of paper. "My office has worked out the translation. That is not so bad for poor, slow Stein."

"My dear chap! Oh, my dear chap!" Reggie soothed him. "Splendid."

The telegram was instructions to a broker to stop selling rubber shares, and buy.

Stein chuckled. "And now Sir Ulyett shall explain to me why when his friend is dead he seizes his friend's papers and goes from them quick to change his game on the Stock Exchange."

"Yes. Yes. Very interestin' question. What's the theory?"

Stein sat up and laid a finger on his arm.

But Reggie went on dreamily. "You mean Butler knew something Ulyett wanted? Yes."

"Pst!" Stein warned him.

But Reggie did not notice. "Yes. So Ulyett had Butler killed in order to get hold of his papers. Yes. You could work on that."

"Ach, righteous God!" Stein muttered.

"By all means." Reggie gazed at him. "But why?"

Stein waved empty hands. "Have you no ears, then?" he said. "No senses?"

"Oh, I hope so. I think so."

"I made signs to you. And still you talk! Pardon, my dear Fortune, but it is unfortunate. Ulyett was coming this way. Now he is gone. See."

Sir Samuel was seen to arrive where the others of his party sat by the hotel door. Something was said between him and them. They all went in. "Seems rattled," said Reggie.

"Is it not strange?" Stein laughed angrily. "The man was coming to us—to listen to us perhaps, perhaps to ask what this means that the landlord requires of him Butler's papers—and you let him hear you say he killed Butler. He is frightened, yes. Also he is warned. You permit me to say, it is provoking, my friend."

"Sorry to annoy you," said Reggie.

"But did you not hear him come? Did you not see I tried to stop you?"

"Oh yes. Yes. But I've been in a few cases myself, Stein. I thought you were wrong."

"Wrong! My God! Is it your way in England to let a man know you suspect him?"

"Sometimes. To see what it makes him do. Very interesting and instructive. I want to see what Ulyett will do."

"So. You are very ingenious." Stein shrugged. "Me, I do not like it. I do not tell the suspect what he is to fear. It is for him to make the mistakes, not me. I ask him to explain this, to explain that, while he does not know how much I know, and when he blunders, I have him. But now Sir Ulyett is on guard. It will not do. You have spoilt my affair."

"Oh, I'm sorry about that," Reggie said placidly. "How much do we know, Stein? That Butler was murdered, yes. That Ulyett wanted his papers which have some bearing on a gamble in rubber Ulyett is working, yes. And I've told Ulyett he killed Butler. He didn't like my mentioning it at all. But we don't exactly know it yet."

"God in heaven," said Stein. "That is what I complain of. You tell him what we are not ready to tell him, what we cannot yet act upon, and now while we seek the evidence he can work to guard himself."

"Yes. That's what I'd like him to do. My dear chap, we don't want more evidence. We want to get rid of what we've got. The existin' theory is that Ulyett murdered Butler to steal his papers. But your evidence is that while Butler was murdered, Ulyett was in Zürich. That's rather a difficulty."

"Pfui! I do not know everything, no. If the alibi is right, Ulyett did not do the murder with his own hands. And what then? Do you forget the Mr. Trove?"

"Yes. No. I remember him continuously."

"He also is very much afraid. He also wants to know if we suspect."

"No. Several curious points about Mr. Trove. Well, well. I wonder what they're up to now."

"I can guess what Ulyett is doing," said Stein gloomily. "He is burning Butler's papers. Then he will tell us there were no papers. And we can prove nothing. I must thank you for that, my friend."

"I wonder," Reggie murmured. "Well, let's come and see if there's any ashes." Herr Stein growled and followed.

By the door of the hotel Woodham sat alone. Reggie remarked on the beauty of the night and said he was just going to bed. Woodham was thinking of it. The others had gone some time ago.

"You see!" Stein muttered as they went upstairs. He hurried to Ulyett's door and knocked. There was no answer. He tried the handle and found the door fast. "So." He scowled at Reggie. "If he has gone!" he muttered.

"Well, that'd be very interestin'," Reggie murmured.

Stein knocked again more loudly, and still there was no answer. They waited and listened. Inside the room some one was coughing faintly, stopped, coughed again.

"Oh, my aunt!" said Reggie, and ran into the next room. From the window there he clambered on to Ulyett's balcony. Light shone through the louvre shutters. He dragged them back and went in. Ulyett lay on his bed half dressed, unaware of his visitor; he breathed as if he had a cold; his face was dark. Reggie felt at his brow and his pulse. The arm fell limp as it was let go. He coughed.

Reggie left him and unbolted the door to find Stein defending himself from a girl in a dressing-gown who wanted to know why he was disturbing her father. Reggie beckoned them in and shut the door behind them. She ran to the bed. "Your father has had an overdose of a sleeping-draught, Miss Ulyett."

"It's absurd. It's impossible. He never takes such things."

"So? So!" said Stein, and contemplated the unconscious man.

She shook him, she cried to him, "Father! Father!" but he lay still and there came from him only that faint, choking cough. "Oh, Mr. Fortune——"

"Yes. Be quite quiet, please. What's the doctor's telephone number, Stein? Thanks. I don't want anybody in here." Reggie ran out. When he came back he had a steaming jug and a coffee-pot. "Now, Miss Ulyett, everything's goin' to be done for him.

You'll go back to your own room, please, and say nothing to anybody."

"Oh, but you'll tell me if——"

"I'll tell you when I know." He put her out. "Now, Stein, give me a hand." He took off his coat.

"What is it? What is to do, Fortune?"

"Veronal, I think. Hefty dose. We'll wash him out and put coffee into him. That's all, till the doctor comes along with strychnine and some other little things. Now——" They worked upon the senseless man....

The doctor appeared with a bag panting, flushed, excited. "I come so quick as I can. You make work, Mr. Fortune. What is this, then? Another accident?"

"We'll try strychnine, please," said Reggie stolidly, and the injection was made....

The doctor studied the unconscious body. "It was veronal? How? A suicide?"

"I don't know."

"It is possible; it is very possible," Stein said. He looked at Reggie. "If he was afraid—then——"

"A little digitalin wouldn't do his heart any harm," said Reggie; and again the syringe was used....

"You came to him quickly?" the doctor said.

"Yes. Yes." Reggie smiled. "We don't generally get to these cases quite so soon."

"Righteous God!" Stein muttered. "Fortune! Did you think this would happen when he heard——?"

"No. I thought something might happen."

"You meant this?"

"I didn't know," Reggie said slowly and felt Ulyett's pulse. "I don't know now, Stein...."

It was towards morning when he left the bedside. Though Stein shut the door quietly, somebody heard. The girl sped out of her room, a fluttering ghost in the gloom of the corridor. "Mr. Fortune?"

He led her back into her room. "I think he's coming through, Miss Ulyett."

"You think!" The white face trembled.

"Yes. You can sleep now."

"I want to see him."

Reggie shook his head. "He isn't conscious yet."

"You've left him in there alone!"

"Oh no. No. The doctor's with him. We won't risk anything, Miss Ulyett. But he's doing quite well. He has a good heart. Doesn't use drugs much in the ordinary way, does he?"

"Of course he doesn't. It's ghastly. I can't believe he took anything." She shook and sank down on her bed, twisting her hands together.

"Something happened to him," said Reggie quietly. "What do you think it was?"

She flung back her head and he saw her throat throbbing.

"Everything's like a horrible dream," she cried. "Poor Dr. Butler and now father. Mr. Fortune! I believe it was Dr. Butler's death made father like this." Large dark eyes gazed at him in a miserable appeal. "The shock, you know? Couldn't it be?"

"Your father was all right at dinner."

"Oh no, Mr. Fortune. He was wretched. He wasn't a bit like himself. And afterwards when he came in from the garden we thought he was going to faint. They had to get him some brandy."

"Did they though," Reggie murmured. "Who thought of that?"

"I don't know." She pushed back her hair. "Adrian brought it, I think. What does it matter? He was frightfully upset. He drank it and said he was all right. But I had to help him upstairs to bed. I'm sure it was just shock, Mr. Fortune."

"Yes. Yes. It has been a nasty business. But he's in safe hands, you know. And now you're going to sleep, while he's pulling through. Good night."

Outside in the corridor Stein waited. "So? The daughter has something to say?"

"Yes. She says he came back from the garden sufferin' from shock."

"So," said Stein with satisfaction. "That was surprising, my friend."

"And Trove brought him a drink."

"So?" Stein smiled. "Always the Mr. Trove."

"That's surprising too, isn't it?" Reggie was a little shrill. "Good night."

When Stein came down in the morning, he was told that Mr. Fortune had eaten his breakfast. He found Mr. Fortune sitting on the small of his back contemplating the mountains from behind a large cigar. "And how is it now, my friend?"

"'Twas the voice of the sluggard, I heard him complain," Reggie murmured; his round face was pale and languid. "Thank you, we are doing as well as can be expected. Taken quite a lot of nourishment. But still prostrate. Lucky beggar. Doctor's gone. Grenadier of a nurse in charge." He lowered his voice. "Have you got a nice quiet man about? Sort of fellow that can follow a fellow and not show up. Good. Tell him to look after me. I'm thinkin' of takin' a little walk."

"So. You fear something more?"

"Oh Lord, yes. We aren't done yet."

"So. You shall be guarded, my friend. But I beg of you, no more like last night. That was too rash."

"My dear chap! Oh, my dear chap!" Reggie sighed. "It didn't do any dam' thing. Run away." He saw Trove and Woodham at the door of the hotel. They watched him hungrily, and as Stein faded away approached him.

"This is a bad business about Ulyett, sir," Woodham began. "I hear you were up all night."

"No. No. Lost my beauty sleep, that's all."

"What is it?" Trove blurted out. "What's the matter with him?"

"Well, Miss Ulyett thinks it's shock." Reggie considered him dreamily. "You wouldn't wonder, would you?"

"Good Lord, no," said Woodham. "Poor old Ulyett! I'm afraid Butler's death hit him rather hard."

"Yes, a bad business. I wonder." He stood up and stretched himself. "I was just going for a walk. If you two fellows have got time, there's one or two little things I'd like to ask you."

"Rather," said Woodham heartily. "Come on." Trove made no objection.

The road was populous in the village, and even beyond the shops had too many tourists for confidences. Reggie explained the beauties of nature to silent companions. After a while he turned off into a path across half-mown pasture and coming between them urged them to analyse the separate scents of hay in the making. Woodham with a certain condescension assisted. Trove made noises and at last exploded. "You wanted to ask us something, didn't you?"

"Well, it is rather a complex case." Reggie stopped. A man who was trudging after them went into a shed. They were close to the base of the mountain wall which shut in the valley. Reggie turned away towards the gorge by which in roaring falls the river came down. "Of course, you fellows know much more about it than I do," he murmured.

Trove gave him a fierce, puzzled stare. Woodham laughed. "I say! That's rather startling. I'm afraid I don't know anything that I know of."

"Oh yes. Yes. I was thinking about these two men. What exactly is the connection between Butler and Ulyett?"

Trove looked at Woodham. "Why, they were very old friends," Woodham said. "Surely you knew that."

"Yes. So I've heard. And Ulyett makes chemicals, and Butler's a consulting chemist. Any business connection?"

"Hadn't you better ask Ulyett?" said Woodham coldly.

"I hope to. But Ulyett's unfortunately out of action. Rather curious conjunction. One old friend comes to see another. And one gets killed before they meet and the other is knocked out. Any business reasons?"

"I'm afraid I can't help you," said Woodham. "I'm not in their confidence, Mr. Fortune."

"You were, weren't you?" Reggie turned to Trove.

"I was Butler's assistant. You know that," Trove said sullenly. "Look here, what is all this, Fortune? You came into the business as a doctor. You're talking like a policeman."

"Yes," said Reggie, and paced on. They were climbing the steep path into the gorge. "I am a policeman. Didn't you know?"

"I know who you are," Trove growled.

"Steady, Adrian," Woodham said gently. "Not quite playing the game, is it, Mr. Fortune? When a fellow calls in a doctor he doesn't expect to get a detective."

"No. It was a bit of luck."

"So that anything Adrian says can be used as evidence against him. Oh, very lucky—for Adrian." Woodham turned, laughing. "I think Mr. Fortune had better go on walking by himself, old man."

But Trove stood fast. "What the devil do I care?" he cried. "What do you want to know? Ulyett often consulted Butler, I can tell you that. He'd been consulting him about a process for making synthetic rubber, and Butler was going to report to him here."

Reggie walked on slowly, and the roar of the falling water rose about them. "What was Butler going to say?"

"I don't know."

"Ah, pity." Reggie paused and looked down through the spray at the foam which boiled about the rocks in the gorge. "Whose process was it?"

Woodham laughed. "I suppose it was mine, eh, Adrian? If you'd asked me what I had to do with Ulyett I would have told you at first, Mr. Fortune. I submitted a process for synthetic rubber to Sir Samuel Ulyett. And what then?"

"Well, that's that," said Reggie. "Now about Butler's death." He turned to Trove. "You started off with him up that way," he pointed above the gorge.

"I was with them." Woodham smiled.

"Oh yes. Yes. You and Miss Ulyett saw them off." Reggie drew from his pocket-book a little map on tracing paper. "Let's get this clear." Holding it by the corner, he gave it to Trove. "You went up the valley and Woodham left you about—where?"

"I don't know. Somewhere there."

Reggie took the map by the corner again and passed it to Woodham. "What do you say?" He smiled.

"About there, yes. An hour's walk. What's the use of this? I came back to the hotel with Miss Ulyett and went off to Brigue."

"Yes. Yes. Thanks very much." Reggie smiled and took the paper again delicately. "I'm afraid it was rather greasy." He put it away with care. "Sorry. I wanted your finger-prints."

Woodham shrugged. "You seem to prefer dirty tricks, Mr. Fortune."

"What do you want my finger-prints for?" Trove cried.

"Would you be surprised to hear there were finger-prints on Butler's clothes?"

"His own, I suppose," said Woodham.

"No, I didn't see his own."

"They might be mine," Trove muttered.

"Yes, they might have been."

"Oh, my God! You mean he was murdered?"

"Steady, Adrian," Woodham said. "You've had enough, old man. Don't say anything now. Better get back. You're not fit for any more of these dirty tricks."

Trove stumbled away. Then Woodham turned upon Reggie. "So you found finger-prints, did you?" he said, and his face was white.

"Do you mind?" Reggie smiled.

"Wasn't it luck?" Woodham approached. "Wasn't it damned luck you came?" and sprang at him.

Reggie dropped and caught at his knees. He fell and went on falling down into the gorge, bounded from rock to rock into the rushing foam.

Reggie rose from the ground to meet the rush of a sturdy Swiss who chattered German at him. "Lord God, you are safe, you are not hurt? The villain, the murderer. I saw all. He would have killed you."

"Oh yes. Yes. That was the idea." Reggie smiled.

"He is gone! He is gone!" The detective peered down into the foam.

"Yes. You'd better look for him."

The detective gasped. "As the gentleman says," he muttered, and stared at the placid gentleman with goggling eyes.

Reggie wandered back to the hotel languidly.

He was received by Herr Stein with every sign of excitement. "My friend, there is news. The guides they find marks that a man has been up above the couloir where the stones start from."

"Yes. That was Woodham," said Reggie. "Don't worry. He's dead."

"Righteous God! What is this, then?"

"He tried to do me in. He fell into the Kander. Your man is fishing him out. What's left. Come and have some lunch."

"God in heaven!" Stein muttered and rushed away.

Some time after lunch Mr. Fortune came out of Ulyett's room and went to his own and rang for a waiter and asked him to find Mr. Trove and Herr Stein. Trove came quickly. "Well, what now? Are you going to give me in charge?"

Reggie held out his hand. "My dear chap!" he said. But Trove did not take it. "Oh, my dear chap! That little game wasn't meant for you. I had to make sure of Woodham."

"What have you done with Woodham?" Trove cried.

"When Woodham knew I knew, he tried for me too. But I was ready, you see. He went down into the gorge."

"He's dead?"

"Yes. Yes. The best way."

"You mean he killed Butler?"

"My dear chap!" Reggie said gently. "Hadn't you ever thought of that? You're rather loyal."

Stein came in. "So!" He looked at the pair of them.

"My God!" Trove was saying. "Loyal! I hated the fellow."

"Yes." Reggie smiled. "So you had to be fair to him. But Miss Ulyett won't really miss him, you know."

Trove was all a blush. "So," said Stein. "Now we hear all about it, yes?"

"Oh, quite clear, isn't it?" Reggie murmured. He dropped into a chair. "Woodham invented a process for making rubber and took it to Ulyett. Possible sort of process. I fancy the original idea was that he could force the pace and marry Miss Ulyett before it was tried out. The lady didn't oblige. Ulyett sent the process to Butler for investigation and report. But he was rather taken by it and he began a little gamble in rubber shares and took Woodham in. Quite a nice bit of business. Synthetic rubber coming—slump in the market. Only Butler decided the process was no good."

"He never told me that," said Trove.

"It was in his papers. Woodham may have guessed. Probably he always knew it wouldn't stand examination. He stuck to Miss Ulyett, but he couldn't make anything of her, and Butler was due. Something had to be done about it. He got Ulyett to go and talk to the Zürich chemical works about subsidiary work for his precious process and so had Butler to himself for a night. I take it he made sure Butler was going to turn him down. Further action was necessary. When Butler took you off over the mountains he saw his chance. He went off to Brigue and put up his alibi. That was his only weak point. That made me take notice of Mr. Woodham."

"So?" Stein said.

"Quite a nice alibi. But too simple. Brigue's about an hour from Kandersteg. Quite easy to book a room there and be here when you want to. Woodham was up above the couloir waiting for you when you came back. He started the stones on you. And then the luck began to run against him. If you'd both been killed, he could have got back and abolished Butler's papers and kept Ulyett in play and made something of the rubber gamble. And with you eliminated Miss Ulyett might have been easier."

"I say, keep Miss Ulyett out of it," Trove growled.

"Sorry. He didn't, you know. Well, he didn't kill either of you. He found you both stunned. He rolled Butler away and stifled him."

"My God! That was it, was it?"

"Oh yes. Yes. Stifled him with a coat. Butler didn't suffer. But meanwhile you came to and ran off for help. Second bit of bad luck. Still it looked all right to Woodham. He'd got his alibi. And if there was any talk of foul play you'd be suspected. But then you bumped into us at Interlaken. Third bit of bad luck. That was finally fatal. I'm afraid he didn't realize it till to-day. He rather underestimated other people. These clever chaps do. Well, I think we played up to Mr. Woodham quite nicely. No nasty questions. Not a word about him. Ulyett made the trouble. When he heard Butler was dead he went for Butler's papers and found out the rubber process was no good. Hence the hasty telegram, Stein. That annoyed Woodham, who wanted to go on with the gamble and use the sham process to frighten the market. Hence a strain in their relations that night, Stein. Poor old Ulyett heard us talking things over in the garden, and instead of butting in and telling us what he knew, which was what I was playing for, he nearly fainted. Unfortunate reaction. Woodham saw him knocked over and didn't know why. Very disconcerting. It seemed the best thing to Woodham to eliminate Ulyett. Then Ulyett couldn't blab, and if it looked like suicide, it would look as if Ulyett had been up to something dirty. So Woodham went off for brandy, put some veronal in it, and gave it to you to take to Ulyett. He very nearly won that game too. Which made it obvious that something had to be done good and quick to deal with Mr. Woodham. Hence our little altercation this morning."

"But, I say, what about those finger-prints? If you found finger-prints on poor Butler, why——"

"My dear chap! Oh, my dear chap!" Reggie smiled. "There weren't any finger-prints. That was only a little device to bring Mr. Woodham up to the scratch."

"Good God!" Trove stared at him.

"Yes. Yes. These little things are confusing to the layman. Well, that bein that, I'll just go back to my wife . Good-bye" And he went.

Trove looked at Stein and Stein looked at Trove. "So!" said Stein "So. You see now, my friend. It is quite simple. But what an artist!"

Mrs. Fortune strolling under the trees at Interlaken was surprised by a hand coming under her arm. "My dear child!" she smiled.

"Come on, Joan," said Mr. Fortune. "I want a hazel ice."

RAZOR EDGE

ANTHONY BERKELEY

Anthony Berkeley Cox (1893–1971) wrote whodunits as Anthony Berkeley, and novels about the psychology of crime, such as *Malice Aforethought*, as Francis Iles. Under both names, he wrote books of distinction that have stood the test of time. He founded the Detection Club, and although he effectively stopped writing crime fiction after a remarkable career lasting no more than fifteen years, he continued to review the genre with intelligence, perception, and occasional acerbity, until the end of his life.

'Razor Edge' seems to have escaped publication until 1994, when it appeared in *The Roger Sheringham Stories*, an edition limited to a mere 93 copies. Sheringham, a 'great detective' who often proves to be far from infallible, is in characteristically jaunty mood, and I am delighted to bring this story to a wider readership.

* * * * *

THE BATHING around Penhampton is notoriously dangerous. In consequence the mortuary of the local police force is larger than usual, for swimmers are obstinate people, and though the wide sandy reaches of Penhampton beach itself are well guarded, the few miles of rocky coast in either direction, with its many coves and little bays, are impossible to supervise.

It was therefore no surprise to the borough police when a body was reported among the rocks of Sandymouth cove on a sunny July afternoon. The usual routine was set in motion, the body collected and brought to the mortuary, and the temporary assurance obtained from the police surgeon that death was due to drowning. A careful description of the body was taken, but any enquiries as to its ownership were made unnecessary by a visitor to the police station.

It was five o'clock, and Superintendent Thomas, having signed all the documents awaiting his attention, was thinking of going home when his sergeant clerk told him that a woman was in the charge-room reporting that her husband had gone bathing in Sandymouth cove that morning and had not returned.

"I'd better see her," sighed the superintendent, thinking of the garden he wanted to water, and put his hat back again on the rack.

The woman had given her name as Mrs Hutton. Particulars of her husband's name, profession and address had already been taken, and these were laid discreetly on the superintendent's table as the sergeant showed her into the room. The woman was fair and a somewhat faded thirty-five though still with traces of a youthful prettiness, and she was in a state of some agitation.

"Sit down, Mrs Hutton," soothed the superintendent. "Now – you're worried about your husband?"

The woman nodded, choked, and said: "Yes. He went out bathing this morning. I was to join him later. His clothes were on the beach, but – oh, I'm sure – I'm sure –"

"Now, now," said the superintendent mechanically, and asked for further particulars.

These took some minutes to obtain, but finally reduced themselves to the following facts. Mr Edward Hutton, described as a financier with an office in the City and a home in Streatham, was staying with his wife at Ocean View Boarding House in the little village of Penmouth, about five miles west of Penhampton. He had left his lodgings at about half past ten that morning, telling his wife that he was going to bathe, probably in company with a certain Mr Barton, who was camping alone on top of the cliffs of Sandymouth Bay: a Mr Michael Somerville Barton, whom Mrs Hutton vaguely believed to be a writer and novelist, from London. Mrs Hutton was to join the two men at about noon; but when she arrived, though their wraps were still on the beach, no sign of either man was to be seen. She had called and searched, and then returned to her boarding house. In the afternoon, being now thoroughly worried, she decided after discussing the matter with her landlady to come into Penhampton and report to the police.

The superintendent nodded. "And the description of your husband, madam?"

Mrs Hutton leaned back in her chair and closed her eyes. "My husband is five foot seven inches tall, not very broad, thinnish arms and legs, thirty-four inches chest measurement, rather long hands and feet, medium brown hair, clean-shaven, grey-green eyes, and rather pale complexion; he has an old appendicitis scar, and – oh, yes, and there is a big mole on his left shoulder-blade."

The superintendent could not restrain his admiration. "Upon my word, Mrs Hutton, you reeled that off a treat. Very different from some of them I assure you."

"I – I was thinking it out in the bus," said the woman faintly. "I knew you'd want a description."

"Yes. Well –" Surreptitiously the superintendent studied the description of the body now in the mortuary. It tallied in every particular. He became aware that the sergeant was speaking.

"Excuse me, sir, could the lady give us a good description of Barton, the other gentleman?"

"No, I'm afraid –" Mrs Hutton hesitated. "I've only met him once, for a few minutes. I can't really tell you – he had a long moustache."

"We can get a description from Mr Turner, sir," interposed the sergeant tactfully. "It's in one of his fields that Mr Barton was camping."

The superintendent nodded and then, with much sympathetic throat clearing, proceeded to the distasteful task of warning Mrs Hutton to prepare for a shock. He was very much afraid that in the mortuary now – if Mrs Hutton would come along for a moment....

He sighed again as the woman gave every sign of imminent hysterics.

"He's here already? Must I see him? Must I? Won't – won't the description do?"

It took five minutes to get her into the mortuary.

But once there she regained her calm. A curious dead-alive look came into her own face as she stared down into the other dead one from which the superintendent had gently withdrawn the sheet.

"Yes," she whispered, tonelessly. "That's my husband. That's – Eddie."

Then she fainted.

* * * * *

Roger Sheringham was staying a week-end with Major Drake, the chief constable of Penhampton. They were old friends, with a common interest in crime.

So far, however, Roger had been disappointed. The Penhampton police was a very small force and his host, though a bachelor, had been unable to enliven the previous evening by tales of grisly murder in his district, for the good reason that his district had never had a murder. When therefore the major announced that on their way to the golf-course he had to call in at Police Headquarters to take formal view of some poor stiff who had got himself drowned the day before, Roger pricked up his ears.

"And by the way," added the major, "you may be able to help us a bit. Ever hear of a chap called Barton in your line? Writes books and things, y'know. Michael Somerville Barton. Hey?"

"Yes, I've heard of him, but I don't know him. A bit too Bloomsbury for me, I fancy. Why?"

"Because he's probably dead."

"What, murdered?"

"No, *not* murdered. Just plain drowned."

"People have been murdered by drowning before now," Roger pointed out mildly.

"Well, this one wasn't. Good lord, Sheringham, you amateur detectives! A corpse in every cupboard, and every death a murder, eh? Haven't you ever heard of such a thing as an accident?"

"Very well: how did Michael Somerville Barton meet his accidental death by drowning?"

"Oh, went bathing with another fellow yesterday morning. Lonely bit of coast. Neither of them seen again. Damn fools, they will do it, in spite of our notices. It's the other fellow's body I've got to look at. Very humdrum and ordinary, I'm afraid. Hurry up with that coffee."

"I've finished."

"Then come on. Got your clubs?"

"They're in the hall."

"Not they. They'll have been put in the cupboard under the stairs by this time. A place for everything and everything in its place in this house, my boy."

With pride the major threw open the cupboard door and extracted his own clubs. Roger's were not there. They were finally found standing in a corner of the hall.

"Come Drake," Roger said. "The house isn't so bad as you make out."

It was only a few minutes' ride to the police station, where on the steps a plainclothesman greeted them respectfully. The chief constable introduced him as Detective Inspector Clarke, in charge of the small C.I.D. section. Roger was childishly pleased to note the look of interest on the inspector's face as they shook hands.

The little party went through to the superintendent's office, where they picked up the large and comfortable man and also the police doctor who happened to be in the building; and after the details of the case had been recited on one side and duly absorbed on the other, a move was made to the mortuary.

"Pasty-faced beggar, eh?" was the chief constable's comment, as they stood in a circle round the slab that bore the dead man.

"He's certainly no advertisement for you," Roger agreed. "'Penhampton for Bonnie Sunshine', eh? Perhaps you haven't had any bonnie sunshine lately?"

"Hot and sunny all the week," retorted the major. "He can't have been here long, that's all."

"The Huttons arrived on the 12th, sir," put in the inspector. "That's about ten days ago."

"Then this fellow was no sun-bather," Roger commented. "Or else he wore a panama. Queer how some men actually prefer hats."

"Come now, Sheringham," said the chief constable impatiently. "Don't begin making difficulties. His forehead's got a bit of brown to it."

"And the skin on his nose looks as if it might have begun to peel at any moment. What more could Penhampton want?"

"Well, Superintendent, if that's all –"

The major's intention of escaping was however temporarily frustrated, for at that moment the sergeant clerk arrived to say that he was wanted on the telephone, by Scotland Yard.

"Scotland Yard, eh?" repeated the major, obviously gratified. "What on earth do they want? Some dam' red tape, no doubt." He went, followed by the superintendent who obviously took no chances.

Roger felt it up to him to make conversation. "You've made your examination, doctor? Death due to drowning all right."

"Oh, yes," the doctor nodded. "No doubt about that. His lungs were chock-full of water."

"Why, did you notice anything, Mr Sheringham?" the inspector asked eagerly.

"Afraid not, this time," Roger laughed. "Except that Mr Hutton wasn't so spruce as he might have been."

"How do you make that out?"

"He hadn't shaved yesterday morning."

"Sorry, but he had," corrected the doctor with a smile. "That cut's fresh, at the side of his mouth. If it had been made the day before, it would have been half healed."

"And yet there's plenty of stubble on his chin. Queer."

"Oh, if you're interested in queer details," said the doctor, "have a look at the scratches on his back."

"What scratches?"

The doctor signed to the inspector, and the two of them turned the corpse over. Roger saw that the skin on the back was badly lacerated, from the shoulders to the small of the back, while the elbows were almost raw.

"Barnacles," explained the doctor shortly.

"There are barnacles on the rocks here?"

"Covered with them. And it was among the rocks that the body was found. Still –"

Roger nodded. "I see what you mean. If the body was washing about, why did it only get lacerated in that particular area? It is queer. Very queer."

"But there's a simple explanation, after all," the doctor smiled. "The man who found him pulled him by the legs to where he could pick him up more easily. That's all."

"No, sir," put in the inspector respectfully. "The body was wedged under a big rock at the side of a pool. Trewin, the farm hand who happened to find him when he went down for a pail of sea-water, says he picked him straight up from the pool."

"There's an abrasion on the front of the right thigh, where he was wedged," supplemented the doctor.

"Yes, but that's natural. Those scratches aren't."

"And there's another thing, though I didn't put this in my report because I'm not certain. I've an idea those lacerations were made during life. There were signs of free bleeding – freer than I should have expected after death."

"That clinches it," said Roger.

"Clinches what, sir?" asked the inspector.

The return of the chief constable prevented Roger from answering. Major Drake wore an air of triumph.

"Well, it seems we've caught a Tartar," he announced. "This fellow was wanted by the Yard for share-pushing. They've arrested his partner, but didn't know Hutton was here. They saw the report of the accident in this morning's papers."

"Well, fancy that," observed the inspector.

Roger stared down at the dead man. "You never know, do you? He doesn't look like my idea of a share-pusher. Those long hands. Weak chin, too."

"Yes, yes: criminal type, obviously," pronounced the major. "Well, doctor, this is bound to raise the question of suicide. Fellow wanted by the police and all that. Any chance, do you think?"

"I shouldn't have said so. But of course he may have swum deliberately too far out and drowned himself."

"And Barton got drowned trying to save him," suggested the superintendent. "The papers might fake up something like that."

Roger broke into the discussion.

"Look here, I'd better tell you. This man Hutton didn't commit suicide, or get drowned by accident. He was murdered."

There was a pause.

"Really, Sheringham," observed the chief constable with disgust. "Didn't I warn you, Superintendent? Sheringham, this is no time for joking. We're due on the golf-course in ten minutes."

"What makes you think he was murdered, Mr Sheringham?" asked the superintendent, more temperately.

Roger explained, calling on the doctor for support. The chief constable was not convinced.

"Scratches! Nonsense! Bathing dress, that's all."

"Do you mean, he wore a backless swimsuit, as I believe the loathsome term is?"

"He was wearing a pair of slips," said the superintendent. "They were a goodish bit torn at the back, but not in front."

"It's murder," said Roger with finality. "And I think I know how it was done. I want Inspector Clarke to take me to where the body was found, and help me look round."

"Inspector Clarke has his work to do," barked the major.

"This is his work. And I warn you, if you don't take up an investigation of this case, I'll write an article for *The Daily Courier* showing how the murder was done, and blame the Penhampton police for obstruction."

"I believe you would, too," admitted the baffled chief constable. "Very well. You can have Clarke for an hour or two this afternoon to help investigate your mare's nest. In the meantime –"

"Oh, I'm not playing golf," Roger retorted. "Come on Inspector. If we hurry we can reach the major's car before he does."

It was only a few minutes run in the car from Penhampton to the place where the body had been found, about a mile and a half from Penmouth on the Penhampton side. The inspector took Roger down by a cliff-path, and showed him the place on the rocky shore.

"Very convenient," Roger commented. "Would you say that a body washing about on the incoming tide could possibly wedge itself there?"

The inspector considered. "Well, now that you mention it, sir – "

"Exactly. It was put there. Probably in the hope that it wouldn't be found for days. Now let me see, was the murder committed here, or not? Probably not, but certainly within a short distance. He wouldn't want to carry the body far."

Roger looked around. The coast at this point consisted entirely of rock, with a short fringe of shingle round the cove; of the sand implied in its name there was none. The rock was tolerably flat, but sprinkled lavishly with heavy boulders and broken up by innumerable pools, big and small. Floor-rock and boulders were alike plastered with barnacles and seaweed.

"What exactly are you looking for, sir?" the inspector asked.

"A pool. Not as big as this one, but not too small. A pool that may not show any traces at all, for two tides have been over it already; but this time yesterday the pool I want was pink."

"You think that he was murdered in a pool then, sir?" said the inspector curiously. "Well, I don't see why, but there's one just over there."

"Too big."

"There's a smaller one just beyond it."

"Too small." Roger looked round carefully. On the seaward side of a particularly large rock was a medium-sized, oblong-shaped pool. "That's more like it. And hidden from the shore, you see. Let's have a look at that one."

They slithered over the seaweed and rock and looked down into the serene water. There was nothing to be seen but the floating seaweed and the barnacles over the flattish bottom.

"Well, there's nothing else for it," Roger sighed. "I must get in. Any regulations here against bathing in the nude?"

"If there are, sir, I've forgotten them," promised the inspector.

Roger undressed, balancing with difficulty on the seaweed, and stepped into the pool. The water came just to his knees.

"What do you expect to find, sir?"

"Probably nothing. I hoped there might be some signs of a struggle – seaweed torn off or something. As it is –" He began to grope carefully among the thick bunches of seaweed that lined the sides.

The inspector watched for a few minutes then let his eyes wander towards the shore. He could take advantage of the visit at any rate to obtain Barton's description from Mr Turner, the farmer. As to the murder, what on earth would a man like Barton want to murder Hutton for? Why, according to the information he had collected, they had only known each other a couple of days, after a chance encounter in the cove here. Then an idea came to him.

"You mean, Barton might have been one of Hutton's share-pushing victims, Mr Sheringham? Perhaps he followed him down here, to do him in."

"There are all sorts of possibilities," Roger said abstractedly, from the depths of the pool. "But I think – hullo! What's this?"

He groped for a minute, and then drew out a shining object through which a strand of seaweed still ran.

"A ring. A man's wedding-ring." He peered inside. " 'E.H. – B.G. 18 November 1933'. E.H. What was Hutton's Christian name, Inspector?"

"Edward, sir. Well, that proves it right enough." The inspector did not withhold his admiration. "A smart bit of work, sir, and that's a fact."

"I thought I was on the right tack," Roger said modestly and scrambled out of the pool.

While he dressed they discussed the next move. A visit to the farm was indicated, and another to the Hutton's lodgings. In the end it was decided that the inspector should go up to the farm and get Barton's description and any other particulars, while Roger had a look through the man's tent.

"And find out what clothes he usually wore," he instructed the inspector.

"Yes, sir. Well, if you're ready – why, bless my soul, you've never told me how the murder was done."

"As I suspected from the beginning. And," Roger grinned, "if you'd care to step into the pool with me, Inspector, I'd guarantee to murder you too, in less than two minutes, though you're a bigger man than me. No? Well, have you ever heard of the Brides in the Bath case?"

A light broke over the Inspector, and shone in his face.

"Exactly," Roger nodded. "He got the man into the pool somehow – perhaps called his attention to that bunch of red anemones – then grabbed his ankles, hoisted his legs in the air so that his head went under the water, and in two minutes or less the job was done."

"And but for those barnacles, sir –"

"Exactly. He'd have got away with it."

*   *   *   *   *

The inspector was longer at the farm than Roger, waiting in the car, had expected, but when he returned he was brimming with news.

"The woman's in it, sir."

"Ah! You've discovered that?"

"Did you know, Mr Sheringham?"

"I had a strong suspicion. Well, what have you learned?"

"Why, sir," explained the inspector, "by a stroke of luck I found a man who was working in this field yesterday afternoon. He says he saw a woman on the beach about half past three, and the clothes he describes her as wearing tally well enough with Mrs Hutton's when she got to the station."

"Mrs Hutton didn't mention being on the beach in the afternoon?"

"No, sir: she did not. But that's not all. There was a man with her."

"The deuce there was!"

"Yes, sir. By the looks of it, they came out of a little cave under the cliff here. (I must have a look there later.) Manders – that's the farm-hand – thought they might be a larky couple, so he watched; but after talking a minute the man went back into the cave, and the woman went off along the beach. Manders didn't see either of them again."

"I see. And Barton's description?"

"Well, Mrs Turner couldn't tell me much. Average sort of height, she thought; not a big man. When she saw him on the day he arrived, the nineteenth, he had on a blue suit; afterwards he always wore a pullover and grey trousers."

"A blue suit?" Roger repeated with interest. "There's no blue suit in the tent now."

"Ah!" said the inspector. "And about Barton's moustache –"

"Barton has no moustache now," Roger said impatiently.

"No, sir. Just what I was going to suggest. Because the chap Manders saw – he hadn't got a moustache either, but he was wearing a blue suit."

Roger nodded, as if the news hardly surprised him.

"What do we do next, sir? This is your case."

Roger thought.

"We go to the Hutton's lodging," he said briskly.

"To interview Mrs Hutton?"

"No, no. Not yet. To look for a razor. You see, Barton's razor is here."

The inspector looked puzzled. Then he beamed intelligently. "I get you sir. He ought to have taken it with him, but he couldn't risk coming back to the tent after he'd done the murder. He had his blue suit in the cave all ready, but he forgot his razor to shave off his moustache with. So Mrs Hutton –"

*   *   *   *   *

Mrs Wainwright, the stout, motherly lady who kept Ocean View, was garrulous. She also wiped her eyes a great deal on her apron. Hutton had evidently been her star boarder. Roger listened with patience to her praise of him while the inspector was professionally busy upstairs.

"... a *real* gentleman, he was. So spick and span, and always ready with a joke. Oh, dear, it's sad to think he's gone. Not that he didn't like having things his own way: well, you can't blame a gentleman for that, can you? Not that she ever complained; not the complaining sort, Mrs Hutton isn't. And so well they got on. Never a cross word, that *I* heard. Of course he used to lay down the law a bit, but Mrs Hutton didn't mind that. One of the quiet ones, Mrs Hutton is. (But what she'll say if she comes now and finds the other police gentleman in her bedroom, I don't know. No lady would like that.)

"Upset, sir? Well, it's funny you should ask that, because to tell you the truth she does puzzle me a bit. In fact I'm blest if I've seen her cry yet. Well, it doesn't seem natural somehow, does it? Goes down to the beach with a book or some knitting, just like she used to. 'You have a good cry,' I tell her, 'it'll do you good,' but –

"Yes, she went back to the beach yesterday afternoon. Said she was just going to have another look round before she went to the police, poor soul. What's that, sir? No, no parcel. Just her beach-bag, like she always carried; and –"

The arrival of the inspector cut short the flow.

In the car the two men exchanged results, and the inspector reported at once that no razor was to be found.

"That's what she went back to the beach for," he said with satisfaction. "To take him the razor. You see, Manders being in the field above, Barton couldn't get back to his tent. – Sir!" exclaimed the inspector, aghast at his own perspicuity. "Were they lovers, her and Barton? Is that why Barton killed Hutton?" His face fell. "Oh, but she said they'd only met once." He sighed, and then brightened up again. "That's what she *said*. But suppose they'd been lovers before? They both come from London, you see. What do you think, sir?"

Roger smiled. "What do I think? I think you had better find out whether Hutton was insured. That's a more likely line of enquiry."

"Insured, eh?" The inspector whistled. "You mean, Barton was hard up, and she promised him a share of the insurance money – ? Pretty quick work, with a comparative stranger."

"Nevertheless," Roger persisted, "if Hutton hadn't been insured, I'm pretty certain there'd have been no murder."

*   *   *   *   *

At the police station the superintendent was still waiting for them. On hearing their news he actually summoned the chief constable from his sacred golf-course.

With professional gallantry the latter first swallowed his own words and then showed himself in such an amenable state of mind that Roger was able without difficulty to obtain permission on two points: that for the moment Mrs Hutton would be kept in her state of happy ignorance, and that the London police should be asked to bring down on Monday morning Hutton's partner, now in custody, to answer a few questions which Roger promised should be of the first importance in solving the case.

"But what about Barton, sir?" the superintendent wanted to know. "We must put out an enquiry for him."

"Well, make it a confidential one, to the police only," Roger conceded. "The great thing is that Mrs Hutton must not be alarmed."

For the rest of the weekend he refused to say a further word about the case, to the disappointment of his host.

The inquest had been fixed for Monday morning, but in view of the new developments only formal evidence of identification was taken and Mrs Hutton was the sole witness called, the coroner then adjourning the enquiry for three weeks. After the proceedings Mrs Hutton was invited to the police station to answer a few questions.

"What are you going to ask her?" Roger inquired of the superintendent, as they walked together from the schoolroom which had formed the Coroner's Court. The chief constable had not attended the inquest.

"Oh, just a few questions which she may find some difficulty in answering, Mr Sheringham."

"Are you going to tell her that you know it's murder?"

"No, no. Not yet, sir. That would never do. We don't want to put the two of them on their guard."

Mrs Hutton seemed nervous. She denied that she knew anything about the warrant issued for her husband's arrest, about his share-pushing activities, or about his insurance arrangements; she admitted having visited the beach in the afternoon of Friday, but strongly denied she had met any man there, or even seen one; she denied with equal vehemence that she had known Barton in London, or had ever had any conversation with him alone; she knew nothing about any missing razor of her husband's. But much of her denying lacked conviction, and her hesitations and evasions were obvious. Then she suddenly went hysterical, demanded to know why all these questions were being asked of her, and announced that she would answer no more. The chief constable sent her under the care of a sergeant into another room to recover.

"Pity, sir," remarked the superintendent drily. "She'd have spilled the beans in another minute."

"Must play a game by its rules," pointed out the chief constable. "Well, Sheringham, what about her? She's in it, eh?"

"Oh, she's in it all right," Roger agreed. "Has that partner of Hutton's arrived, by the way?"

"Field? Yes. They've put him in one of the cells."

Roger thought for a minute. "Can we have Mrs Hutton back in about ten minutes? I should like to ask her just one question myself. In the meantime –" He scribbled something on a piece of paper which he gave to the superintendent.

The latter read it, raised his eyebrows, scratched his head, shrugged his shoulders, and then nodded; after which he rose and went out of the room. The chief constable, in confabulation with Inspector Clarke on the other side of the room, had noticed nothing. A minute later the superintendent slipped into his chair again.

The ten minutes passed slowly. At the end of them Mrs Hutton was brought back. She looked pale, but more composed and even defiant.

Roger leaned towards her.

"Mrs Hutton, you have identified the body you saw in the mortuary as that of your husband. Did you know that he had been brutally *murdered?*"

There was a moment's pandemonium. Mrs Hutton shrieked, the police officials gave utterance to indignant protests.

Roger waved the latter aside. "It's part of my case," he explained, "that Mrs Hutton knows nothing of the murder."

"I don't, I don't," screamed the obviously distraught woman. "It's not true."

"It is true." Roger went to the door and beckoned. A constable brought in a small man with a sharp, rat-like face.

Roger looked at him. "You're Field? Well?"

"That's not Eddie Hutton, that stiff," affirmed the ratlike stranger. "Never seen him before in my puff."

Roger signed to the constable to take him away.

"Well, Mrs Hutton?" he said.

This time the beans were were well and truly spilled.

* * * * *

"I don't believe Hutton came down here intending murder," Roger said, when the sobbing woman had been removed again.

"But the chance meeting with Barton was too much for him. He certainly had murder in his mind when he left his lodgings on Friday morning, with the razor to cut off Barton's moustache all ready in his pocket. (He ought to have shaved the chin too, by the way; that was what first made me smell a rat.) It was easy to deceive his wife into believing that both of them had got into difficulties in the water, and Barton had been accidentally drowned. Then he sprang the news of Field's arrest on her and the warrant for his own, and pointed out that this was his one chance if she would identify the body as his. He taught her the description of Barton, and she learned it by heart. There wasn't much risk, you see, in a place where he was a complete stranger; and as you know, it very nearly came off. Really, almost the only risk Hutton ran was in going up to Barton's tent to get that blue suit. It was clever, and so simple. The life insurance Mrs Hutton was to claim may not be huge, but it would be a nice sum to begin –"

The telephone-bell cut him short.

The superintendent listened, expressed his satisfaction, and hung up. "They've got Hutton," he announced. "Just where she said he'd be. She gave him away properly, I'll say."

"We caught her at the right moment," Roger commented. "Half an hour later, when the reaction set in, she might not have been so ready to give him away. By the way, what are you going to do with her?"

"Do with her? Why, we shall –"

"Exactly. What can you do? You can have her up for perjury, or conspiracy, or obstructing the police, but if she pleads coercion she'll certainly get off. Why not let her go?"

The chief constable snorted indignantly. The woman had led them all down the garden path, and it had taken a confounded amateur to –

"Let her go," repeated Roger.

They let her go.

HOLIDAY TASK

Leo Bruce

Leo Bruce was the pen-name of Rupert Croft-Cooke (1903–1979), a gifted journalist, biographer and broadcaster whose career was blighted when, in 1953, he was sent to prison for six months. He was convicted of indecency offences at the height of a crackdown on homosexuality. He made his home in Tangier for the next fifteen years before returning to his native Britain after the law had been liberalised.

Bruce's first detective novel, the much-praised *Case for Three Detectives* (1936), introduced Sergeant Beef. A longer series, featuring amateur sleuth Carolus Deene, began in the mid-Fifties and continued until 1974, which saw the publication of *Death of a Bovver Boy*. Although, as that title suggests, Bruce tried to move with the times, in spirit his work belonged to the Golden Age of detective fiction.

* * * * *

Sitting on the rocks under some of the highest cliffs on the coast of Normandy I watched Sergeant Beef deliberately enjoying his holiday. With a floppy canvas hat on his head and trousers rolled up to the knee, he was prawning.

The sun was high when Beef proposed that we should go up the cliff path for a drink and I readily agreed. We were crossing the beach when to my surprise he hailed one of three men approaching us.

"It's old Léotard," he said aside to me. "One of the best detectives in the Sûreté. I worked with him on the Mr G. case. Hullo, Leo!"

"It is my friend Beef!" he said in English, and a string of introductions followed.

Beef, redundant as ever, had to explain that he was on holiday, and Léotard said that he wished he were. He was very much on a job.

"Body washed up?" Beef grinned.

"No, no," said the Frenchman with a half smile. "Not washed up. Cast down."

"What, off the cliff?"

"You come and see if you like," Léotard invited, and we all moved off in the direction in which the Frenchman had been going when Beef hailed him.

Léotard explained a little as we went. That morning some boys had reported the wreckage of a car at the foot of the tall cliff known as the White Bear, and a policeman had gone down to investigate.

He had found that "wreckage" was a mild word to use for the shattered bits of metal which were all that remained of a Renault car. He had also found a corpse.

"Identified yet?" asked Beef.

"Oh yes," said Léotard. "It hid the body of a M. Henri Poinsteau, the newly appointed governor of the largest prison in Normandy, and reputed to be the most detested man in the French prison service."

"Ah!" exclaimed Beef.

"Not 'ah,' my dear friend. There is no 'ah' that we can find. The car was Poinsteau's. It had been driven at speed straight over the cliff edge—a case of suicide."

"Daresay you're right," conceded Beef. "It's not the way I'd choose, though. You know his reason for it, I suppose?"

"Not yet. The case was only reported this morning. I arrived an hour ago. The body, or what was left of it, was, of course, photographed, measurements taken of its situation and drawings made before it was removed."

We were approaching a tangle of metal and upholstery which had once been a car.

"We must see what we can now," said Léotard, "for in another hour the tide will be in."

The third man began taking finger-prints, and Léotard himself examined the beach near by. Beef scarcely glanced at the wreckage or the beach but kept gazing up at the cliff-head above us. He was the first to speak.

"I don't believe this was suicide," he announced.

"We shall see," snapped Léotard.

During the next few days Sergeant Beef continued to spend his mornings prawning and to eat gargantuan meals at our little hotel. But in the evenings he and Léotard seemed to enjoy talking shop, and I listened.

If Beef was right in his almost psychic dismissal of the suicide theory and consequent belief that Poinsteau had been murdered, then, admitted Léotard, it would not be hard to find motives. In the criminal world he had countless bitter enemies, men who had suffered from his savagery and sadism.

But beyond this admission Léotard would not go. He could see nothing connected with the death which could be called evidence of murder.

The finger-prints found on the steering wheel were Poinsteau's and the car expert believed that the engine was running when the car hit the ground. It seemed certain that Poinsteau had driven himself over the edge of the cliff.

But why? Nothing that Léotard could learn about the dead man gave any indication of this. He was a bachelor who lived alone; his financial affairs were in order and he appeared to enjoy his position. Besides, he had just been appointed to one of the most important posts in the service.

"He only moved in on the day before the body was found," explained Léotard. "He had spent the afternoon in supervising the arrangement of his furniture which had just arrived from his last quarters. He had some fine furniture, large Empire pieces, and they suited the new house admirably.

"He had arrived at the prison in his car at lunch time and all the afternoon he had been with the moving men, while his car had been in the garage which adjoins his house. Later that evening he must have decided to go for a drive, for when one of his assistants came to his house he found that Poinsteau was not at home, and the garage empty."

Beef nodded.

"You have one advantage," he told Léotard. "Its happening in a prison makes it easy for you to check up times, and so on. The gatekeeper must have seen him go out. What time was it?"

Léotard frowned.

"Now we come to a rather funny thing," he said. "The gate-keeper swears he never did come out. He was on duty from twelve noon till midnight. He remembers Poinsteau arriving in his car, but he is quite certain that he had not left when he went off duty.

"The man who took his place says the same. Poinsteau's was the only car in the prison premises, and it did not pass the gate that evening."

"That's odd," said Beef. "What other ways out are there?"

"None," said Léotard. "Of that you can be certain. There is no other exit from the jail."

"Then," I put in, "if Poinsteau was murdered it must have been a widespread plot in which one of the gatekeepers was involved. Perhaps his murderers came from the inside, drove him to the cliff's edge in his own car and pushed him over."

"Or murdered him first," suggested Léotard, "and merely set the engine running with a corpse at the wheel. The injuries were such that no one could possibly tell if he had been killed by a blow on the head, for instance.

"But the trouble with that theory is that the two gatekeepers are most reliable men who seem to be speaking the truth. His subordinates in the service for the most part respected Poinsteau. It was the prisoners who hated him."

It amused me to notice how absorbed Beef had become in this case.

He seemed able to think and talk of little else but the rival theories of suicide and murder, weighing the points in favour of each. So far as Léotard's investigations went, there was no motive for suicide, for it had been found that the dead man had no money worries and the most persistent inquiries could not bring to light any private intrigue or complication.

On the other hand, for murder there were plenty of motives, and suspects as well. The chief obstacle to the murder theory was the fact that Poinsteau must have somehow driven through the gates himself, or have left his car outside the prison earlier in the day—at all events made a voluntary exit.

Unless the gatekeepers were involved it seemed impossible that the murderers, however many or however powerful they may have been, should have spirited the governor and his car from a closely guarded prison.

Then, a few days before our holiday would end, Léotard made an exciting discovery. Two men who had served long sentences under Poinsteau had arrived in the nearest large town a fortnight before the governor's death and left on the morning after it. Léotard had a dossier for each of them and they were certainly well qualified as suspects. The elder one, known as The Ace, had been sentenced for manslaughter and the younger for robbery with violence.

They were both sworn enemies of Poinsteau and the younger brother of The Ace was doing a sentence of three years' hard labour in the jail to which Poinsteau had been appointed and would have come under his authority that day.

Besides, the movements of the two men had been secretive during their time in the town and too many curious people were eager to swear that they had never left a certain dockland cafe on the night of Poinsteau's disappearance.

"But how can I arrest them?" demanded Léotard. "Nothing to connect them with the crime."

Next morning I again accompanied Beef on his prawning expedition. Beef had just lowered all his nets when I heard him shouting excitedly.

"What was it that Greek said?" he yelled.

"Which Greek?"

"The one that jumped out of his bath because he'd just thought of what he ought to have seen years before."

"Eureka," I told him.

"Well, that's me. Come on!"

I knew him in this mood and meekly watched and followed while he threw his prawns back into the sea, left his nets at a café near the cliff-head, and without waiting to change his highly informal clothes sat himself in the only car in the village which was for hire and told me to get the driver to take him to Rennes.

When we approached the city I asked where he wanted to go. He consulted his notes and mispronounced the name of a firm of removal and storage contractors. I gave it to the driver and after some dangerous swerves through the streets we drew up at an office door.

"You wait here," Beef said, "unless they don't talk English, in which case I'll call you."

It seemed that there were no language difficulties, for Beef was absent some twenty minutes. When he joined me to drive home, I tackled him.

"Was that the firm which moved Poinsteau's furniture?" I asked, rather unnecessarily as I thought. But Beef had a surprise for me.

"No," he said, and closed his eyes.

When we were back he hurried to Léotard's hotel.

"Of course," was his greeting, "we ought to have seen it days ago. I must be slipping. You can arrest your two men. You'll have to fill in the details, Leo, because after all I'm on holiday, but I don't think you'll have much difficulty.

"I've just been over to see the people you told me had the order to move Poinsteau's furniture. Well, they didn't."

"Didn't have the order?"

"No. Didn't move it. They got a telephone message saying the job was off. See it now? Who else had access to him that afternoon? Who could come in and out without anyone thinking twice? The two moving men, of course. I think your gatekeeper will pick them out in any identification parade.

"Easy for them to kill Poinsteau and leave the jail as quietly and comfortably as you please. Easy for those two men to hire a van from somewhere else—or even buy one if they were in funds and determined enough. Easy job altogether."

"I am sure that it was," said Léotard. "No difficulty at all in cracking Poinsteau on the head. And then, I suppose," the Frenchman had grown very sarcastic, "the dead man sat in his car, passed the gatekeeper, went to the cliff and was still at the wheel when the car went over?"

Beef did not smile.

"Yes," he said. "That's just what happened."

Léotard prolonged the game.

"The gatekeeper could not see him because he was already a ghost, perhaps?"

"No, Leo," said Beef seriously. "The gatekeeper couldn't see him for the same reason that nobody else could. Him or his car.

"I can't think why I never thought of it before—perhaps it seems funny to have one car inside another. Yes, that's what they did. Drove it, with the corpse and all, straight up a couple of planks into the pantechnicon. That's how the governor left his prison in his own car—like Jonah in the whale's belly.

"Now you fill in the bits and pieces and go and catch your men. I want some prawns for tea."

A POSTERIORI

Helen Simpson

Helen de Guerry Simpson (1894–1940) was an Australian-born Renaissance woman who moved to England but never lost her love of her native country, which supplied the backdrop for some of her fiction. She applied her talents effortlessly to occupations as diverse as literature, broadcasting and cookery and invariably seemed to meet with success. In collaboration with Clemence Dane (the pen-name of the Academy Award-winning playwright Winifred Ashton) she wrote three detective novels, one of which was filmed by Alfred Hitchcock as *Murder!*

Simpson contributed dialogue to Hitchcock's *Sabotage*, and her historical novel *Under Capricorn* was filmed by him after her premature death from cancer. She was a close friend of Dorothy L. Sayers, whose admiration for her vivacious and warm personality was unbounded. This is one of her very few short stories, and is marked by her characteristic humour and lightness of touch.

* * * * *

AT about one o'clock on the last night of her stay in Pontdidier-les-Dames Miss Charters was awakened by indeterminate noises sounding almost in her room, and a medley of feet and voices in the street. It was not the first time this had happened. Pontdidier had belied the promise, made by an archdeacon, that she would find it an harbour of calm. The fact was, the town was too near a frontier, and too unsophisticated. When politicians in Paris, to distract attention from their own misdeeds, began to roar of treason, Pontdidier believed them, and the Town Council—"nos édiles"—set up a hue and cry for spies. Miss Charters had not failed to observe this nervousness, and to despise it a little, without ill-humour; but to be roused by other people's unfounded terrors at one in the morning was a little too much, and she said so, in her firm French, to the landlady as she paid her bill next day.

"Je ne suis pas sure que je puis vous recommander à mes amis. Votre ville n'est pas tranquille du tout."

The landlady sank her head between her shoulders, then raised and swung it deplorably to and fro.

"Las' naight," said the landlady, practising English, which reckoned as a commercial asset, "it is a man escape from the police. A spy that makes photographies. They attrape him, but the photographies—gone! Nobody know."

"Un espion!" repeated Miss Charters coldly, as one who had heard that tale before. "Esperons qu'il n'échappera pas."

With that she walked upstairs to her room for a final inspection. Her hot-water bottle, as usual, had been forgotten in the deeps of the bed, and this she rescued thankfully. Going to the washstand to empty it, she set her foot on some round object, and came to the floor with no inconsiderable bump. The object, obeying the impetus she had given, rolled to rest against a chair-leg, and Miss Charters, turning to eye it with the natural resentment of one tricked by the inanimate, instantly recognised it as a spool of film.

Her mind, with a gibbon-like agility which unhappily never comes at call, leapt from the spool to the noises in the night; linked these with her own wide-open window, probably the only one in the entire façade of the hotel; and came to the conclusion that this spool had reached her floor by the hand of the suspected spy now in custody; flung as he fled. But there had been, her subconscious seemed to think, two noises in the room. She looked for another possible missile, and perceived, under the bed, a flat wallet of some kind. It was quite inaccessible, the bed's frame hung low, she had no umbrella to rake for it, and some vague memory of criminal procedure insisted that the police must always have first cut at a clue. It was her duty to go downstairs, display to the landlady the spool, which she had picked up instinctively, and ask that the authorities should be informed.

She set foot on the stairs, and even as she did so, halted. It became apparent that she would have to give her evidence in person, swear to the noise in the night, to the morning's discovery. This would involve missing her train, and its subsequent connection, with the expense of warning domestics and relatives by telegram. More sinister considerations succeeded these. The French were hysterical. They were spy-conscious. They would refuse to believe that she and the fleeing man were strangers. As an excuse for open windows a plea of fresh air would not satisfy.

Halting on the stairs, she rehearsed these reasons for holding her tongue, and came to the conclusion that silence, with a subsequent letter from England, would meet the case. To roll the spool under the bed till it lay by the wallet, and so depart, would be the dignified and comparatively honest course of action. But the turmoil of the morning had let loose in Miss Charters' mind hordes of revolutionary desires, which now found a rallying ground in the fact that she had not, in her forty-odd years, had one single unusual experience. She had never held unquestioned sway as chief talker at any party; she had never come within hail of being the heroine of any incident more lively than the spoiling of a Guide picnic by rain. The spool of film, now safe in her bag, tempted her; to take it home as proof of the adventure, to hand it over in the end, perhaps, to somebody from the Foreign Office or Scotland Yard! She hesitated, and the revolutionaries in that instant had her conscience down. No word of any discovery found its way into her farewells.

At the station she became aware of two things. First, that she had twenty minutes to wait for her train; second, that amid the excitements of the morning she had omitted a visit to that retreat which old-fashioned foreign hotels leave innominate, indicating it only by two zeros on the door. She cast a prudish but searching eye about her. The word "Dames" beckoned; Miss Charters bought a newspaper and, apparently purposeless, drifted towards it.

The usual uncleanness greeted her, and to protect herself from unspeakable contacts Miss Charters sacrificed a whole sheet of her newspaper. It was newly printed, the ink had a bloom to it. Miss Charters, accustomed at home to entrust to newspaper the defence of musquash against moth, vaguely supposed that it might prove, on this analogy, deterrent to germs. She emerged without delay, glanced to see that her baggage was safe, and paced up and down reading what remained of *Le Petit Journal*. There were fifteen minutes still to wait.

Seven or eight of these had passed in the atmosphere of unhurried makeshift that pervades all minor French stations, when a commotion was heard outside, chattering of motor cycles and shouting. Through the door marked "Sortie" three policemen in khaki and kepis made a spectacular entrance, followed by a miraculous crowd apparently started up from the paving-stones. The three advanced upon Miss Charters, innocently staring, and required her, none too civilly, to accompany them.

"Pourquoi?" she inquired without heat. "Je vais manquer mon train."

They insisted, not politely; and their explanations, half inarticulate, contained a repetition of the word "portefeuille." At once Miss Charters understood; the wallet had been found. (Who would have thought the French swept so promptly under beds?) She must give her account of the whole matter, miss her connection, telegraph her relations. Bells and signals announced the train to be nearly due; with a brief click of the tongue she summoned resolution for a last attempt at escape.

"Je suis anglaise," she announced. "Mon passeport est en ordre. Voulez vous voir?"

She opened her bag, and immediately, with a swift fatal motion, made to shut it. On top, surmounting the handkerchief, the eau-de-Cologne, the passport, lay the damning red spool, so hurriedly, so madly crammed in. The foremost policeman saw it as soon as she did. He gave a "Ha!" of triumph, and caught the bag away from her. His two companions fell in at her side, the crowd murmured and eddied like a stream swollen by flood. As she was marched from the station, out of the corner of an eye she saw the train come in; and as they entered the Grande Rue she heard the chuff and chug of its departure. Hope gone, she could give undivided attention to her plight.

It became evident, from the manner of the policemen, and from the fact that she was taken to the Hotel de Ville, that matters were serious. She made one attempt to get her bag; certain necessary words lacked in the formula of defence she was composing, and the bag contained a pocket dictionary. Her request was denied. A cynical-looking man at a large desk—mayor? magistrate?—fanned away her protests with both hands and listened to the policeman. So did Miss Charters, and was able to gather from his evidence that the wallet found in her room contained papers and calculations to do with the aerodrome near by. Could anything be more unlucky? The one genuine spy that had ever frequented Pontdidier-les-Dames must needs throw his ill-gotten information into her bedroom!

The functionary asked at last what she had to say. She replied with the truth; and despite a vocabulary eked out with "vous savez" told her story well. The functionary noted her explanation without comment, and having done so asked the inevitable, the unanswerable questions.

"You found these objects at 10.45 this morning. Why did you not immediately inform the police? You insist that they have nothing to do with you. Yet you were actually attempting to carry out of this country one of the objects. How do you account for these facts?"

Miss Charters accounted for them by a recital, perfectly true, of her desire to shine at tea-parties. It sounded odd as she told it; but she had some notion that the French were a nation of psychologists, also that, being foreign, they were gullible, and sympathetic to women in distress. The cynical man listened, and when her last appeal went down in a welter of failing syntax, considered a while, then spoke:

"I regret, mademoiselle. All this is not quite satisfactory. You must be searched."

The French she had learned at her governess' knee had not included the word he employed, and it was without any real understanding of his intention that she accompanied a woman in black, who suddenly appeared at her side, looking scimitars. They progressed together, a policeman at the other elbow, to a small room smelling of mice. The policeman shut the door on them; the woman in black ejaculated a brief command; and Miss Charters, horrified, found that she was expected to strip.

In her early youth Miss Charters' most favoured day-dream had included a full-dress martyrdom, painful but effective, with subsequent conversions. She now learned that it is easier to endure pain than indignity, and amid all the throbbing which apprehension and shame had set up in her temples, one thought lorded it: the recollection that she had not, in view of the dirty train journey, put on clean underclothes that morning.

The woman in black lifted her hands from her hips as if to help with the disrobing; there was a shuffle outside the door as though the policeman might be turning to come in. With a slight scream, at speed, Miss Charters began to unbutton, unhook, unlace her various garments; as they dropped, the woman in black explored them knowingly, with fingers active as those of a tricoteuse. At last Miss Charters stood revealed, conscious of innocence, but finding it a poor defence, and ready to exchange the lightest of consciences for the lightest of summer vests.

The woman in black was thorough. She held stockings up to the light, pinched corsets; at last, satisfied, she cast an eye over the shrinking person of Miss Charters, twirling her slowly about. Now the words of dismissal should have come. Instead, at her back Miss Charters heard a gasp. There was an instant's silence; then the one word, ominous: "Enfin!"

The woman in black ran to the door and shouted through it. Miss Charters heard excitement in the policeman's answering voice, and his boots clattered off down the corridor, running. Her imagination strove, and was bested. Why? What? The woman in black, with a grin lineally descended from '93, informed her.

"And now, my beauty, we'll see what the pretty message is that's written on mademoiselle's sit-upon!"

The next few moments were nightmare at its height, when the sleeper knows his dream for what it is, knows he must escape from it, and still must abide the capricious hour of waking. An assistant in blue was vouchsafed to the woman in black. One deciphered such letters as were visible, the other took them down, pesting against the artfulness of spies who printed their messages backwards. In deference to Miss Charters' age and passport some decency was observed. Policemen waited outside the half-open door; there was much noise, but no threatening. The women heard her explanation (conjectural) of their discovery without conviction and did not even trouble to write it down.

At last the message was transcribed. The woman in blue compassionately gave Miss Charters back her clothes, a gesture countered by the woman in black, who refused to allow her to sit down lest the precious impression be blurred. With a policeman at her elbow and the two searchers at her back, her cheek-bones pink, and beset by a feeling that this pinkness ran through to her skeleton, Miss Charters once more faced the functionary across his table. The transcription was handed to him. He considered it, first through a magnifying glass, then with the aid of a mirror. The policeman, the two searchers, craned forward to know the fate of France, thus by a freak of Fortune thrust into their hands:

"Et maintenant," they read in capital letters, "j'ai du cœur au travail, grâce aux PILULES PINK."

The functionary's eyes appeared to project. He stared at Miss Charters, at the searchers; with a start, at his own daily paper lying folded, with his gloves upon it. He tore it open, seeking. Page 7 rewarded him. "Maladies de Femmes," said the headline; underneath, the very words that had been deciphered with such pains, accompanying an illustration of a cheerful young woman, whose outline appeared in transfer not unlike the map of a town. Silently he compared; his glass was busy. At last he looked up, and Miss Charters, meeting his eye, perceived something like comprehension in his glance, a kind of gloating, a difficult withholding of laughter—"Rabelaisian" was the word which shot across her mind like a falling star. It was a hard glance to face, but all Englishness and spunk had not been slain in Miss Charters by the indignities chance had obliged her to suffer. She had one magnificent last word:

"Je rapporterai le W.C. de la gare aux autorités sanitaires!"

It was the best she could do. The larger threat which at first inflamed her mind, of complaints to the Ambassador in Paris, of redress and public apologies, would not do; both she and the

Rabelaisian eye knew why. She could never, to any person, at any time, confide the truth of an experience so appalling. So far as vicarage conversation went, the thing was out of the question. Hateful irony! Something, after forty-odd years, had happened to her, and it had happened in such a manner that mere decency must strike her mute. In the words of a ceremony she had often in younger days read over fondly, she must hereafter for ever hold her peace.

Miss Charters held it. The relations who welcomed her a day later were of opinion that her holiday in France had not done her much good. They found her quiet, and discovered that what she wanted was to be taken out of herself. So they arranged little gaieties, at which Miss Charters listened silently, now and then pinching in her lips, to travellers' tales of those who had been seeing life in London and by the sea.

"But then," as a relative remarked, "poor Aggie never did have much to say for herself."

WHERE IS MR MANETOT?

Phyllis Bentley

Phyllis Bentley (1894–1977) was the daughter of a Yorkshire mill owner, and she is most famous for her *Inheritance* trilogy. These books made excellent use of the development of the West Riding textile industry as a background, and were successfully televised in the Sixties with a cast including John Thaw.

Her detective fiction is much less well known, but a string of short stories featuring Miss Marian Phipps appeared in *Ellery Queen's Mystery Magazine* after the Second World War, although the character made her debut in 1937. 'Where is Mr Manetot?', published a year earlier, is rather different in mood and style, and first appeared in a long-forgotten anthology called *Missing from Their Homes* which contains interesting 'missing person' stories from writers as different as Anthony Berkeley and Graham Greene.

* * * * *

"*MISSING* from his home, 54 Wharfedale Terrace, Hudley, Yorkshire, since Thursday, January 12th, William Quarmby Manetot. Here is a description of Mr. Manetot, who by profession is a schoolmaster. Age 47, height 5 feet 8 inches; very slender, stoops considerably; thick brown hair turning grey, brown beard; complexion pale, eyes brown; wears tortoise-shell spectacles with very thick lens; walks with a limp as a result of a shrapnel wound. When last seen he was dressed in grey tweed suit, grey pullover, soft grey felt hat, dark tweed coat, black shoes, and was carrying a small suit case and a black leather satchel. Any listener who has information about any person answering to this description should communicate at once with the Hudley police, telephone Hudley 60006. Mr. Manetot, whose studies in the economic history of his native county are well known in academic circles, has been working under great pressure of late, and it is feared some ill may have befallen him."

*   *   *   *   *

In the Audley Private Hotel, Northerley-on-Sea, the loud-speaker stood on a high shelf in the lounge, just opposite the reception office. As the reading of the police notice concluded, a sallow young man with dark hair and a black tie, who was lounging by the office window, took out from his pocket an envelope which was stamped but bore no postmark. He turned it over once or twice thoughtfully, then suddenly jerked out the several sheets it contained and began to read. The creases in the sheets were deep and soiled, as if they had often been refolded, the writing was small, but decided and the writing of an educated man.

*   *   *   *   *

"My dear Matthew," read the young man, "I am writing to give you an account of a very extraordinary experience I have just had, and to ask your advice as to what I ought to do. It seems to me that my plain duty is to communicate with the police—yet what have I really to tell them, after all? The whole affair is so slight, so subtle, so far from obvious, that I really dread the thought of trying to explain my doubts and suspicions to a sergeant or inspector or whatever it is, in a seaside town of this kind. A sharp, shrewd bustling man, accustomed to petty pickpockets and confidence tricksters, I expect he would be; and such a man would think me mad! And how does one frame a statement of that kind? How convince an unknown policeman of one's honest motive? Who does one ask for? How begin one's tale? Besides, I don't know either the name of the first person concerned, or the face of the second.

"On the other hand, you know, Matthew, I strongly suspect that murder has been committed here. Yes, the whole thing really looks very fishy to me. And as a decent law-abiding citizen, I can't just pass by on the other side and risk leaving a murderer at large, now can I? So here I am, in the lounge of the Audley Private Hotel, scribbling it all down for you to read. I shall post this to you on my way to the station, and I want you to give it your serious consideration, and telephone me exactly what you think I ought to do. Give me a proper legal opinion, in your capacity as my solicitor, rather than as my friend. I shall go back to Hudley by to-morrow afternoon.

"Meanwhile, I confess, Matthew, I'm taking very good care not to be alone in any room here. The reason for this will appear in the course of my story; but I can assure you that I'm very glad of the company of the two thin spinsters by the lounge fire. I certainly shan't venture upstairs to my bedroom. Indeed, I'm not sure that it's wise of me to stay here at all. But then, if I went to the station I should have an hour to wait, and somehow after yesterday I'm not fond of waiting at stations. Besides, I want to see if they find poor Mrs. Whitaker. And whether she's alive or dead when they find her—I've not much doubt which it will be, myself. But I'm wasting time and paper, and not getting to my story. So here goes.

"Yesterday afternoon (that is, the afternoon of Thursday January 12th) I was sitting at my desk at home in Hudley, just finishing the proofs of my new book on weavers' guilds in the 14th century, when the telephone rang. It was one of those 'personal' trunk calls, and after I had assured the operater several times that I was myself, I was put through to Sir Thomas Cadell. Of course I needn't enlarge on Cadell's identity to you, Matthew; he's one of our greatest economists, and if his advice had been followed earlier, Europe wouldn't be in the mess it is to-day. I knew his son well—the one who was killed in the War—and Sir Thomas has always been kind enough to take a fatherly interest in my work. I was delighted, but surprised, when he rang me up from his country home; for I couldn't imagine any circumstances arising between myself and Sir Thomas, which should necessitate such urgent communication. However, it was all quite simple really. The poor old boy began by telling me he wasn't at all well.

" 'I have a cold, Will,' he said, in a querulous tone. 'I keep coughing—peck, peck, peck, a silly dry cough, it is. It came on last week and it doesn't get any better, in fact, to-day I'm not too clever, as you say in your part of the country, not too clever at all.'

" 'I'm very sorry to hear it, Sir Thomas,' I said, and meant it, for I like the old chap—he's so simple and good and modest—as much as I admire his work, and that's saying a good deal. 'Is there anything I can do to help you, sir?' I said, for I was troubled about him, he sounded so shaky and unlike himself.

" 'It's your holidays, isn't it, Will?' he said. When I told him yes, he seemed to hesitate, and then went on: 'How is your book going, lad?'

"'I'm just correcting the last eight pages of the proofs,' I replied.

"'Then could you do a job of work for me?' said Sir Thomas eagerly.

"'I could!' said I with emphasis. 'Tell me what it is, and the thing's done.'

"When I heard what it was I didn't feel so sure, however, especially as I was a bit fagged with the effort to finish my proofs before school began. It appeared that Sir Thomas was booked to give two lectures on the history of silver currency, in a Lancashire town—one that very evening at seven-thirty, and another at the same time the following day. Cadell wasn't fit to travel—'or so my wife says,' grumbled the old chap—and would I do the lectures for him. He sounded so worried and ill and mournful that in spite of some misgivings I replied at once that I certainly would do the lectures, though what the audiences would think of the substitution I could by no means guarantee.

"'You'll do it better than I—my working days are over,' said Sir Thomas, in a high, peevish tone.

"I told him with conviction that he was talking nonsense. The old boy seemed pleased, and his voice was more cheerful as he gave me details of the place, time, and subject of the two lectures.

"'Shall I telephone or wire to announce my coming!' I asked.

"'No; what's the use? It's too late for the change to be made public. Just turn up and talk,' said Sir Thomas, with a chuckle. I believe he rather hoped the audience would mistake me for him, and the notion of such a leg-pull cheered him.

"He rang off. I looked at my watch and saw there wasn't much time if I were to be punctual to the hour named—railway traffic through the Pennine hills is not quick work. I snatched up my notes and writing materials and hurriedly threw a few clothes into a case. Old Mrs. Ingram, my landlady, had gone out, and I was alone in the house, so I scrawled on a piece of paper: *Back on Saturday*, and hurried off. As I went down our little terrace I thought I saw Mrs. Ingram sitting chatting in the bay window next door, and waved to her. I don't know why I report all these minor details so carefully, Matthew—or yes, perhaps I do, it's because I'm so anxious to be absolutely accurate about what may have to be police evidence.

"In the train I busied myself preparing notes for the two lectures. When I came to consider, it seemed rather odd to lecture twice, on consecutive evenings, presumably to the same audience, on the same rather limited and specialist subject, and it did just occur to me as I worked, to wonder, in some anxiety, whether Sir Thomas had not been mistaken in his details. And of course he had, though not, as I thought, about the subject.

"When I reached the hall—a large brick erection belonging to a chapel—it was all dark and silent, and there was nobody about; Sir T.'s name was announced on a big board outside, certainly, but only one lecture was advertised, and the date given was Friday, January 13th. It was easy to see how Sir Thomas might have fallen into the blunder; there had, perhaps, been some discussion about the date, and he had made a second entry in his diary and forgotten to erase the first. Easily done, and I couldn't find it in my heart to curse the old fellow; but still, there it was. And there *I* was, stranded in a dreary industrial town, with an engagement there twenty-four hours hence, and nothing to do there before. I returned promptly to the station to ask for trains back to Hudley, but was snubbed by the booking-clerk, who seemed insulted that anyone should wish to do such a foolishly devious journey. A porter was more sympathetic, but all our poring over a well-thumbed time-table which he took from his waistcoat pocket only confirmed that the journey, in the evening was highly tedious, not to say tiresome. Why should I toil back to Hudley, I began to reflect, only to toil here again next day? My proofs were in my satchel; I could work on them anywhere. I was not expected at home. Why not stay here?

"I suggested this to my sympathetic porter, but he seemed not to like the plan, and shook his head over it doubtfully.

" 'Why not go on to Northerley instead, sir?' he suggested. 'Now there's a place! Northerley-on-Sea! Don't tell me you never heard of Northerley,' he said with a grin, 'and you from Yorkshire?'

"I grinned back, for Northerley is one of the pleasure cities of the industrial north—the lads and lasses of factory and mill live the year through on the memories of the joyous week they spend there. Seeing me incline to the project, the porter pressed it; there was a fine train to Northerley in half an hour, he said, a club train, an express, softly cushioned, brilliantly lighted, a really comfortable train. Twenty minutes by that train would see me in Northerley, with hotels and picture palaces——

" 'And the sea,' I said.

" 'Aye—and t'sea,' agreed my porter. 'If you like sea in winter.'

"I felt I liked the sea at any time, and particularly just now after my long bout of close work; so I booked a ticket for Northerley

Central from the supercilious clerk, and began to pace up and down the station, waiting for the express.

"Doesn't it seem strange, Matthew, that all these small unimportant incidents should have combined into this; that I can help to hang a murderer? They might so easily not have happened! If that porter had not been on duty, for instance? But he was; and so I waited for the train to Northerley.

"The station was by now very quiet. My porter friend, scorning the sombre covered way sloping up to the bridge, had swung himself down to the rails and crossed to the ticket office on the opposite platform, and there seemed nobody else about at all. It was a cheerless gloomy scene; the paving stones beneath my feet were dark with grime, the remote glass roof over my head was dark with grime, the supporting metal pillars were dark with grime, the very air seemed grimy too. The ticket office across the rails was the only building to show a light; on my side all was dark and silent and empty; I tried the handles of one or two doors, but they seemed locked. A quiet depressing rain had begun to fall; the drops could be seen gliding silently to earth in the light of the rare and dirty station lamps. Across the rails, in the ticket office, someone now shouted: 'Good night!' A door slammed cheerfully, steps receded, silence fell again; the station seemed even gloomier than before. I shivered, turned up my coat collar, quickened my step.

"It was at this moment that I heard the whispering.

"You know my habit of mind, Matthew; you know I'm an incredulous, questioning sort of fellow, not easily convinced that something odd is happening, not easily impressed. I tend always to seek a natural explanation before having recourse to an extraordinary one. And so that night—strange to think it was only last night—as I could see nobody about who might be whispering, my first reaction was to decide that the sound could not be that of human voices, but must proceed from some other cause. It must come from the wind whistling through the telegraph wires, or stirring a shred of paper, or driving the rain on the roof. But there was no wind; the rain fell soft and straight; no torn corner flapped among the newspaper placards round the closed bookstall. I spent a few minutes trying to trace the sound thus to its origin, but having failed, made an effort to shake off the obsession and resumed my pacing. But the whispering went on—soft, sibilant, continuous, it was never broken by a laugh or a pause such as enliven normal cheerful converse.

"As I paced up and down I began to locate the sound, it seemed to come from above my head, whenever I passed one of the locked waiting-rooms. I halted on the spot, yes, the hissing sound certainly was strongest there. I looked up, and saw that one of the grimy panes leaned backward in its grimy frame, open. Ah! The air hisses out through there, I decided, for the moment satisfied with this explanation. But as I stood there, close to the ventilator, the whisper seemed to become human; I even thought I caught a definite word: *sand*. Yes; *in the sand*, I heard, *in the sand*. I moved away at once, uncomfortable, if that was a human conversation, then I had been eavesdropping. Ashamed, I walked briskly away, to the far end of the platform, where it dipped and tailed off into nothing. The prospect here was even more dismal; just a yard of gleaming metal in the light of the last station lamp, and then endless darkness and rain. And the whispering seemed to have followed me; *sand, yes, in the sand*.

"I shook my shoulders angrily, annoyed with myself, for allowing my nerves to be so easily upset and limped briskly back, determined to settle the matter once and for all. If there were people inside that waiting-room, then I could go inside too. I marched up to the hissing ventilator, halted there and tried to peer through the window, below, but the panes were of opaque glass for the purpose of privacy, and nothing was to be seen. I strode up to the door, tried the handle and shook it violently, it did not yield. The whispering, however, stopped at once.

" 'There *is* someone within, then!' I thought, and shook the door again.

"Just then I observed that one of the door panels had been broken, and replaced with plain glass. Irritated into bad manners by thwarted curiosity, I stooped and peered through this pane.

"The hanging lamp outside threw a shaft of light obliquely across the little room on to the far wall. The surrounding darkness was so black, and the shaft of light so narrow and so clearly defined, that for a moment I was not sure whether what I saw was a framed picture or a reality. Then the girl became aware of my presence; she turned her head quickly, and shot me a viperish glance from her beautiful eyes. Yes, what I saw was the head and shoulders of a real girl; a beautiful creature, brilliantly fair, with a black velvet cap perched on her small neat head. She sat erect with a defiant air. Her pale hair shone, her rounded cheek had a delicate bloom, her lips were rich and shapely, her rather broad tip-tilted nose gave her face character. Only her eyes, which shone out in the dark like those of a tigress, were displeasing; they were—well, they were like a tigress's eyes: golden, gleaming, inhuman.

"I see I've just compared her to a viper, and now to a tigress! Well, and perhaps I'm not far wrong. That's the trouble, you see. At this moment she was certainly very angry, and not without cause. I know too much of the difficulty experienced by young people of the poorer kind in finding a place and time for courtship, to blame a pair of lovers for any expedient they may adopt to secure solitude; I forgave these two the jammed door at once, and felt a real mortification for having disturbed them. Yes, there was a young man beside the girl; but—and this is the whole point of the story, Matthew—I saw *only his hand*, which lay caressingly on the girl's upper arm. It was a rather unusual hand, however; long and sallow, with very thin fingers, very wide apart; and on the first finger was a ring with a large green stone. In the shaft from the lamp the green stone gleamed like a cat's eyes in the headlights of a car. I saw nothing else of the pair, Matthew; just the girl's fair head, her velvet beret her rather solid white throat, some rough dark fur below, the man's curving fingers, the gleaming ring. For a moment I gazed in at them, forgetting myself in my admiration for the Rembrandt chiaroscuro effect, and thinking what a good shot it would make for a camera, then with a start I remembered my manners, and stepped backward out of sight.

"This might have been a signal for which the whole station was waiting, for at once everything began to be perfectly ordinary and cheerful. A door swung open again on the opposite platform, and out came my porter, his peaked cap perched on the back of his head; whistling cheerfully, he swung himself down to the rails and came across to me.

"'She won't be long now, sir,' he said; he nodded reassuringly and began to make a considerable noise throwing parcels on a heavy truck.

"From the dark slope leading to the bridge there now came the sound of footsteps and cheerful voices; a group appeared—father, mother, two children walking and a babe in arms—then a single man alone, then another group of four; suddenly the platform seemed full of passengers, all talking and laughing, and the station was no longer grim and desolate, a place of eerie shadows and mysterious whispers, but just a normal industrial station, peopled by jolly, sturdy north-country folk. The pair in the waiting-room had evidently resigned themselves to an end of their privacy and released the door, for the woman with the baby in her arms pushed it open and went in without any difficulty.

"The train roared in; a long, fine, fast, comfortable train, brilliantly lighted and sumptuously upholstered, as my porter had promised me; it was so crowded that the windows were all steamed, but after my lonely wait I was not averse from company, and took the only vacant seat in a smoker without dissatisfaction. In the bustle of entraining I did not observe Tiger Lily and Green Ring, as I called them, on the platform; I cannot swear, Matthew, either that they took the train or did not take it, or that one took it and the other not. If I could give definite information on this point, my duty would be clearer; but I cannot.

"Well! I reached Northerley and walked out of the station towards the sea. My satchel and case were not at all heavy, and

I decided to stroll along the front until I came to a hotel I fancied, for at this season of the year there would be no difficulty in securing accommodation at any hostelry I chose. The scene was just the kind I liked. A sea breeze was beginning to blow— somehow there is always a sea breeze at Northerley—and the surf rang out in those short heavy barks which so often presage a rising wind and a falling glass; clouds sailed steadily across the sky, rain lashed my face. To my right the lights of Northerley lay strung out like diamonds on a black velvet thread, with pendants of coloured stones here and there, where a cinema sent out its orange or purple glow. On the left, the lights tailed away after a few hundred yards, and the sand dunes on which the place was built resumed their sway, looming vaguely against the dark sky. I put down my case and stood a moment, considering. The more expensive and luxurious hotels lay to the right, but the unbridled sea to the left; my right promised more creature comforts, my left, more romance.

"While I hesitated, the sharp tap-tap of a woman's high heels sounded to my left; I looked in that direction and saw Tiger Lily, swinging briskly along on very high heels. Her back was towards me, but it was Tiger Lily without a doubt; that pale glossy hair, that velvet beret, that shoulder curve, were hers. Amused by my own decision, I nevertheless decided to let her appearance settle my question for me; I picked up my case and at a discreet distance followed her along the promenade. She continued for a few hundred yards beyond the last high-powered lamp, then suddenly dived down a narrow lane at the side of one of the buildings, which continued here, though more sparsely than before. I walked along and looked up at the front of the place. A large brass scroll over the façade announced it as the Audley Private Hotel. It looked cheerful, with plenty of white paint and glass about it, and spring flowers on the tables by the dining-room windows. I went in.

"The interior of the Audley Private Hotel did not quite live up to its outside appearance, but it was a pleasant place enough; a homely, comfortable, cosy boarding-house, run by a good solid north-country woman who believed in blazing fires and plenty of nourishing food. The wireless was allowed to stay on rather longer than I liked, and the numerous oil-paintings of stags at bay and waterfalls in thunderstorms made the lounge a little pompous; but the arm-chairs were deep, the linen spotlessly clean, the mattress on my bed (I punched it as a test) well-sprung; they gave me a fire in my room and the hot water was boiling. There was a slight delay in showing me to my room because, it appeared, my chamber-maid was not on duty; but as soon as she remembered this, Mrs. Whitaker, the proprietress, a stout buxom kindly soul with white hair and a wheeze, in purple silk, bustled upstairs herself and saw me comfortably installed.

"When I came down again she bustled out of the office to ask me, with her kindly smile, whether I was hungry. It was long past the dinner hour, and I was loath to give trouble, especially on an evening when as it seemed they were short-handed, so I asked merely for coffee. It came promptly, steaming hot, with a fine plate of sandwiches besides; Mrs. Whitaker put it down by me herself, beaming. She was now wearing a fur coat over her purple, and a velvet hat; I know little of women's clothes, but I saw that her gloves were fur-lined and her neat shoes new and well-polished, and from her whole air, as well as that of the Audley, I judged that her banking account was what we in the north call a 'warm' one. (Meaning, my dear Matthew, that no financial draught blows chill upon it.) She bade me good night, and went out by the front door, letting in a great gust of sea air as she did so. From the remarks the other guests in the lounge exchanged after her departure, it appeared that she always took 'a constitutional' thus, at this hour.

"The other guests, Matthew, as they emerged from their newspapers and began to talk, had little that was striking about them. Tiger Lily was not amongst them, at any rate for the moment. There were two thin neat spinsters, permanent residents at the Audley and rather apt to stand on their dignity on that account. There were several middle-aged mothers of families who had obviously come to Northerley to convalesce after a tiresome bout of influenza, and several fathers of families ditto; these all seemed rather desolate without the families aforesaid, and discoursed at length about their children. I listened perforce, and heard the beginning, crisis or end of many domestic dramas of which their recounters rarely perceived the real significance. They were sharp enough about each other's affairs, however, and sharpest of all about the widowed Mrs. Whitaker's; they put their heads together and lowered their voices lest the receptionist, a prim lady with piled-up black hair and high cheekbones, who was now making out bills in the little office, should hear them, but could not refrain from the topic of Mrs. Whitaker's wealth and Mrs. Whitaker's son.

"A little difficult, Mrs. Whitaker's Alfred, I gathered; she spoiled him; he never had worked as he should; a fine hotel like this waiting for him, and he preferred to live in Manchester and do something or nothing in an insurance office; ah, but did he prefer it, or was it his mother who made him go? This last question was canvassed hotly, so that our voices rose rather beyond discretion, and Miss McCorquodale thought it best to come out to us. In a dry Scots tone she made detailed inquiries about our comfort, which effectually stemmed the flow of scandal, and finished us off by asking if we would care to have her mend the fire. She gave us such an accusing glance as she spoke that it was plain she meant to have a negative reply to such an extravagant suggestion. Accordingly we all gave repudiating murmurs and shook our heads, and as soon as we could, shuffled off to bed.

"I slept splendidly, without a dream, though I was dimly conscious of wind and rain; I awoke only when the chambermaid came in next morning to raise my blinds. As she stood there with her arms, in their grey print, raised above her frilled cap and neat fair head, the sunshine poured in, turning her milky cheek to rose, her pale hair to gold. She turned, and I started; for those were the wide nostrils and golden eyes of Tiger Lily. She moved about the room, arranging towels and hot water, and I watched her covertly. She no longer wore her angry tigress look, or if she still had a feline air, it was of a tigress full-fed. She finished her duties, and left without a look towards the bed; I watched the muddied heel of her strong shoe vanish, and felt surprise that she should appear contented in those shoes and those clothes.

"The dining-room of the Audley was a cheerful place this morning, with its row of windows looking out over the now blue and sparkling sea. There certainly had been heavy rain in the night, for the Promenade still gleamed wetly, and the iron seats, outlined in drops, glittered in the sunshine. Mrs. Whitaker did not appear at breakfast, which seemed to cause the guests of longer standing than myself some surprise. As they passed the little table laid for two, demurely hidden behind a palm, where Miss McCorquodale was just finishing her last cup of tea, they all greeted her and asked for the proprietress in varying tones, which yet all showed that Mrs. Whitaker was wont to share her receptionist's early meal. The breakfast provided for the guests was solid and enjoyable; we all had nothing to do all day, so we did not hurry; we were still sitting over our first smokes and our newspapers in the lounge when the clock was well on its way towards eleven. Miss McCorquodale was busy in the office, with her everlasting accounts; of Mrs. Whitaker I had as yet seen nothing this morning.

"Suddenly a strong gust of wind rustled all the newspapers; we looked up, annoyed, and saw that the front door had been burst open by the onslaught of a young man in a considerable hurry. He was thin and dark and wiry, with drooping lids and an unshaven chin which gave him a dissipated air; he wore the usual tweed overcoat and soft felt hat of the young provincial clerk of to-day, with the addition of a long white muffler, much rumpled and rather dirty, twisted carelessly round his throat. He was certainly in a great state of excitement, for he tripped and almost fell over the rugs as he rushed across the lounge.

"'Corky!' he shouted, putting his head in through the little window. 'Corky!'

"'Good morning, Mr. Alfred,' replied Miss McCorquodale without enthusiasm.

"So this is Mrs. Whitaker's son, I thought with interest; the difficult one, who is spoiled and lives in Manchester.

"'For God's sake, Corky!' cried Alfred, his dark eyes glittering and his fingers twitching with excitement. 'How did it happen?'

"'How did what happen, Mr. Alfred?' demanded the McCorquodale repressively.

"'Hasn't anything happened? My mother's all right? It was a hoax, then?' cried Alfred. 'Thank God! But who could have sent it? *You* didn't send it, Corky, surely?'

"'If you'll tell me what you're talking about, Mr. Alfred, I'll tell you whether I had anything to do with it or not,' said Miss McCorquodale severely. 'At present, I just can't make head or tail of you, and that's the truth.'

"She gave a pointed glance towards his hat; Alfred impatiently snatched it off, then leaning back against the office wall, pulled out of his overcoat pocket the torn orange envelope of a telegram.

"'Look, Corky,' he said in a hoarse tone. 'I got this shortly after eight o'clock this morning. Read it.'

"The receptionist took out the telegram. Her change of expression as she read was so startling that all the guests, who for some time had been keenly if covertly interested in the dialogue, now cast all pretence aside and listened shamelessly. What we heard was sufficiently surprising.

"'*Come at once, your mother is dying*,' read out Miss McCorquodale. She stared at the young man for a moment in horrified silence. 'But, Mr. Alfred!' she broke out then: 'It's all ridiculous—your mother isn't ill—she's safe and sound in her room. At least, I think she is!' cried the good creature, suddenly blanching. She ran out of the office and climbed the staircase in a stumbling sprawl, calling: 'Lucy! Maud! Lucy! Mrs. Whitaker!'

"There was a scurry of feet above, but no cry of reassurance. Alfred Whitaker went to the foot of the stairs and stood there, looking up eagerly, waiting; without quite meaning to do so we all clustered about him. Footsteps sounded in every direction above our head, and fragments of conversation clamoured at our ears. 'But, Lucy, surely you saw her. ... No, madam. ... Yes, madam. ... No, Miss McCorquodale, she wasn't there when I took her tea.'

"Miss McCorquodale appeared at the head of the staircase, her good decent face a blotched and contorted mask. Tiger Lily, and another maid in uniform, came behind her.

" 'She isn't here,' whispered the receptionist. 'She isn't anywhere. Her bed hasn't been slept in. Nobody has seen her since she went out for her walk last night.'

"She sat down on the top step and burst into tears.

" 'But the telegram!' cried young Whitaker, turning towards us, his sallow face lined with worry. 'The telegram! Who can have sent it? It isn't signed. My landlady brought it up to me in bed, this morning. I'd been at a dance last night, you see, that's why I was a bit late this morning, and she brought it up to me in bed. It seems as if somebody must have known something about my mother's— disappearance, if that's what it is.'

" 'May we see the telegram?' demanded one of the spinsters, eagerly.

" 'I think you should inform the police immediately,' I said.

" 'I suppose we should—yes, certainly,' replied Alfred in a dazed tone, drawing the telegram from his pocket again and holding it out for all to see.

"We all crowded to look over his shoulder. I too had taken a step and bent towards him, when I heard a stifled exclamation from the head of the stairs. I looked up; Tiger Lily was glaring at me with the same fury in her lovely eyes that I had seen the night before. She has recognized me, I thought, by my limp and glasses, I suppose; but why this anger now? I looked down at the telegram, which read, in the tapes of pale print these new machines inflict on us:

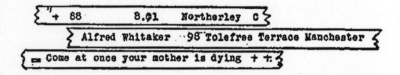

```
+ 88         8.91     Northerley C
    Alfred Whitaker  98 Tolefree Terrace Manchester
Come at once your mother is dying + +.
```

"And as I looked, I knew, in one lurid flash, why Tiger Lily was angry at my presence.

"For the thin first finger of Alfred Whitaker's long sallow hand bore a ring with a green stone which I had seen before.

* * * * *

"And that, my dear Matthew," read the young man, beginning the last sheet, "is my whole story. You'll say there's absolutely nothing in it? Perhaps not. But it all fits so well, doesn't it? Put it this way: Alfred is in debt, and needs money. Mrs. Whitaker has already given him too much, and won't give him more. There is the usual entanglement with the girl—he would see plenty of his mother's maids if he lived at the Audley, and it would be easy enough to get entangled with Tiger Lily. Mrs. Whitaker begins to suspect this entanglement, though not its full extent, and sends her Alfred to Manchester to be out of Tiger Lily's way and do some work. But Alfred has debts, and Tiger Lily is difficult, and—though I shrink from writing this—they decide to murder Mrs. Whitaker, who is old and wheezy, on her evening walk. (I can't forget how often I heard them say: *sand, in the sand*.) In the morning Tiger Lily sends the telegram—with a false name on the back, of course, and from the station, at one of those little wooden pigeon holes through which only the hands can be seen—and Alfred's landlady brings it to him while he is still in bed. Which is meant to prove, don't you see, one, that somebody else, presumably the murderer, knows that Mrs. Whitaker has been done in; two, that it happened in the night; and three, that Alfred has been in Manchester throughout that period. Alfred makes a great fuss, rushes off to Northerley, demands to see his mother, thinks the telegram may be a hoax; oh, decidedly it is not Alfred who can have done this deed! That is what he wants us to think, Matthew. He has a well-faked dance alibi for last night, you notice, and takes the trouble to tell us about it at the first opportunity. But it is faked, Matthew, because you see, *I can break it*. He was at a station distant only twenty minutes from Northerley, between eight and nine last night. And I can prove it. Or can't I? That's what I want you to tell me, Matthew. Am I just being a fool? Allowing a dark station and a whisper and a ring and my own overworked nerves to make a fool of me? But in that case, why should Tiger Lily hate me so? No— I think murder's been done, Matthew. The police have been notified, and are searching high and low for Mrs. Whitaker; they'll find her in the sand dunes, I believe. Dead, certainly. Very probably strangled by that long white scarf.

"Meanwhile, as I write this, Tiger Lily passes often through the lounge, and her eyes are more the tigress eyes each time they rest on me. I wish I were well out of Northerley. I'm leaving by the first possible train. Alfred is supposed to be helping the police in their search; but is he? I'd give a good deal to know the whereabouts of that young man, for I'm greatly afraid that he's a murderer.

"Well, that's the whole story, Matthew; you shall advise me on it to-morrow. It's not yet quite time for me to catch my train; but I think I shall leave now—I'm tired of Tiger Lily's eyes—and per-haps take a little snoop round those sand dunes, myself. If she is found there, strangled, poor Mrs. Whitaker, that would decide me to tell the police what I know, at once.

"Till to-morrow, then. What sort of a show I shall make at lecturing to-night, I really do not know!

"Ever yours,

"W.Q.M."

* * * * *

The sallow young man in the reception office of the Audley Private Hotel refolded the letter, and gave a quick look round him. The lounge was empty. He stepped out of the office, crossed the lounge, and halted by the fire which blazed on the hearth. With another furtive look about him, he suddenly threw the sheets he had been reading into the brightest flame. He took up the poker and rammed them viciously home, beat at them and scattered them to make them burn the faster. When they were ashes he stood erect, and laughed.

At this moment a fair young girl in maid's uniform brought in an evening paper on a tray. Her face was mutinous, and she seemed about to make some fierce complaint; but a door opened upstairs, at the sound the young man shook his head vehemently at her, and she was silent. The young man, hearing footsteps on the stairs behind him, opened the newspaper and glanced at it with a casual air.

A name caught his eye. "Sir Thomas Cadell," he read, "is making excellent progress towards recovery from his recent attack of influenza, and hopes by next week to be able to resume his university duties. During his illness Sir Thomas, we are told, was not informed of the disappearance of his friend Mr. William Quarmby Manetot, as he was not in a fit state to receive any bad news. It is now thought possible by the police that Sir Thomas may be able to shed some light on the movements of Mr. Manetot, for it appears he was in communication with Sir Thomas the day he disappeared."

The newspaper dropped from the young man's hand, and he stood silent, staring in front of him.

"What are you looking at, Mr. Alfred?" demanded the girl in a petulant jeering tone.

"Sand!" said the young man hollowly.

THE HOUSE OF SCREAMS

GERALD FINDLER

Gerald Findler is, by a country mile, the most mysterious of the contributors to this anthology. This story was rescued by Robert Adey from the highly obscure *Doidge's Western Counties Annual*, an illustrated publication combining fiction with a directory of people, places and services. Adey is the world's leading expert on 'locked room' and 'impossible crime' stories, and he was so impressed by Findler's tale that he included it in *The Art of the Impossible*, co-edited with Jack Adrian.

Adey discovered that Findler had published at least one other story, but nothing more. To this meagre horde of information, I can add only that Findler was responsible for a pamphlet called *Ghosts of the Lake Counties*, published by Dalesman Publications in the 1970s. It seems that Findler lived in, or was at least very familiar with, the Lake District, and it would be pleasing if publication of this anthology leads to the discovery of more information about him.

* * * * *

I had been on a walking tour through Cumberland when I discovered this House of Screams.

Hidden among a clump of trees—there it stood: a mysterious looking building ... windows and doors overgrown with green creeper ... garden and lawn badly requiring attention.

The nearest house must have been two miles away, and I can quite understand the 'To Let' board not appealing to those who were on the look-out for a residence near the Cumberland lakes and fells.

To me, however, this house did appeal. Here was a house wrapped up in solitude—far from the noise and bustle of industrial Britain. Here was the very place I had often searched for, and had now found.

By spending three months alone, I could write the book which I intended to be my great success. No noise—no servants—no conventions to upset my work—just to write, write, and write.

I made my way back over the course I had come, and found the owner of the house was abroad, but his agents were in Penrith. By going on another mile I should be able to phone from a village Post Office.

I reached the Post Office and General Store, and phoned the house agents in Penrith, who seemed delighted to accept my own terms as to rent. They informed me that the house had never been occupied since the owner had left to go abroad some years ago. It was well furnished, and they would send the key out by messenger immediately.

I arranged to stay the night in this old world village, and then take possession of my newly acquired house. First thing next morning, I engaged two women to go out and clean and air the rooms, so that I could occupy it that evening.

The village store also were asked to deliver groceries and necessaries every three days—and not being used to sudden increases in trade they willingly complied with my request.

At 5 o'clock the cleaning and airing (such as it was) of the house was finished, and after tipping my two cleaners sparingly, I was left alone to commence my work.

As I had previously stated, the house was hidden in a clump of trees—and except for an occasional bird pouring forth its twilight song, the world was quiet.

I made tea, and ate up a portion of cake I secured in the village, and then I settled down to work writing my book.

It is surprising how time flies when one is deeply interested in some work or hobby and what appeared to me to be a few minutes was close to five hours, because my watch said it was ten minutes past eleven o'clock.

The day to me had been a busy one so I decided to give up my writing and toddle off to my bed.

My chosen bedroom was large, but contained rather too much furniture, and the only means of lighting the room was by an old fashioned oil lamp, the glass of which was unusual in shape, very finely made, and of a peculiar green shade.

You can imagine, then, how dull a bedroom would look—green lights—large ugly furniture—crowding any available space. Two windows were draped with heavy curtains, which I had drawn to the side, for the air seemed damp and thick. I tumbled into bed and left the lamp burning, for I have lately got into the habit of waking in the early hours, and reading a chapter of some favourite book.

Outside, the wind was blowing a little stronger than it had done for days—and the dark skies foretold of a coming storm.

As soon as my head touched the pillow I was asleep, and I remembered nothing more until I was awakened by a horrible scream which seemed in the very room where I was lying. The lamp still threw its flickering green light about the rooms and I felt every limb of my body shaking nervously.

I got out of bed and slipped on my dressing gown, lit a cigarette to steady my nerves, and looked around the room for the person whose persistent screaming was unbearable, but not a sign of anyone could I see.

I plucked up courage and started to search every room in the house, thinking perhaps some poor girl had got lost and had entered the house in fright, but room after room only contained horrid shadows that seemed like ghosts flying past me. I have never believed in things supernatural, but now that belief was getting badly shaken. The perspiration was standing like beads on my forehead.

Towards the front of the house I made my way, and in the hall I lit another lamp—much the same kind of lamp that was still burning in my bedroom.

No sooner had I left the hall than a second lot of screaming started. It seemed to me like a girl in mortal agony—but where she was I could not tell.

The wind was whistling through the trees—and the two lots of screaming seemed to delight in making every sound.

I had searched every nook and corner, with the exception of an attic room, of which the door refused to open. I made up my mind to explore that room at daybreak—to solve the mystery of this House of Screams.

After half an hour enduring this ghostly serenade, the storm outside began to break, and strange though it may seem, the screaming started getting fainter too, until it gradually died away.

It was now 4 o'clock and the strain of this haunted house was telling on me, so I wrapped a rug around myself and quickly went to sleep in an easy chair. I did not waken until 10–15, and found the sun peeping in through the window. My head throbbed—as though I had a horrible nightmare after too great a supper—but the peculiar green lamps still burning were sufficient proof to me that my experience was more than a ghostly dream.

I made a jug of coffee, but could not eat anything, for my appetite had deserted me with my courage. After my necessary toilet, I found a large hammer and a wood chopper and made my way upstairs to the attic—the only room I had not been in.

For ten minutes I battered and hammered at the door, until slowly it moved under the weight I had applied. When the door opened, a terrible sight met my eyes—for sitting on a chair by a small table was a skeleton.

Had I solved the mystery of those screams? I walked nervously towards the table, which was thickly covered with dust. I picked up a small bottle from the floor, and faintly written on a red label was the word 'Arsenic.'

A leather wallet lay on the table, and I opened it. An envelope first caught my eye, and it was addressed 'To the finder of my body.' I opened the envelope with shaking fingers, and pulled out the letter which I now have in my possession. It is getting worn with being continually shown, but it reads thus:—

'To Whoever You May Be.'

'My end is drawing near, and the screams of my late wife continue. I have stood this horror as long as I dare, and now my brain is on the verge of snapping. My lawyer believes me to be going abroad, but the last few hours the spirit of Muriel will not leave me—but still goes on screaming—screaming—screaming. Before I die I must confess that my jealousy caused me to ill-treat my wife, who was both young and pretty.

She was 21 when we married, and I was in my sixtieth year, and because of the many admirers she had, I bought this house and brought her here.

Most of my time was spent in drinking—and when under the influence of liquor, I have thrashed her unmercifully.

No wonder her ghost screams. She died a year after our marriage—a broken heart was the cause of it, but the village doctor said it was lung trouble.

I thought that when she was gone that I would be rid of her incessant screams—but no, she has left them to torture my very soul.

This attic is my only refuge, and I have boarded up the door—and now intend to prepare for my . . .

Screaming again.—My God how she screams.'

* * * * *

The letter remains unfinished, but it unfolds both romance and tragedy.

Somehow I felt that the late owner of that skeleton had earned his deserts. His own actions had brought about his own end.

* * * * *

Surely after hearing the screams of the ill-treated girl the previous night—and finding the skeleton of her brutal husband—no man could settle to write a book. So I packed up my few belongings, and walked into the village to notify a somewhat dull constable of my experience.

He laughed at my idea of a screaming ghost and enquired the number of drinks it took to get like that, but when I told him of the skeleton in the attic, he thought he had better ask his Sergeant to come through.

I had kept the wallet in which the letter was found, and in searching among its various contents, I came across a portrait of a beautiful girl. Her eyes seemed to be dark and bewitching, her face full of noble character and beauty, her lips were lips that most men would move heaven and earth to kiss. Was this the young girl who was the victim of that brute who believed in torture instead of love.

This girl's face has fascinated me ever since. Perhaps it is because I have heard her screams, and know her story, that one will understand how a few years ago I made my way back to the House of Screams.

The building was in a bad state of repair, the furniture all removed. An old road-mender told me the house was haunted, and how the villagers imagined ghosts flitted through the trees every night at twelve o'clock.

At the village where I had previously stayed the night, I was informed about the young bride who was ill-treated, and how she was buried in the little churchyard nearby. The village postmaster described her as a girl with dark eyes that fascinated man and beast, and I concluded from his description that she and the girl of the photograph were one and the same.

I made my way to the churchyard, and found a stone bearing the name of Muriel Dunhurste, aged 22 years, over a small grave. A lump seemed to swell in my throat—I again pictured such a sweet innocent girl being ill-treated by such a drunken sot as he confessed to be.

I made up my mind to leave the place forever; it seemed the uppermost thought in my mind. Just as I arrived at the little white gate of the churchyard, a big touring car pulled up and a young man got out, and made his way into the churchyard. At first I was filled with surprise, for this young man was the very image of the dead girl whose grave I had just visited.

He made his way to the very spot where a few minutes previous I had stood, and I noticed he placed a small wreath of white lilies on the grass mound. By this I concluded that he must be the girl's brother—and this proved to be correct, for when he came back to his car, I asked him if he was going towards Penrith, and if so would he give me a lift. He replied he would be delighted with my company.

We had not gone far on our journey, when I showed him the portrait from the wallet. He recognised it immediately, and inquired from where it came, as it was a portrait of his late sister, whose grave he had just visited, taken before she married.

I told my story carefully, and after thinking for a few minutes he smiled. 'Well, friend,' he said, 'I owe you an apology. But let me tell you my side of the story—that of a self-confessed murderer.

'I always loved my sister, and she wrote to me after her marriage and told me of her husband's brutality—well, I arrived too late— for she had died.

'Now I acted in a friendly way to her husband, and one night he admitted when under the influence of drink, that her screams upset him. I left him alone in his house, only to return a fortnight later, with two peculiar shaped lamps which I said were keepsakes of my late sister.

'At that time I was on the variety stage as an Illusionist, and these lamps I had specially made to my requirements. They were manufactured so that if the lamps were lit these peculiar shaped lamp glasses would get hot. Now by making a whistle or scream of a special range nearby these lamp glasses would act as reproducers, and throw out a weird increased volume of the original sound.

'A day or so before I gave him the lamps, I experimented with them in such a way that it was only when the wind was very rough—and caused a high whistle through the trees that surrounded the house—that the lamps screamed. By filing little bits of the lamp glass, I was able to get a sound as near to my sister's scream as possible.

'The lamps evidently did the work intended, and drove my sister's husband to take his own life.

'As for your experience, my friend, I regret you spent a night under such weird circumstances, but I gathered from your conversation that you were an author. If that is so—why not write a true description of the House of Screams.'

COUSIN ONCE REMOVED

Michael Gilbert

Michael Gilbert (1912–2006) was one of the most distinguished male British crime writers of the second half of the twentieth century. He combined a prolific career as an author of books, short stories, plays and screenplays with a busy life as a partner in a prestigious Lincoln's Inn firm of solicitors. His clients included his friend Raymond Chandler.

Gilbert's facility for writing readable, well-plotted mysteries was matched by a fondness for varying the type of stories that he wrote. His work ranged from traditional whodunits and novels of psychological suspense to spy stories and international thrillers. Every now and then, he drew on his legal knowledge for plot material, and this story is a typically assured example.

* * * * *

When Kenneth Alworthy said to his cousin Arthur, "I've fixed to take a little fishing holiday in early June. I'm going to a farm in Cumberland. It's got two miles of fishable water and I'm told it's as lonely as the Sahara Desert," Arthur (himself a fisherman) felt that peculiar thrill which comes when, after the casting of successive flies, each gaudy, each attractive, each subtly different, the big trout is seen to rise ponderously from the peaty recesses under the river bank and cock his eye at the lure.

Arthur had wrought hard and long for this moment.

Almost a year ago he had mentioned Howorth's Farm to his cousin. He had done it casually—so casually that Kenneth had already forgotten who had told him about it. Twice thereafter he had mentioned it to friends who, he guessed, would pass it on to Kenneth. Then, in March, at the time when the first daffodils look out and far-sighted people plan their holidays, he had sent a copy of a Cumberland newspaper to his cousin. In it he had marked for him an account of the newly discovered rock fissure below Rawnmere, for Kenneth was an amateur of speleology.

But it was not only the marked paragraph that he had counted on Kenneth seeing. Immediately below it was the five-line advertisement which the owner of Howorth's Farm put into the local press each spring.

After that Arthur left it alone.

If a trout will not rise there is no profit in thrashing the water.

*   *   *   *   *

If you were asked, why was it so important to one cousin that the other cousin go apparently of his own free will, to a particular farm in Cumberland, then you would have to cast widely for the answer.

First you would have to examine the will of their common grandfather, Albert Alworthy, who had made his money out of quarrying, and tied it up tightly.

His solicitor, Mr. Rumbold (the father of the present senior partner), had drawn the will, and his client's instructions had been clear. "Tie it up as tight as the law allows," said the old man.

"To my children, and then to their children, and the survivor can have the lot. I dug it out of the earth by the sweat of my brow. Let them sweat for it."

Fifty years later Mr. Rumbold, Junior, had attempted to explain these provisions to Arthur.

"Two wars thinned you out a lot," he said. "Your father and your cousin Kenneth's father—that was your Uncle Bob—were the only two of old Albert's children who had any children themselves. And you and your cousin are the only two grandchildren left."

"And so it goes to Kenneth and me?"

"To the survivor of Kenneth and you."

"How much?—about."

The solicitor named a sum, and Arthur Alworthy pursed his lips.

He wanted money. He wanted it badly, and he wanted it fairly quickly. Not next week, or even next month, but if he didn't get it in a year he was done for. Certain bills were maturing steadily. He might borrow to meet them, but borrowing more money in order to meet existing debts is an improvident form of economy, even for a man with expectations. And even borrowing could not keep him afloat for more than a year at most.

A second reason for the selection of Howorth's Farm lay in a personal tragedy which had befallen Arthur some years before, when walking in the neighbourhood. He had lost his dog, an attractive but inquisitive cocker spaniel, down a pot-hole in the moor. It was a deep, ugly-looking hole, partly masked by undergrowth and surrounded by a rusty and unstable wire fence. Had it existed in a less lonely spot its dangers would have led to proper precautions being taken. As it was, it was fully three miles from Howorth's Farm, and the farm was five miles from the nearest village. A few of the shepherds knew of the pot-hole's existence and it was to one of them that Arthur had hurried, hoping there might be some way of saving the animal.

The shepherd had shaken his head with the quiet firmness of a man who tells an unplesant truth.

"Nothing come alive out of that pot," he said. "Poor little beggar, but you can reckon he'll be dead by now. It's not a dry pot, you see, Mister. There's a scour of water at the bottom." Twenty years ago, continued the shepherd, a party of experts had gone down to explore. They had found a sheep, which had fallen in a month before. At least, they thought it was a sheep. The icy current and the jagged rocks had done their dissecting work very thoroughly and the evidence was by then inconclusive.

"Another month," said the shepherd, "and there wouldn't have been nothing left at all."

"They ought to put a proper fence around it," Arthur had said, angrily.

"So they ought," the shepherd had agreed, but he had said it without much conviction because, rusty and rickety as it was, the fence was now strong enough to stop a sheep, and that was all he really cared about.

*   *   *   *   *

The day after Kenneth packed up his fly rods and left for the north, Arthur went on a walking tour. He went a certain distance by train, and after that he used youth hostels on some nights, and on others nothing at all, for he was an experienced camper, and could make shift for days by himself with a sleeping bag and a small primus stove. Four days later he passed the night in a tangle of thickets just above Howorth's Farm. He had walked twenty miles the day before without putting his foot on a man-made road. He had provisions for seven days with him, *War and Peace* in the three-volume edition, and a strong pair of field glasses. Luckily the weather remained fine.

On the fourth day he saw Kenneth, a walking-stick in his hand instead of a fishing rod, coming up the hill by the path which ran past his encampment.

Hastily brushing himself down he slid out of the undergrowth, and made a detour, striking the path higher up.

Thus the cousins met, face to face, on a turn in the track, out of sight of the farm.

When greetings had been exchanged, Arthur said, "I'm based on a hostel over at Langdale. I thought I'd take a walk in this direction and watch you catch some fish."

"Not today," said Kenneth. "The dry weather has sucked the life out of the stream. The old boy down at the farm swears it's going to rain tonight, and that I'll get some sport tomorrow. Today I'm giving it a rest. Have you any ideas on what it would be fun to do? I don't know the countryside myself."

Arthur pretended to consider.

"It's the best part of three miles," he said, "but let's go and look at that pot-hole I found five years ago."

His cousin was agreeable.

It took them an hour, and Kenneth's life depended solely upon whether they happened to meet anyone. A single shepherd, seeing them from a distance, would have made it necessary for Arthur to choose another time.

They met no one, and no one saw them.

Presently they were gazing down into the hole.

"You can almost hear the water running," said Arthur. "Look out, man—don't lean too far—!"

*   *   *   *   *

A month later Arthur sat again in the room of Mr. Rumbold, the solicitor.

"Tragic," said the lawyer. "I don't suppose we shall ever know the truth. He must have gone out for a walk and fallen down one of those holes. There are a lot of them in that district, I understand."

"Dozens," said Arthur, "and it would take a month to explore a single one of them thoroughly."

"You were on holiday, yourself, when it happened?"

"I was on a walking tour. I may have been less than forty miles from the accident when it happened," said Arthur. He never lied unnecessarily.

"A tragic coincidence," said the lawyer.

Towards the end of the interview Arthur broached what was in his mind.

"I suppose," he said, "in the circumstances—I know the formalities will take a little time—but might I be able to have a little money?"

"Well, I'm not sure," said the lawyer.

"But—" Arthur took a firm hold of himself. "You said yourself," he went on, "that it all went to the survivor."

"Can you prove that you are the survivor?"

There was a long pause.

"I suppose not. Not *prove* it. Everyone assumes—I mean, he left all his things at the farm. No one's heard a word from him since."

"The law," said Mr. Rumbold, "is very slow to assume that a man is dead. If, in all the circumstances, it appears probable that a man has died, you will, after a suitable time has elapsed, be permitted to deal with his estate—"

"A suitable time?" said Arthur hollowly.

"Seven years is the usual period."

"Seven years—but it's crazy! Mr. Rumbold, surely, in a case like this, where it's obvious that an accident—"

"*If* Kenneth is dead," said Mr. Rumbold, "and, as I say, the law will presume no such thing from his mere absence, but *if* he is dead, then I am not at all sure that it *was* an accident."

When Arthur had recovered his voice he said, "What do you mean?"

"I tell you this in confidence," said Mr. Rumbold, "as it was told me. But your cousin has been suffering, since the war, from a deteriorating condition of the spine. One specialist had gone so far as to say that he was unlikely to live out the year. I'm afraid he may have made his mind up, perhaps on the spur of the moment, to end himself. So you see—"

Arthur saw. He saw only too clearly.